THE DETECTIVE & THE CHINESE HIGH-FIN

ALSO BY MICHAEL CRAVEN

The Detective & The Pipe Girl: A John Darvelle Mystery

Body Copy

THE DETECTIVE & THE CHINESE HIGH-FIN

A JOHN DARVELLE MYSTERY

MICHAEL CRAVEN

HARPER

NEW YORK • LONDON • TORONTO • SYDNEY

HARPER

This book is a work of fiction. The characters, incidents, and dialogue are drawn from the author's imagination and are not to be construed as real. Any resemblance to actual events or persons, living or dead, is entirely coincidental.

HarperCollins books may be purchased for educational, business, or sales promotional use. For information please e-mail the Special Markets Department at SPsales@harpercollins.com.

FIRST EDITION

Title page spread photograph by Joseph Sohm/Shutterstock, Inc.

Library of Congress Cataloging-in-Publication Data has been applied for.

ISBN 978-0-06-243937-6

16 17 18 19 20 OV/RRD 10 9 8 7 6 5 4 3 2 1

THE DETECTIVE & THE CHINESE HIGH-FIN

1

On a recent Tuesday morning, I was using one of the cinder-block sidewalls in my office as a backboard for Ping-Pong practice. I'd hit the ball against the wall, and before letting it drop to the slick concrete floor I'd pick it out of the air and send it back. I'd pop a few backhands in a row, then hit the ball so that it would come off the wall at an angle, over to my forehand side. After some forehand work, I'd angle it back over to my backhand side. And then I'd do the whole cycle over again. And again. And again. Truthfully, this exercise probably wasn't doing a whole lot for my game, but I was enjoying it immensely. Keeping the ball in the air, never letting it drop, popping it back and forth, making it look like it was on a string.

My office is a warehouse in west L.A., in Culver City. And not too long ago, I'd installed some pretty nice speakers in my space. So as I practiced I was listening to a playlist, at fairly high decibels, of some of my favorite Replacements songs. The music was loud and full, bouncing off the walls and coming right at me, just like the Ping-Pong ball. The sound really filled up the space, and it filled me up with a wild range of emotions. Like, when "Alex Chilton" came on, I felt like dropping to the ground and firing off push-ups. And yet when "Skyway" played, I wanted to drop to the ground and sob uncontrollably.

At some point I looked over at my desk and saw my phone shaking, shivering, frantically moving around like a small, terrified animal. It was ringing too, but I couldn't hear it. The new speakers doing their job. I killed the music, let the Ping-Pong ball drop to the concrete for the first time in a while, and answered my phone.

"John Darvelle."

"Um, Mr. Darvelle? Um, hello, my name is Peter Caldwell."

This guy was a nervous wreck. I could tell after one sentence.

"Hi, Peter. What can I do for you?"

"I got your name from another lawyer I know. Um, let me back up. I'm a lawyer. But the other lawyer is Franklin Beverly."

I'd done some work for Franklin in the past. "Sure," I said. And then, again, "What can I do for you?"

"Well, I'm the lawyer for the estate of a woman named Muriel Dreen. Mrs. Dreen is old. Quite old. And she, well, she has an . . . *issue.* At first she didn't ask me to try and help, to try and figure out the problem. This kind of thing is really outside my duties as an estate lawyer . . ."

I thought, If I had a lawyer who had this much trouble getting to the point, I'd probably get rid of him. Or her. But that's just me.

"Peter," I interrupted. "Are you looking to hire me on behalf of Muriel Dreen?"

"Yes."

"Then let's meet in person so I can do two things: tell you how much I cost, and then, if we're in business, find out what's going on."

"Right. Great. Actually, that's what I was going to ask you. To see if you were willing . . . Um, Mrs. Dreen wants to tell you the situation herself. So can you come over? That is, if I give you the address, can you come over? I'm assuming you'll be able to find it, you know, if I give you the address."

I wondered, Is he done? Is he done with his rambling series of questions? And, more important, am I supposed to answer all of them?

Instead of doing that I just said, "Yes. Give me the address. I'll head over now."

I lowered and locked the big metal sliding door that is the entrance to my space—I keep it open almost any time I'm in my office—then got in my car and headed toward Beverly Hills. Muriel Dreen's house was in that section between the shopping area and the actual hills. The flatlands. The flatlands of the Hills. Oxymoronic. Or maybe just moronic. But a nice area, that's for sure. Big, wide streets lined with palms, a lot of older mansions that, while still quite large, don't take up too much of the lot. There's nothing more desperate-looking than a house too big for its lot. It's like, either fork out the dough to get a bigger lot, or build a house that actually fucking fits. You know what I mean? Man, seeing that, it upsets me. It really does. Anyway, as I was saying, there are no hills in this section of the Hills. You could see some up ahead, but right here? Flat as Kansas, babe.

I pulled into the semicircular driveway that sat in front of Muriel's large, cream-colored French château–style house. There was an old white Rolls parked in an open garage and a new BMW 3 Series parked in the semicircle. A man who looked to be about thirty-five got out. I summoned my greatest detective skills to determine that this was Peter.

I got out of my car and walked over to him. He stuck out his hand. "Peter Caldwell."

I nodded, and we shook.

He continued, "Thanks for coming over, Mr. Darvelle."

I thought about telling him to call me John but decided against it. It was fun to be called "mister" every now and then.

I looked at Peter. Thin and tall, maybe six-two, an inch taller than I am. But one of those people who, despite some height, stand kind of hunched over, permanently looking at the ground. He had sandy blond sort of messed-up hair, balding a bit, and a nervous, uncomfortable look in his eye. But a nice, sensitive, even hurt look in his eye as well. This was a decent guy, with manners. If you hired him, he'd probably do right by you. He'd be a stammering, indecisive wreck at times, and maybe drive you crazy eventually, but he'd probably do right by you.

Probably. In my line, it takes a whole lot more than a first impression to make me trust someone.

I liked him. For now. But, man, just visibly uncomfortable in his own skin. I pictured him unzipping himself, his skeleton stepping out of his body and then dancing around in front of me, smiling, moving its shoulders around, kicking its feet like it was at a hoedown, happy as hell to be freed from the prison that was Peter.

I think I smoked too much weed in college.

Peter looked at me and said, "Let's go meet Mrs. Dreen, okay? That's what Muriel prefers to be called, Mrs. Dreen."

He furrowed his brow a bit and then said, "Wait. We should talk about your fee—what you charge—first, right?"

"Right," I said.

I told him my rate and how I bill: by the hour. I told him what counts as a business expense and what doesn't: Dinner with someone I'm talking to on behalf of a client? Counts. Dinner at home during the course of an investigation? Doesn't count. I also told him what information I put on the actual invoice when I send it in: client's name, invoice number, date, amount. That's it.

As I went through my spiel, his eyes widened and he started nodding. His already-nervous expression was now exaggerated, which I hadn't thought possible.

When I was finished, he said—referring, I thought, to my rate—"Really?"

"Really," I said.

He nodded some more, and some light beads of sweat popped up on his already-furrowed brow. And then he just said, “Okay. Okay. Let’s go inside.”

He opened the front door of the house and we walked in to meet Mrs. Muriel Dreen.

2

Inside. An old-fashioned Beverly Hills mansion. Lots of beige and cream. A shiny, pristine piano in one room. A grandfather clock ticking loudly in another. Antiques everywhere. All the rooms we went through were clean and uncluttered and polished. But you got the feeling that no one had spent any actual time in them in years. And not just because there were vacuum tracks in the carpet. There was an eerie emptiness, a palpable stillness.

We got to a back room that most people would probably call the den. Peter went in first, I followed. The room was pretty small if you compared it to the other rooms we'd just walked through. But not small if you compared it to a similar room in a house in a neighborhood with a less desirable zip code. There was a large flat-screen TV in one corner broadcasting a stock-analysis-type show, but with the sound off. Some more antique-type furniture was neatly positioned around the room. There were little tables with pictures in silver frames on them. An olive green couch that perhaps had never been sat on lined one wall. And in the corner farthest from the doorway, a comfortable-looking navy blue chair housed Muriel Dreen.

She wore eyeglasses, a burgundy dress, a white cardigan over her shoulders, and deep blue shoes that matched the chair. I'm pretty sure she got everything from the Talbots catalog, maybe even the chair. She had the TV remote in her left hand and a lit cigarette in her right. On a little table next to her: a mostly empty ashtray, a Bic lighter, and a just-opened pack of Carltons.

"Mrs. Dreen," Peter said. "This is the detective. This is John Darvelle."

Muriel Dreen switched off the TV. Then she gave me a big, charming smile and said hello. She knew how to engage someone quickly. She'd probably done it a lot at fabulous parties when she was in her twenties and thirties, two or three hundred years ago.

She told me to have a seat on the couch and charmingly dismissed Peter. Then she just kind of stared at me, her big eyes magnified through the lenses of her thick glasses.

She stabbed her cigarette out in the ashtray, then grabbed the pack and tapped out a fresh one. She went through a whole ordeal of lighting it. She held the lighter up to the end longer than she needed to, and then she puffed and puffed, creating a big cloud of smoke in front of herself and getting a bright orange cherry going.

I just watched. It was, I'd say, mildly entertaining.

Finally she took a long, full drag, exhaled a roomful of blue smoke, and stared at me some more, with those exaggerated eyes and that charming and, I could now see, manipulative smile.

Seeing that the show was over, I put my hands up and said, "So, what's up?"

Quickly she said, "One of my workers has stolen from me."

"Okay," I responded cleverly. "Stolen what?"

"My engagement ring. It wasn't even that valuable, not like the tacky rings girls want today. But it was valuable to me. And that Heather stole it. I'm sure of it."

Man, that big, charming smile she'd shot me was gone. Her magnified eyes had narrowed to magnified slits, and her mouth had twisted into a viperlike sneer.

She continued. "Heather Press is her name. She tended to the plants before I fired her. A common little girl with a common little face. And a common thief too. She took my ring. I know she did. I filed a police report, and some policemen went over and talked to her, but they said Heather denied it and there wasn't anything else they could do. I don't think those policemen were very good at their jobs, because I know that common little girl took my ring. I *know* she did."

Just like that, Muriel had riled herself up. She was breathing heavily. Shifting a bit in her chair. Maybe even starting to perspire. And showing me through all this involuntary agitation that it wasn't so much the ring that she was upset about. It was that someone had defied her.

"Okay," I said. Man, I was really on a roll with the clever responses that day. "How do you know it was her? Don't you have other staff?" What I wanted to add was: Are you sure *you* didn't lose the ring? You know, because you're a hundred and twelve? I mean, look, Muriel—or Mrs. Dreen, as you prefer—I'm in my late thirties and I found my lost cell phone in the freezer the other day.

But I didn't add any of that. Instead I just asked the aforementioned, more respectable question.

She answered, "Because the rest of my staff has been with me for years, forever, so it had to be her. And it's not possible that I lost it, because I don't wear it. A few years after my husband, Inman, died—and Inman died ten years ago—I started keeping it in a box in a drawer in the dresser next to my bed. Close to my heart, you see. But not on my hand. So it's not as if the ring ever moved. It just sat in its box. Before it was taken—stolen, that is."

Hmm. She'd addressed the question I asked and a couple I hadn't. Those being: Do you wear it? And: Do you keep it somewhere specific when you aren't wearing it? Sharp as a tack, this nonagenarian appeared to be.

Right then a thought occurred to me, and I'm a little bit embarrassed to share it, but I'm going to anyway. Here's what I was thinking: What the fuck is this case? I'm getting hired by a little old lady to find her stupid ring that her gardener took? Excuse me, but I've solved murder cases that the cops couldn't figure out. In Los Fucking Angeles, no less. I'm not Encyclopedia Fucking Brown. I'm John Fucking Darvelle. But then I realized that that attitude is terrible. That's arrogance. And arrogance is what gets you in trouble.

Arrogance isn't just ugly, it's stupid. Because right when you start strutting around like a peacock, spreading your feathers and claiming you're too good for things—that's just the moment when you get burned. And the sting hurts twice as bad because you said you were too good for the thing that burned you in the first place. I'll be guilty of arrogance again at some point in my life, for sure. Maybe even pretty soon. I hope not, but maybe. But right now? I'm not going to let it get the best of me. Look, I'm not dying to investigate this case. But, bottom line, I'm a detective for hire. I was hired at my rate. I accepted the case. And now I was going to find out what happened to that fucking ring.

I said, "All right, Mrs. Dreen. You seem like you've thought this through. Why don't I go talk to Heather Press. If you're right, if she took your ring, I bet I can get it back."

"Oh, she took it, all right. You'll be able to see it written all over her common little face."

"Does Peter have a picture? A phone number? An address where I can pay her a visit?"

"Yes, he does, Mr. Darvelle."

Again with the "mister." Again, I let it ride.

"Great," I said. "I'll be in touch."

I got up, and even though her right hand was free—she was no longer using it to handle her smoke; she'd housed it in one of the ashtray slots a few seconds ago—she extended her left hand. You know when people do that? Maybe they're holding something in their right hand, or even have an injured right hand? Except she wasn't holding anything, and she didn't appear to be hurt. Maybe it was her way of exhibiting refinement or charm or something. I didn't know. Anyway, she held it almost like she wanted me to kiss it. I imagined myself getting down on one knee and giving her extended hand a soft, wet, almost erotic kiss. I have no idea why. Don't worry, I didn't do that. I just grabbed it and gave it a little shake. It was soft, fleshy, I could feel the loose skin under my thumb. And it was cold, just like those magnified eyes.

I walked out of the room and found Peter sitting in a chair just off the front foyer. He was looking out a window, trapped in some kind of daydream, I guessed. But then I noticed he wasn't daydreaming. He was looking at a squirrel nervously scurrying around a tree. The squirrel stopped on a dime—upside down, by the way, his claws stuck to the bark—and, while still sort of shaking all over, looked right at Peter. Did these two creatures see themselves in each other? Was Peter thinking, Man, my nervous disposition would sit better with me if I could just dart around a tree all day, collecting acorns? And was the squirrel thinking, Shit, sure I'm a trembling mess, but I could still get into the field of law with a specialty in estate management?

Peter, I think feeling my presence in the room, turned to look at me. Right then the squirrel, still upside down, craned its head up to look at me too.

I stood there face-to-face with not one but two shivering creatures, shivering like my cell phone earlier.

"Peter, I need a couple of things from you."

Instinctively he stood up and said, "Absolutely."

The squirrel took that as its cue to split, zipping down and out of my eyeline.

"Heather Press," I said. "What does she look like, what's her phone number, and where does she live?"

3

Heather Press lived not too far away, corner of Charleville and Elm, in a less high-dollar section of the Beverly Hills flatlands. Heather's section was rows of apartment buildings, eightplexes, tenplexes, twelveplexes, all packed in right next to one another just south of Wilshire. Still nice, treelined streets, not a lot of riffraff, very livable, just no mansions with white Rollses in their garages.

From Muriel Dreen's, I drove south down Rodeo Drive for kicks. I could have taken a less hectic street, but I wanted to look at all the spray-tanned, surgically altered people milling about, going in and out of the famous, fancy stores, dropping thousands. At one point I saw a lady walking along, with a little dog sticking out of her purse. Not so unusual for this crowd, but, thing is, the little dog had its own little purse. I was still marveling at this sight as I veered left onto Wilshire Boulevard, leaving Rodeo in my rearview.

Three minutes later I was at Heather Press's place. Nice little eightplex on the corner. Probably had good molding and hardwood floors. The lawn in front of the building was well manicured, but underneath the front left bay window was a full-on garden. It contained some bright flowers I didn't know the names of and some sort of exotic-looking plants, even a little row of tomatoes. And at the end, right by the door, some flowers I *did* know the name of. Some California poppies. Those small yellow cups with a hint of gold that, while far from rare, are quite fetching and very evocative of California.

My detective's intuition told me that this little garden belonged to Heather, because, you know, she was a *gardener.* I was really earning my money so far. A redbrick sidewalk took you up to the central entrance to her building. I parked my car across the street and down a bit, got out, hit the sidewalk. The door at the end of this charming little walk wasn't locked, so I went right in. Inside was a dark, carpeted alcove with an apartment door on the left, one on the right, and two just like it down the hall, and, I guessed, four matching ones up the stairs right in front of me.

From Peter, I knew that Heather lived in apartment A, and I now saw that A was the apartment to my immediate left, the one with the garden. Hey, I was right. But I have to tell you, you do have to be careful, because it's just that kind of assumption that trips you up in my game all the time. You go, She's a gardener, so the place with the garden *has* to be hers. And then it turns out not to be. And then you go, Shit, *really*? But this time I had confirmation. All right, moving on.

I knocked. Nobody home.

I walked back outside. I put my face right up to the front bay window. Nice Crate and Barrel–type apartment. Nobody inside sitting there petulantly, refusing to answer the door. I walked around to the side of the building and looked in the bedroom windows. Had to look through a crack in the blinds to discover—drumroll, please—nothing. Nobody home.

I went back around front, got in my car, and sat there.

What to do? What to do?

Call her? Nope. Won't recognize the number. Won't pick up. And even if she did, she might not answer my questions. And even if she did answer my questions, I wouldn't be able to read her. Also, she might not agree to see me today, and I wanted to see her today. Wanted to try something on this one that I thought might work. No. Not calling her. Might have to call her later, if she doesn't show up eventually. But not now. Not yet.

And then I thought: I know, I'll go get some lunch, then sit here and wait. Now that, *that*, is a plan. I walked over to Beverly Drive—not Beverly Boulevard, which is also close by, but Beverly Drive. It's very easy to mix up the two, even if you've lived here forever. Yes, it's annoying. And confusing. But either way, Beverly Drive was two blocks away and lined with a bunch of coffee shops and lunch spots, so it was for sure the place to go to complete my mission. I walked over, hit a little deli, and picked up a turkey-

and-Swiss with spicy mustard, mayo, lettuce, and pickles and a cold, canned Fresca. I know what you're thinking. Seriously, I really think I know what you're thinking: Was it Peach or Original Citrus? It was Original Citrus, unfortunately. Still delicious, but not truly sublime. Not that mix of citrus and peach that somehow tastes, in the best possible way, like baby aspirin. My Original Citrus Fresca was, however, ice-cold, so that worked. I walked back over to my car, got in, and took down the sandwich and the beverage.

And then I sat there. And waited. I put my seat back a bit. Yeah, might be a long wait. Music. Time for some music. I put on Cheap Trick's first album. I listened to "Hot Love" twice in a row, with some volume, then turned it down a bit and let the album play. I was at ease, relaxing a bit while on the job, enjoying the comfort of my still-pretty-new car. I lease a new car every three years or so. I always get random, borderline-generic American cars that nobody really notices. Helps in my line. Really does. Thing is, the cars I lease are still pretty nice, and, like I said, comfortable. Right now I'm driving a 2014 Ford Focus hatchback. You've rented one. Mine's Oxford White, which in plain English means: white. The Focus also comes in White Platinum, which in plain English also means: white. For some reason I love the fact that it's a hatchback. I'm not sure why. And I *really* love telling people that it has five doors. That is the highlight of my day every time someone asks me how many doors my car has. Which is rare. But it does happen.

Two hours later a new pickup truck, with a woman

behind the wheel, drove right by me. The driver didn't notice me or my Oxford White Ford Focus. As the truck slid by, then disappeared into the alley behind Heather's apartment, I noticed some gardening tools in the bed of the truck. About a minute later, a young woman who looked an awful lot like the driver of the truck walked around from the back of the building and headed up the little path I'd been on a couple of hours earlier. She was wearing a white T-shirt, shorts, bright blue socks, and brown work boots. She had a backpack over one shoulder that made her tilt, just slightly, to one side. I liked her outfit, liked her style.

I quickly got out of the Focus and walked over.

When the woman had just about reached the main entrance I said, "Hello. Excuse me. Heather?"

She turned to look at me. She was probably forty, attractive, tan from working outside, dyed-blond hair tied up, and pretty, catlike green eyes. Her face held the emotional scars of a tough childhood, disappointment, parents who made her unsure and uneasy. It made her more attractive. Was it a common little face? A little, perhaps, but I realized now that that was just Muriel Dreen insulting Heather in a way that Heather couldn't really defend against. Muriel was wellborn and Heather wasn't. It was a fact, not defendable, really, so Muriel used it to hurt her. Bitch.

Heather said, "Yes?"

She was smiling. She wasn't worried. Maybe she was used to being approached as she worked outside, by people who wanted to hire her or ask her about plants. Or maybe she just wasn't that freaked out by a stranger saying hello. I hoped it was the latter.

"Hi, Heather. My name is John Darvelle. I'm a detective. I was hired by your old boss, Muriel Dreen. She thinks you stole a ring from her."

Very quickly, almost without missing a beat, she smiled in a knowing way and said, "Oh god, this again?"

"Yes. This again. Except this time, it's not going to be a couple of tired cops looking through your drawers, not finding the ring, then closing the case. It's going to be me figuring out what happened."

It came out hot. Which is what I wanted.

She frowned and shrunk into herself a bit and said, "What does that mean?"

It was a curious response. It wasn't: There's *nothing* to figure out. It was: What does that *mean*? It was a good question. I liked it.

I softened my tone and said, "I'll explain. But first, here."

I took out my wallet. I showed her my detective's license and my driver's license. I handed them both to her. She looked at them quizzically and then handed them back.

I said, "So here's what it means. Heather, if you took that ring, I'm going to find out. If it's hidden around here somewhere, I'll find it. If you sold it, I'll figure out who you sold it to. But I doubt you would have done that. Maybe, but I doubt it. Too soon. Paper trail.

"Anyway, it's not going to be like when the cops came by. With a case like this, they just want to check a box and go back to the station house. With or without the ring. But more important, they have to play by rules that I sometimes don't have to play by. Like, I can break into your house when you're not home. Or I can break into your truck when you're at Home Depot, buying some new gloves or something. And I would do that. I will do that. And then I have ways to make it look like nothing illegal ever happened. Or I'll just tell the cops—who I know, by the way—my version of the story. You know what I'm saying? *My* version of the story.

"But I don't want to do any of that. Because if I do, in the end you'll get in trouble. Maybe serious trouble. And I don't really want that. You seem like a nice person. I don't know, there's just something about you. I'm on your side. I'm not sure why, but I'm on your side. People do things they shouldn't do. Like steal rings. And sometimes—not all the time, but *sometimes*—those people deserve a pass. So if you did steal it, just give it to me. You won't get in trouble. I will make sure you don't get in trouble. I promise. Muriel Dreen won't even know you took it. But if you did steal it and you don't give it to me, I will find it. I *will* find it. And in this version of the story, you *will* get in trouble. I promise that too. Okay? I just want to be done with this. I want to go back to my office. I've got a Ping-Pong table in it, and some really good speakers. I like being there. And I want you to be able to go back to your job too. I want you to be able to go make some other mean old lady's yard look nicer."

After a long pause she smiled and said, "You've definitely met Mrs. Dreen."

"Yeah," I said.

Then, after another long pause, perhaps she was thinking of her next move, she said, "I need to put this bag down."

She took the backpack off her shoulder and put it on the bricks right in front of the main door. Then she looked at me again. Thinking. Thinking about what to do. I was pretty sure of it now.

I said, pointing to the California poppies in her garden, "Those are California poppies."

She smiled and said, "Very good!" I think she was glad that I had a tiny bit of knowledge about her field, and that I was helping her kill some time. But I think, I really think, it was more the former.

"It's the state flower, right?"

"That's right. Do you know what the other yellow flowers are called, the ones with the black center next to the tomatoes?"

"I do not. I'm afraid I've given you most of my flower knowledge."

"They're called black-eyed Susans."

"I've known a few of those."

"Ha," she said. "They're pretty, but I like the name more than I like the flower."

She kneeled down and adjusted a few of the black-eyed Susans. Untangled them a bit to make them look more presentable. Then she stood up and looked at me again. Thinking. Thinking again.

"The ring," I said.

Without directly addressing what I'd just said, she asked, "Do you want to talk inside?"

"Yeah, sure."

She grabbed her bag and we went in the main door. Outside her apartment door she said, "Do you mind taking off your shoes?"

"No problem." I took off my brand-new black Adidas running shoes and put them by the door. She took off her boots and did the same. And we walked in. Her apartment was astonishingly clean. I mean absolutely perfect. And she must have done it herself. She wouldn't have a staff like Muriel Dreen.

She said, "Would you like something to drink?"

"Do you have any beer? Like, Bud Light? Coors Light? That type of beer?"

"Really?" she asked.

I couldn't tell if she was saying "Really?" because now this stranger in her house was asking for alcohol. Or because it was only about three in the afternoon. Or because of the kind of beer I preferred. Light, cheap, American. As opposed to, you know, a pumpkin amber ale with hints of pine made by a guy with a three-foot beard in his backyard in Portland.

So I just said, "Yeah."

Heather walked from the main room through a little dining room, into her kitchen.

I sat down, carefully, on the very clean, cement-colored couch.

Heather reappeared with a bottle of Bud Light. Before, I had been pretty sure I liked her. Now I was certain. She sat down in a chair across from me.

I said, "This might be the cleanest apartment I've ever seen."

"I like to clean," she said.

And I thought: That really is the trick. Learn to like things you're not supposed to like. Learn to embrace them, enjoy them.

I took a big swig of the beer. It was cold, light, delicious. I wanted to have eleven of them and listen to Heather tell me more about her apartment-cleaning concepts.

She said, finally ready to talk, to address what I'd said, "I have a question. You think I took Mrs. Dreen's ring. Otherwise you wouldn't have said all that stuff. Why do you think I took it?"

"I don't know," I said. "Why did you?"

"Ha," she said, for the second time since I'd met her. "That's not what I meant. I meant . . . You know what I meant."

I took my third sip of the beer, almost finishing it. "Truth is, Muriel's the one who convinced me. The ring doesn't move, so she didn't misplace it, and the rest of her staff has been there a while. Simple, but it makes sense. I think she's right. I think you took it."

"Well, because I don't really want you to break into my house or my truck, let's say she's right and you're right. Would I really not get into trouble?"

"You really would not. I'd return it to Muriel and Peter, and I wouldn't tell them that it was you who took it. I'd tell them something else."

"Why? Why would you do that?"

"Because that's the deal we're making."

"Hmm," she said.

"Why don't you give me the ring, Heather."

She looked at me. She stared at me. And then she smiled and held the smile on her face for a long, long time. I think she was contemplating again, maybe for the final time, whether she could trust me. I got the feeling that she had trusted people before and it hadn't worked out all that well.

"Okay," she said. "Follow me."

We got up and walked out the door into the little central alcove. We put our shoes back on and went back outside.

Heather walked into the garden beneath her bay window. She dug her hand down into the soil next to one of the tomato plants and pulled out a small plastic ziplock bag. She walked back over to the sidewalk where I was, then brushed the soil off the bag, opened it up, and pulled out the ring. She handed it to me. I looked at it. A square diamond, emerald cut, I think, about one and a half carats, with deep blue triangular sapphires on either side of it.

I had to side with Muriel Dreen on this one. It was pretty. Classic. Classy.

Heather Press said, "The police didn't look in the garden."

"The place that makes the most sense, yet somehow is ignored. There's some kind of poetry to that."

She didn't respond. She just looked at me again. Giving me the green cat eyes, her mouth now a straight, serious line. And her face now saying "I trusted you" as she said, "I'm not going to get in trouble."

It was a statement, not a question. But it was still a question.

"Scout's honor," I said.

I'd never been a Boy Scout. I just said that for some strange reason. You ever do that? Just say a saying that you never really say, or maybe have never said even once? It just basically emerges out of freaking nowhere and it feels weird coming out of your mouth and sounds even weirder? Have you ever done that? You've done that. What is that?

I looked at Heather and said, "Thank you. For the beer . . ." I held up the ring. "And for this."

She nodded. I turned, walked over to the Focus, and got in. I buckled up, then cranked her up. Then I looked to my left, and there was Heather's face. Inches away from mine, framed by my window. I powered it down.

"You know how you asked me why I took the ring?"

"Yeah."

"Well, I think I know why. Muriel Dreen is the meanest person I've ever met. She's so mean to all the people who work for her. All the people who have been there *forever*, as she likes to say. And she was mean to me too. She would threaten to not pay me. And, see, she always talked about her ring. She would go on and on about how tacky everyone is nowadays, and for some reason she would always bring it back to how tacky everyone's engagement rings are today and how her beloved engagement ring from Inman was the kind of ring a classy girl gets. And she'd say it to me like I was the kind of girl who would never get a ring like that. I've never stolen anything in my life. It was an impulse. Just this out-of-the-blue impulse. I thought if I took her ring . . ."

I looked at her. Her face darkened with shame. But also defiance. And the beautiful vulnerability I'd seen right when I met her.

She continued, "I thought if I took her ring it would hurt her. Hurt her back. For hurting her staff all the time. And for hurting me."

I nodded and said, "She won't know you took it."

She nodded just a little bit, and I said, "Bye, Heather."

I powered up my window and took off, headed for the Dreen house, Muriel's ring sitting in the empty cup holder next to the one holding my empty Fresca can.

4

I called Peter Caldwell and said I was headed back to the house. He said he was running an errand but that he'd head back too. I got there first, then waited thirteen minutes for Peter to pull up in his BMW. Outside the front door, I told Peter I had an idea and that I wanted to look in Muriel's bedroom. He nervously agreed, then escorted me inside.

We walked through the house to the bedroom. I went over to the dresser next to the bed, the one that had housed the ring. I put my hands on top of the dresser and gave it a long, pensive stare. Then I got down on the floor and looked underneath it. I scooted my whole body over and looked underneath the bed. Unlike most beds, there was nothing, nothing, underneath it. No dust. No spare blankets or linens. No boxes filled with old, cracked coat hangers and half-filled photo albums. Nothing. I reached my arm way back under the bed and then, in a dramatic show, got my head, and then the whole top half of my body, under there too. Then I reverse-scooted out, stood up, opened my hand, and showed Peter the ring.

"There you go," I said. "Under the bed. Problem solved. Case closed."

"I don't understand. You're saying you just found the ring under there?"

"That's right."

"Um, Mr. Darvelle, we looked everywhere in here. Including under the bed. The ring wasn't there."

I handed the ring to Peter. "Didn't look hard enough."

On the way out, we walked by the den, Muriel's room. I poked my head in. She was in her chair, sitting just like she had been when I was talking to her, only now she was asleep. Her magnified eyes were closed behind glass.

Even asleep, she looked . . . *mean.*

Outside, as I was getting into the Focus, Peter said, "Mrs. Dreen's not going to believe this story."

"Well," I said. "*That's* the story. Okay? I'm going to go home, write up an invoice, print it out, and mail it to you."

Snail mail. Better than e-mail. For invoices in my line, anyway.

Peter looked at me for a long time with those nervous but kind eyes and said, "Okay."

"Want to give me your card so I know where to send the invoice?"

Peter reached for his wallet.

Back in the Focus, back on the road. It was a terrible time to be driving in Los Angeles. Five bells. If you're on the road at this time in L.A. you're either a rookie or an idiot.

I thought, I have three choices. One, fight traffic and go to my office in Culver City. Two, fight traffic and go to my house in Mar Vista, which was a bit farther away. Three, go park somewhere and just sit in my Focus and wait. And fume. Fume in the Focus.

I chose option one, but with an asterisk. I'd take some pro-level side streets and try to beat the system. Which I did, sort of. By taking Beverly Drive into Beverlywood and winding through that perfectly nice, but a tad random, neighborhood sitting just south of Beverly Hills. I popped out the back of it onto Venice Boulevard, then stuck out a few depressing, stifling sections of traffic until I was free and clear in the warehouse district of Culver City.

Back at my desk, highly proud of myself for getting there reasonably unscathed, I wrote up my invoice, printed it out, envelope-d it, addressed it, stamped it, and put it on my desk to send out tomorrow. I still hadn't burned enough time to drive home in peace, not really even close, so I just sat there. Put my feet up on my desk and sat there.

As I mentioned, I work out of a warehouse, a pretty nice-sized one. Before it was mine, a movie producer used it to store a couple of midlife-crisis cars, thus the aforementioned cinder-block walls, slick concrete floor, and big sliding door. Late afternoon is one of my favorite times to have it open. Cool air coming in; slanting, fading sunlight reflecting off the floor; the lot out in front of me that people use to access the other warehouses going from a sparse few folks to almost none.

Inside my space, I've got my desk, two chairs in front of it, two filing cabinets behind it, a sink, a bathroom, a little fridge, a coffeemaker, and, most important, an electric-blue Stiga indoor-only Ping-Pong table.

And before you ask: yes, there's enough room *around* the table to actually play. One of the things you see all the time, drives me crazy, is a Ping-Pong table stuck in a space without enough room around it. To properly play Ping-Pong, you have to be able to back up, away from the table, significantly. To properly defend shots. To properly position yourself for certain swings. And if you can't do that, if that's not an option, then it's not really Ping-Pong. It would be like having no room behind the baseline of a tennis court. That wouldn't be tennis. It would be some other form of cramped bullshit. Which would be a good name for what so many people end up playing when they think they are playing Ping-Pong: Cramped Bullshit Ping-Pong.

The other thing you should know about my Ping-Pong table is that I never use it as a table-table. I never empty my pockets and put the contents on it. I never put beverages on it, unless I'm playing beer pong, of course. Which I actually play later on in this story. But anyway, I never sit and eat at it, either. When I see any of this behavior, you know, when I walk into a house and see a bunch of shit on top of someone's table—bills, keys, a cookie, clothes, I swear, *clothes*—and I see this a lot—I always think: That is a fucking crime. And I often say to the perpetrators of that crime: Have a little goddamn respect.

Moving on. Like I said, I was back at my office, sitting there at my desk, waiting for traffic to die down, feet up, kind of scanning my space, just thinking a bit about the little case I'd been on.

When my phone rang.

I looked at the caller ID: the Los Angeles Police Department. For a split second I thought, Did Muriel Dreen call the cops because she doubted my story? Did Heather Press call the cops because I told her that if she didn't give me the ring I'd use some unorthodox tactics to find out whether she had it? Nah, highly doubtful on both counts.

Far more likely they just wanted something. I work with the police department from time to time. And I know quite a few of the cops around town, as I'd explained to Heather Press. And I think that some of them are good at their jobs. Quite good. Certainly not all of them, not even close, but some of them. And I'm even moderately friendly with a few of them. All that being said, I like to give all of them, every last one of them, a little shit from time to time.

Which is why I answered the phone. "Yes?"

"Darvelle, this you?"

"It is."

"It's Ott. You got a second?"

Homicide detective Mike Ott. One of the ones who are good at their jobs. And one of the ones who I like, in a we'll-never-hang-out-socially kind of way. Ott and I have crossed paths quite a few times over the years, most recently on a murder case involving a famous movie director and a high-concept crime ring.

I said, with over-the-top glee, "For you? Of course!"

"Listen. I have some business for you. You interested in taking a case?"

"Yep," I said. "I am."

"All right, you want to come down tomorrow? I'll tell you about it. Give you the case file."

"You want to tell me anything about it now?"

"No. I'm busy. And it's not a rush. It's cold. Been cold for a while. Unsolved murder. Family wants it investigated further and we don't have the men."

Notice how he left out the part where they'd looked into it and come up empty? I did. But I wasn't going to mention that. Not this time. The guy was throwing me business. Sometimes I know when to shut up.

Sometimes.

"Okay," I said. "Tomorrow when?"

"Let me think. You live in Mar Vista. So if I were to ask you to come at 8 a.m., it would be almost impossible for you to avoid sitting in the worst kind of fucking traffic. Which I know you don't like."

Did I mention that some of the cops like to throw shit back at me as well? You give it, you got to take it.

I said, "I'm assuming you're about to say 8 a.m.?"

"That's why I'm giving you this business, Darvelle. You're a pretty good detective. Eight a.m. My desk."

"Great," I said. "Thank you, Mike. I'll see you at eleven."

And I hung up.

And then I thought about the old lady, the plant lady, and the ring again. Maybe taking a case that I wasn't all that interested in had somehow led to me getting this one.

Because sometimes getting going, even in the smallest way, opens up a cosmic window for something bigger to happen. Interesting how that occurs. You know? Whatever field you're in, when you just do *something*, anything, when you just get started, you are pushing a big inert rock, the big invisible wheel of momentum.

The two things don't even need to be tightly connected. You start organizing your office and the phone rings. You're on a case and you can't think of a theory to explain what's happening, so you throw out a first-thought idea, maybe even a terrible, nonsensical one. And then a decent idea pops into your head. You don't have an interesting case on your desk, so you take a not-so-interesting one. And then you get a call from Mike Ott about a murder the cops couldn't crack.

Yeah, you're giving the big rock a little nudge, a little push, and before you know it, it starts to roll down the hill. I wondered, if you looked at specific examples, whether the second things, the better things, actually only appeared if you engaged with the first things. Do you always have to somehow, even if just with an obscure action, press start on the Cosmic Momentum Wheel? Sitting there, I just didn't know the answer to that one. Might need to think about it a little more. What I did know was that I probably wasn't going to get to the bottom of it right then and there. I also knew that I could probably drive home now in relative peace.

So I got up, cut the lights, and cut out of there.

I got in the Focus and headed off the lot. Right at the point where you leave the lot proper but are still technically on the lot, there's a streetlight that kicks on automatically at dusk. It was on now, but because there was still some light in the sky, the beam coming out of it was weaker than it would be later. Sitting underneath it, and glowing just a bit because of the weak light, was a new gray Mercedes S-Class, one of the big-dog Benzes. It sat with its grille pointing conspicuously at the lot's exit. Under a spotlight of sorts, nothing covert about it. I drove—slowly—right in front of it. I looked through its windshield. There was a man sitting behind the wheel. An older man. Mid-, or maybe even late, fifties. He had dark hair slicked back, a trimmed salt-and-pepper goatee, and glasses. Big gold frames, with maybe just the slightest tint of bronze to them.

I looked right at him. I could only just see his eyes behind not one but two walls of glass. He looked right at me. *Stared* right at me. Expressionless.

I wondered, driving home, Was that guy there for me? Again I had one of the thoughts I'd considered when I'd seen "LAPD" on my phone: Muriel Dreen. Sitting there with her ring but not happy with the story that came with it. So she sends someone to look into me. Possible. More likely than her calling the cops about it . . . Or was it something to do with an old case? Somebody sent back to fuck with me? Wouldn't be the first time. Or did this guy in the Mercedes have something to do with my *new* case, the one I hadn't even gotten yet, the one I'd just talked to Mike Ott about? Stranger things have happened. Information travels fast.

Or was it just *nothing*? Just a guy sitting on a lot full of warehouses, minding his own business?

Somehow I doubted that.

5

The next morning after a nice, mostly traffic-free drive, I got to the downtown Los Angeles police station around 10:45. I went up to the detectives' floor and told a tired, cynical female police officer who I was and that I was there to see Mike Ott.

"You have an appointment?"

"Yep. It's for eleven."

She picked up a phone, got Ott on the line, told him that a man named John Darvelle was here for his eleven o'clock.

I mouthed to the officer, "Tell him I'm early."

She ignored me. Then hung up. "Ott says you're three hours late. He's not available now. You're going to have to wait. Sit over there."

She pointed me to an area in front of her desk but also off in a corner that could only be described as cripplingly depressing. Two little blue grammar-school-style chairs, both with cracks in them, and that's it. No coffeemaker. No coffee table. No out-of-date magazines. Nothing.

But I'd known that Ott would make me wait. I was prepared for it. So I went over and sat down in one of the little blue chairs, then pulled out a book I had brought, a book I had already read, a book I like to reread from time to time. It's called *Sizzling Chops and Devilish Spins.* It's a book about Ping-Pong and how to get better at it. I read it for about fifteen minutes, then peered over the top of it and said meekly to the officer, "Can I get some water in a small paper cup?"

She glared at me.

Thirty-seven minutes after that, the officer said to me, "Ott's ready. You can go on back. You know where he sits?"

"I'll just look for the perfect hair."

Truth is, I did know where he sat. I'd been there lots of times. I walked behind the officer's desk, then back through the detectives' floor until I found him. He was on the phone, but he motioned for me to sit down.

Detective Mike Ott was fifty-three. And he did, in fact, have one of those heads of hair that just defy logic. Gray now, but thick, literally as thick as the hair on the head of a teenager. It pissed me off. I looked at the sharp part running down his head, a plethora of hair going one way, a plethora of hair going the other way. I thought, He's probably one of those guys who has a comb at his house. I've literally never used a comb. These days, I zip my hair down with a head shaver to about a half inch all over. Keeps my receding hairline looking tight, as opposed to the other option: sickly and sad. But even before my Oster head shaver became one of my closest friends, I still never used a comb. A brush, maybe, or my hands, but never a comb. Not once.

I watched Ott finish up his call. Below the hair was a face carved out of stone, a face made up of right angles, with smallish gray eyes and bone-dry skin made even drier and older-looking by years of stress and smoking.

He hung up the phone. "You're late."

"I was early. Got here at 10:45."

"You know, I know I asked you to be here early, which was inconvenient for you. But, bottom line, I'm giving you business and you're still a pain in the ass."

Ott looked at me for a long time with that strong but tired stone face. I didn't say anything. I didn't defend myself against his accusation. I just sat there. Eventually he picked up a big file on his desk. "Here's the situation."

He didn't open the file. He put it back on his desk and continued. "Case is over a year old. Well over. Fifteen, sixteen months. You may remember it. It got a little press. Short version is this: Rich guy walks out of his house in Hollywood one morning, about to get into his car, takes a bullet to the chest. Bullet came out of a pistol from seventy-five, eighty yards away. Guy drops dead. Now, that kind of kill shot isn't a heat-of-the-moment thing, some kind of goddamn blowup argument, or anything random. You know that. One shot with a pistol, from a stakeout point pretty darn far away. Premeditated murder. And not easy to pull off.

"Anyway, we looked into it carefully. Turns out, this guy was the worst kind of little shit. A rich asshole who spent his life letting people down and shitting all over everyone. So initially, we thought we'd have plenty of possibilities right off the bat. Thing is, though, everyone in his world, all the people you talk to when somebody gets it, had alibis. Interestingly, and maybe because they had alibis, none of the people in his world was particularly shy about being truthful about the dead man's character. His family barely liked him. Nobody seemed to be hiding anything with respect to their feelings. Well, his parents didn't outright *say* he was a shit. But most of the people we talked to said what I just said. Guy was a shit. So, again, you have all these people who openly didn't like the guy, who had been wronged by him, whatever, so you'd think we'd find a suspect, right? But no. Everybody's story was airtight. Airtight. We never named a suspect. Case went cold."

"I remember this," I said. "He had a pretentious name. Keagon. Keaton."

"Yeah. That's it. Keaton. Keaton Fuller."

"Okay. What else?"

"As I mentioned on the phone, family wants the investigation to continue. But I got to tell you, Darvelle—"

I interrupted, "You've got about three hundred more murders to look into now, and those have a chance of being solved."

He gave me his stone face. "Yeah. That's right." He picked up the file again. "You still want it? Family's open to a private guy. And believe me, they've got the money to pay you."

"Yeah," I said.

He slid the file over toward me. "The parents' names and number are in there. Call them and tell them I referred you."

He stood up. I stood up.

"All right," he said.

We shook hands. I said, "Your niece is an actress, right?"

"Off-fucking-limits, Darvelle."

"No, no. She having any luck?"

"Not really."

"Think I can help. Can probably get her a speaking role on a network show. Buddy of mine's a big TV director. You got a number for her?"

He looked at me. For a brief moment I pictured myself with a hammer and a chisel, chipping away at his concrete face like a sculptor, eyeing my work, chunks of slatelike concrete falling off his face and crashing to the floor. I have no idea why.

Ott plucked a gold Cross pen from the pocket of his suit jacket. He then produced his little spiral notebook from the same pocket, wrote down his niece's name and number, and ripped out the page. He handed it to me.

"Done," I said.

I thought he was going to smile. But I was wrong.

6

I took the case file back to my office. I sat at my desk, slider open, the sun slanting in and popping off the slick blue surface of my Ping-Pong table.

Keaton Albert Fuller, thirty-five, had been shot once in the chest by a Smith & Wesson M&P nine-millimeter handgun. From seventy-five yards away, as Ott had mentioned. The "M&P" stands for "military and police." And a lot of military and police use the weapon. In fact, it's the pistol issued to the LAPD. That being said, it's also available to the general public, and the part of the general public that buys guns seems to like it. A lot. It's one of the best-selling guns on the market.

At 6 a.m. Keaton Fuller had been walking to his car,

when he was shot. His clothing suggested that he had been on his way to the gym.

Keaton's house was in the Hollywood Hills, just a few blocks above the Sunset Plaza section of Sunset Boulevard. An expensive part of town. A lot of celebs live there. And a lot of celebs, wannabe celebs, and people who want to soak in the Hollywood scene in a somewhat obvious, somewhat bridge-and-tunnel way kick around the coffee shops, bars, and restaurants in the area.

The two lead detectives on the case, Rick Harrier and Michelle Martinez, determined that the shooter had been positioned just slightly higher up in the Hills than Keaton's place, in a little clearing off the side of Rising Glen Road, which starts at Sunset Boulevard and twists up the mini-mountain. Crime-scene pictures showed a clear shot right down to Keaton Fuller's driveway.

Harrier and Martinez had interviewed the following people extensively: Fuller's parents, Jackie and Phil; his brother, Greer—yes, definitely also a pretentious name; his ex-girlfriend Sydney Scott, formerly Sydney Frost, who was now married to a man named Geoff Scott; and a former business partner named Craig Helton. They had also talked to a handful of other people less extensively.

As Ott had said, all of them had alibis, airtight alibis, and most of their statements were not particularly sensitive. Keaton, according to everyone but his parents, was a shit.

I looked at a picture of him premurder. Straight, dark hair that he wore kind of long. Blue eyes. And a pretty big guy. The picture was only the top half of him, but I knew from the file that he was just under six feet, so I filled in the rest of him in my mind. He wasn't fat but just sort of soft all over, fleshy looking. Interesting, I thought, that he'd been headed to the gym when he was shot. Maybe he was one of those guys who go to the gym all the time but never seem to get much done. But that softness—it was especially pronounced in his face. He had a little double chin that sat underneath a smug smile, and there was a smug, contemptuous look in his eye.

I put down the picture and called the number for Jackie and Phil Fuller.

"Hello," a cautiously friendly woman's voice said.

"Hi, is this Jackie Fuller?"

"Yes, who's calling?"

"My name is John Darvelle. I'm a private investigator. Detective Mike Ott, with the LAPD, contacted me and told me you were looking for some private help to investigate the murder of your son."

Her voice dropped to a near whisper. "Yes, that's right."

"Would you like to talk? In person?"

"Yes. Would tomorrow work for you? I realize tomorrow is Saturday, but my husband isn't home from work right now and I'd like him to be here when we talk."

"Tomorrow's fine."

I like working on Saturdays. When you work on Saturday, there's an energy present that says: Nobody's working today. In fact, the notion of *you're not supposed to work on Saturday* has essentially been hammered into us. So when you do, it's almost as if everyone around you is frozen. Not literally. People are moving, of course, going to the beach, hitting yoga classes, even *working* on little personal projects, puttering around the house, maybe screwing in a fresh lightbulb or two. But they're not working-working. So when you *do* work on Saturday, it can be quite freeing, even energizing. You've got the day to yourself, and because no one else is doing much, the feeling of progress intensifies. Add to that, people aren't usually calling you, annoying you. You've got this uninterrupted pocket. You've got hours and hours gifted to you. It's like you're stealing time.

"Thank you," Jackie Fuller said. "What time works for you?"

"Any time."

We settled on noon. Jackie Fuller told me that she and Phil lived in Hancock Park, then gave me her exact address.

"See you tomorrow," I said. And hung up.

I called my friend Gary Delmore. Gary's a TV director. A big one. Directs all sorts of shows for all sorts of networks. He's done really, really well in that world. And he's made a dump-truckful of money.

He's also very openly decided to be a lifelong bachelor and use his Hollywood clout to "date" as many actresses, and other attractive women who just might be impressed with his success, as he possibly can before he dies. He's forty-six, tan, and has big, sort of eighties hair and too-white teeth. He's a walking midlife crisis. And he'd be the first to tell you that. And that's why Gary's great. He knows who he is. We hang out from time to time. When we do, it usually involves beer and Ping-Pong. He beat me once. That fact annoys me to an astonishing degree. And that fact gives him an astonishing amount of pleasure. The other thing that's usually involved when it comes to me and Gary is insults. Specifically, insulting each other. We enjoy doing that for some reason.

"Gary, what's happening?"

"The Darv is calling. To what do I owe this distinct pleasure?"

"Oh, before I get to why I'm calling . . . you're not in the middle of a spray tan, are you?"

"Nope."

"Teeth whitening?"

"No again."

"Are you sleeping with a woman who's only interested in you to advance her career?"

"Not right now, no. I will later, but I'm not currently doing that."

"Great. Then you can talk."

"Well, I am in the middle of something. I'm at a toupee store. Looking at a couple of models I think would be good for you."

"I don't need a toupee," I said with a hint, just a hint, of actual defensiveness. "That's why I have a barbershop-level head shaver. When I zip it down, it looks good."

"As good as it can. But I'm looking at a number here I think would look real nice on you. It's called the Ferret."

"Ha," I said. Had to give Delmore that one.

Gary said, "So, what's up?"

"Need a favor. Can you give a part to the niece of a cop

friend of mine? Just a line or something in a show. I owe him one. His niece is a young actress. Probably mid-, late twenties or so. She needs a break."

"Um. Is she *talented*?" Gary added a salacious spin to the word "talented."

"Off-limits. If you sleep with this girl, this guy, her uncle, will shoot me. He literally will. He will sacrifice his badge, his career, his life, and shoot me. He already wants to shoot me. You bang his niece and it will happen."

"Then I might do it just for that."

"I walked into that."

"Yeah, you did. But Darv, truth is, I can't just promise you that I can give this girl a line. I'm going to have to audition her. She has to have some actual talent. I know you like to tell me how bad some of the shows I direct are, but at the end of the day you have to have talent to get a part in one of them."

"Gary. You're currently directing a show that stars MC Hammer as a preschool teacher."

And he was. It was called *Grammar Time!!!* And yes, there are three exclamation points in the actual title.

I continued, "I mean, let's face it, I know some of the shows you do are good. But a lot of them—we're not exactly talking about *Apocalypse Now.*"

"Listen. I'm on set—"

"I thought you were at a toupee store."

"I left and came to set. And while I'd love to listen to you insult me some more, I've got to go print some money while you follow around some guy's wife who's banging her tennis pro. Text me the girl's info. I'll get her in something."

"Thank you, sir. I appreciate it. And you will not sleep with her. Right?"

"I will most likely not sleep with her."

That would have to do for now.

I hung up, sat at my desk, looked out onto the lot, head still, eyes not really focusing on anything, almost in a trance. I'd say that about seven minutes later the trance was broken. The gray Mercedes sedan that had been sitting at the exit to my lot the evening prior appeared, pulling right up in front of my office. The big grille was pointing at me once again. The car wasn't technically in a space; those were around the corner from the entrance—my spot was there, and a couple of guest spots. No, the Mercedes sat rudely right in front of me like it might lurch forward and come at me. It was staring at me, threatening me.

I didn't like it.

The same man I'd seen behind the wheel the night before got out of the driver's side. The slicked-back hair, the goatee, the big, bronze-tinted glasses. I was able to see now that he was on the short side, maybe five-six. He was in pressed gray pants, Gucci loafers, a crisp white shirt, and a thin, expensive-looking brown leather jacket.

The guy who got out of the passenger side of the car was definitely not on the short side. He was large, very large. I'd say six-six. And big, muscular. In jeans, black biker boots, and a white V-neck T-shirt. He had dirty blond, semicurly, longish hair. Nineties hair.

The two men shut their doors simultaneously. I heard the car doors lock and the alarm engage as they walked into my office.

I looked at the older man. Again, no expression. None.

I looked at the big guy. One of his eyes sat just a bit higher in his head than the other. It gave him an inbred, psychotic look.

The older man said, "John Darvelle?"

"Yep."

The older man continued to give me his expressionless expression. The big guy didn't give me much more. A faraway but wild-eyed, almost ravenous, stare.

These two had confirmed who I was.

But I wouldn't say they were glad to see me.

7

The two men walked over to my desk and sat down in the two chairs in front of it. The older man to the right. The big guy to the left.

The older man said, his monotone voice mirroring his expression, "John. I'm Tony Lewis."

I didn't respond.

The big guy didn't introduce himself.

Tony kept talking. "You just did a job for Muriel Dreen. I've known Mrs. Dreen a long time. I sometimes help her out with things. Used to help her husband out too. He was in real estate. Inman. Good man."

He stopped talking. I could mostly see his eyes behind the bronze. He was thinking, contemplating his next sentence, or his next move.

I still didn't respond. Verbally, anyway. The blood in my body, however, began moving around more rapidly.

The older man eventually said, "John, Mrs. Dreen has lived in this town a long time. Her whole life. That's more than eighty years. She's a *very* respected woman. She has a lot of influence. Don't fuck with her, John."

Tony Lewis stared at me.

And still—I didn't respond.

I could feel my heartbeat thumping a bit in my ears.

He continued, "Mrs. Dreen thinks you lied to her about where you found her ring. Nobody likes to be lied to, John. Muriel Dreen especially. I think you lied too. So what really happened? With the ring? You went over to the girl's house and what happened? The girl had it, right? She gave it to you. That's what happened. You need to tell me that. Because the girl can't get away with it. It wouldn't be right. Now, if you tell me the truth, we can tell the proper authorities and move on. But if you don't tell me the truth . . ." He paused and said, "I'll make you tell me the truth."

The way he kept saying "the girl" gave his flat, emotionless delivery a sinister quality. It was clinical, inhuman. Like he could discard her, or anyone, without giving it much thought. Dump a body in a creek, then brush off his hands, brush off his pants, get in his car, drive off, go have dinner.

I looked at Tony Lewis and said, "I told Peter Caldwell what happened. That's what happened."

Now it was Tony Lewis not responding. He just looked at me, I at him. I believed he was a tough guy. I could see him scaring somebody who got in Muriel's way. I could see him, back in the day, making sure Inman got his money after some fucked-up shady real estate deal. Tony was small, but he had confidence, a threatening energy behind the bronze glass.

I broke the silence and said, "Now get out of my office."

He didn't move.

But the big guy did.

He stood up.

Walked right up to the front edge of my desk, then sat down on it. His black boots were on the floor, but he twisted around to look at me, his left hand flat on my desk and his right hand, and arm, free.

The big guy looked at me with his uneven eyes, his removed insanity. In a raspy, almost hoarse voice he said, "Why don't you tell us what really happened."

I looked down at the few things I had on top of my desk. My laptop, sitting in front of me. My landline over to my right. A cup that held some black felt-tip pens. A square glass paperweight about two inches tall that I rarely use but like the look of.

I looked at the big guy and said, "Why don't you get off my desk."

I glanced at Tony Lewis. Nothing.

"Last chance," the big guy said.

My heartbeat was louder in my ears now, making his threat seem like it came from farther away than it actually had.

I said, flatly and this time not to the big guy and not to Tony Lewis but to the space in between them, "Get off my desk and get out of my office."

I didn't expect them to listen to me. I'd said it to trigger the action, and it did.

The big guy moved quickly. With his right hand he

grabbed my shirt at the chest and pulled me toward him.

I grabbed the paperweight with my right hand, pulled it up a foot, then smashed it down onto his left hand, which was still sitting flat on my desk.

Crack. Had to have broken a bone. Maybe two.

The big guy, loosening his grip on my shirt but managing to hold on, took a deep breath and looked down at his hand. I put the paperweight back on my desk and stood up, still connected to him. He was locked in on his hand, giving me his profile. I hit him with a left, hard, in his right ear. Not hard enough to rupture the eardrum, but close. Real close. Ever been hit in the ear? It's excruciating.

The big guy instinctively released my shirt and covered his right ear with his right hand as he went down.

I looked at Tony Lewis. While I'd been going at the big guy, he hadn't moved. I think he wanted me to think he was just watching the whole thing, cool as a cucumber, amused even. But I could tell, even though his eyes were hidden a bit, that he wasn't cool. No, he was frozen, unsure what to do. I moved around my desk and went behind the chair he was sitting in. I grabbed its arms from behind and yanked it backward. Tony Lewis fell to the floor.

I took hold of his leather jacket at the shoulders and dragged him across the slick concrete toward my open slider.

I got him outside, right next to the driver's-side door of his Mercedes. I flipped him over, putting his chest on the concrete. I wrestled the jacket off him and threw it onto the hood of the car. I put my right foot in the center of his back and pressed down, hard. Then I leaned down and grabbed the fat on the back of Tony Lewis's right upper arm.

I pinched it as hard as I could. Tony let out a strange, guttural gasp.

"Leave. Are you going to leave?"

He nodded.

The big guy was on his feet now, leaning against the wall next to my desk, his right hand still covering his right ear and his left hand held gingerly out in front of him. He was unsteady and didn't know what his next move should be, as I now had his boss pinned to the ground.

I pointed to the big guy but spoke to Tony Lewis.

"Tell him to get over to the car."

Tony Lewis nodded.

The big guy walked over and stood next to the passenger-side door of the Mercedes, keeping his hands in the same positions.

I took my foot off Tony Lewis, walked back over to my desk, and sat behind it.

Tony got up, grabbed his jacket off the hood, unlocked the car. Neither one said a word as they both got in.

I'd pull a gun if they came back at me. They'd probably pull one as well. They'd tried the brute-force route; it hadn't worked. And there had to be a gun, or two, in the car. In the glove, under the seat, somewhere.

It didn't happen.

I watched Tony toss his jacket in the backseat, start up the Mercedes, and pull away.

I reached into my fridge and got out a bottled water. I took a few big sips. Then I took a few big, deep breaths.

Then, over the next twenty minutes, taking intermittent sips and breaths, I calmed down a little.

I opened one of my filing-cabinet drawers, pulled out the Muriel Dreen folder I'd put away, then pulled Peter Caldwell's card out of the folder. I looked at it: his firm's name, the address. I closed up my office, got in the Focus, and headed toward Watson, Reese and Lucerne, Century City.

Century City is a small, semifancy district just west of Beverly Hills. It's got a couple of nice, little suburban neighborhoods, but it's mostly commerce and offices: high-end law firms, talent agencies, places where people wear suits, even in L.A.

Was Peter going to be at work? Not sure, but a risk I was willing to take. If he wasn't there, I'd call him and track him down that way. But if he was there, I wanted to surprise him.

I found his building. Parked. Before I went in, I asked a professional-looking group standing just outside the entrance what floor Watson, Reece and Lucerne was on. They were kind enough to tell me. With a smile, in fact. Then I walked into the building, walked right by security, and took the elevator to 22.

I got out, scanned the reception area. Very quiet. And traditional. Lots of dark furniture, a couple of those deep brown leather chairs with the studs all over them. Two pretty receptionists sat behind a big wall of a desk, the firm's name emblazoned in a classic font on its front.

I said to one of them, taking in her sharp business suit and strawberry-blond hair tied up tight in a bun, "I'm here to see Peter Caldwell. He said to come on back." Before she could say anything, I was walking down a long hallway, looking into open office doors.

Six offices down, there was Peter behind his desk, a bright, crisp view of the bright white buildings of Century City behind him.

When he saw me, he looked terrified.

I walked into his office and sat down on a tastefully covered green office chair in front of his desk.

He started to say something. "I told Mrs. Dreen not to—"

I cut him off. "Peter. I told you what happened. I told you the story. And then you send those two over to my office to threaten me? Peter. What were you thinking?"

Stammering and swallowing, he said, "I told Mrs. Dreen not to do that. I told her not to do it. What happened?"

"Why don't you call Tony Lewis and ask him what happened."

Peter nodded.

Right then, the strawberry-blond receptionist appeared in the doorway behind me. "Mr. Caldwell—"

Peter put a hand up and said, "It's okay, Laura."

She quietly vanished.

I said, "Peter. If I see those two again, or anyone like them, and especially if Heather Press ever sees them, or anyone like them, you know who's going to go to jail?"

Meekly he said, "Mrs. Dree—"

I interrupted him and said, "That's right, counselor. Muriel. Muriel's going to jail."

This time he didn't speak. He just sat there, almost imperceptibly shaking. I wondered whether it was my eyes creating the effect or whether it was actually happening. I had a brief memory of the squirrel stuck upside down on the tree outside Muriel Dreen's house.

I let him sit there and take it all in a moment longer. He needed to process, really process, that Muriel would go to jail. Because that's what would end it, would keep Heather Press in the clear.

I said, "Muriel will try to pull some strings to get off the harassment and intimidation charges. But I'll make sure her moves don't work. You know what happens to old, rich ladies in jail, Peter? Here in L.A.? They get fucked with. A lot. Muriel won't be sitting there watching her stock show. She'll be watching her ass.

"Now. You didn't believe me when I told you what happened with Heather. Are you going to believe me this time?"

Peter nodded.

"You sure?"

"John, I told her not to send—"

"Just answer the question."

"Yes, I believe you."

"Good."

I stood up and left. I walked back down the hall toward reception. Right before I got there I had a thought, flipped a U, and walked back to Peter's office.

I poked my head in. "My invoice went out today. Be on the lookout."

He nodded.

I left, this time for real.

8

The next day at noon sharp, I was in Hancock Park at the lovely house of Jackie and Phil Fuller. Phil Fuller. Not a bad porn name. But I digress. Hancock Park is an inland neighborhood east of Beverly Hills where a lot of people in L.A. with old money live. Preppy, East Coast–y types who wear Top-Siders with no irony and who have at some point in their lives spent a significant amount of time on a Boston Whaler.

Their house was a big Tudor on a nice-sized lot. And no, the house was not too big for the lot, which made me happy. Inside, it was tastefully decorated, lots of pictures of family and friends and social gatherings, big rooms that suggested an interior designer's touch but that also had a thrown-together confidence to them: magazines scattered on tables, worn furniture right next to newer things, matchboxes from restaurants in glass bowls.

A few of the photos had Keaton in them, haunting the room a bit.

A couple of big, older, friendly labs wandered around quietly and calmly. Occasionally I'd catch one of their placid eyes.

We were in the living room. Phil and Jackie sat together on a couch across from me. I sat on a straight-backed chair, which I'd chosen over the more comfortable one next to it. Business time.

Jackie was thin, tan, with blue eyes and expensively dyed and cut blond hair. Her hair looked almost shiny, but also soft and healthy. Like it was cared for by a pro often, maybe daily. Her most striking feature, though, was the grief that she still wore on her face. She looked exhausted, her eyes betraying hopelessness.

Phil might have felt just as much grief, but he didn't show it. He was a big man, brown hair going gray, a sweater over his shoulders, big tortoiseshell glasses. And working a comb-over just a bit. I swear, his comb-over looked pretty good. And I thought, Shit, maybe, maybe they'll come back in a kind of seventies-dad kind of way. You know what I'm saying? You know that dad? Out by the pool grilling burgers for the kids, nice Jack on ice in his left hand, slightly ill-fitting burgundy Lacoste shirt over his slightly out-of-shape body. Might mow the lawn later, with a fairly hefty buzz on, then head over to the country club that night for a little dinner and some more cocktails.

You know that dad? You know that dad. I like that dad.

Yeah, Phil's comb-over looked okay, but his overall appearance, for whatever reason, had a slightly contrived quality. Like he was working just a bit to pull off the Hancock Park WASP thing, whereas it came to Jackie naturally. It had probably been Phil's idea to name the kids Keaton and Greer.

We were finishing up the how-much-I-charge conversation. This time, unlike the rattled look I got from Peter Caldwell, Jackie Fuller just said, "Fine."

I said, "I have the case file. I've looked it over. There are a handful of people I want to talk to. I suppose they'll tell me what they already told the police, but I might get something out of their stories that the police didn't. Before I do that, though, I'd like to ask you something. Everyone the police questioned had an alibi. They never named a suspect. They never had a working theory. So, I'm wondering: What do you think happened? Did you ever put together a guess?"

And then, gingerly, I added, "Why do you think your son was killed?"

Jackie nodded to tell me she understood my question, and to tell me she was going to do the talking. She was probably the one who'd conceived of the idea of having the case looked into further, of hiring a guy like me. A mom still looking after her young. I understood it. I respected it.

She said, "Keaton wasn't perfect. He'd made some enemies over the years. Well, I don't know if I'd call them enemies . . . He'd let some people down over the years as a result of his behavior. You probably read that in the case file."

I nodded.

She continued. "He'd broken up with girlfriends. He'd, he'd . . ."

She stopped. She was having a tough time saying the sentence. She moved her eyes over to Phil, who gave her a supportive look. The very beginnings of tears sprouted in her eyes.

She continued, "He'd behaved poorly, very poorly, toward some people. Like I said, girlfriends, but also friends, his brother, business associates. He just didn't act like a stand-up young man in a lot of situations over the years. But did one of those people load a gun and put a bullet in his chest? Did one of those people wait for him to leave his house one morning and murder him? I don't think so, Mr. Darvelle. I really don't."

I nodded, letting her know I'd processed what she'd said. And then I said, softly, "You can call me John."

"Okay," she said. And now that she'd gotten through saying negative things about her dead son, she regained her stride a bit. "So that's why we're so confused. To answer your question, we don't know what happened. We haven't a clue. It's just so random. And . . . *professional.* Six in the morning? Assassinated? And that's what makes it so frustrating. I mean, can you imagine what that must be like? Can you imagine if a loved one of yours was walking out to his or her car one day and just got gunned down out of nowhere? And the police, and Phil and I, and everybody who knew him just have no idea what happened? I still don't sleep at night, John. It's almost like an alien came down from outer space and took our son. It's that strange.

I never thought I'd have a thought like this, but to know who killed my son, our son—and why—would be really comforting in some bizarre way."

I understood what she meant. Must be a pretty unusual, and uncomfortable, feeling. To know that there had to be a reason her son was killed based on the *way* he was killed, but to have zero idea what that reason was.

I said, "Well, I'm going to start with what I have. Going to talk to Greer, the ex-girlfriend, the guy he started the bar with, others." I reiterated, "Sometimes fresh eyes can see fresh things."

We all stood up. I handed Jackie my card.

I said, "I know you know what's in the file. But if there's anything else you think might help me, please tell me. Could be something the cops dismissed. Could be something you just think is out of the ordinary, unusual, interesting, anything. Anything you think might help me."

Jackie and Phil both nodded, and Jackie said, "And please call us anytime with questions, or for any reason, if you think we can help."

Phil spoke for the first time as he stuck out his hand. "Thank you, John. Detective Ott says you're a really good detective."

I thought: Ott. Yeah, good, tough cop. But also, deep down, good guy.

I shook Phil Fuller's hand and said, "I'll see what I can do."

I walked toward the door, escorted by the two big, calm dogs.

9

I got in the Focus and called Keaton's brother, Greer. Halfway through the second ring, a friendly voice said, "Hello."

"Hi, Greer, my name is John Darvelle. I'm a private investigator. Your parents hired me a few minutes ago to look into the murder of your brother. Think you and I could talk?"

"Yeah, Mom told me she was going to do that. And yeah, sure, of course, let's talk. I own a marina in Marina Del Rey. I'm here every day other than Mondays. You can come by anytime. Come by now, if you want."

"Now sounds good to me."

He gave me the name and the address, and I clicked off the phone and hit the gas.

Greer's marina, conveniently named Greer's Marina, was just off Admiralty Way in Marina Del Rey. Not too far from my house in Mar Vista. Ten minutes, maybe, without traffic. Marina Del Rey is one of the more distinctive areas in Los Angeles. That being said, it has absolutely none of the qualities that people think of when they think of L.A. There's no Hollywood scene. And there's no beach scene. There *is* a section on the beach, but it's not a beach that people really go to, it's not the beach you picture when you picture a sunny Los Angeles beach. It doesn't have a funky, hipster feel like its more famous neighbor, Venice, either. But it is, without question, its own thing. Like Gary Delmore, it knows what it is.

What Marina Del Rey *does* have is an enormous man-made harbor that's home to twenty-some-odd marinas. For powerboats and sailboats and yachts and, of course, for boat people. You know? Boat people. People who love boats and talk about boats and often live on boats. Who have at least some amount of alcohol in them at all times, and usually some type of skin cancer on them as well.

Marina Del Rey also has numerous chain restaurants, seventies-style apartment complexes, moderately used tennis courts, often used hot tubs, and, of course, lots and lots of on-the-prowl, wild-eyed cougars.

So, yes, I like it a lot.

As I made my way through Marina Del Rey, I passed a Cheesecake Factory, a Chart House, an Applebee's, and an Outback. Every parking lot was filled. *Filled*.

I got to Greer's Marina, threw the Focus in a spot, then spotted a sort of main building that had an entrance on the side of the parking lot and, it looked like, another entrance leading out to the docks.

I entered from the parking-lot side. Instead of diving into the water, then climbing up onto one of the docks and entering from the marina side. Made more sense to me.

There was a pretty brunette girl, looked to be college age, standing behind a tall counter with a cash register on it.

"Hi there," I said. "I'm here to talk to Greer. Name's John Darvelle."

Before she could say anything, a door opened to my right and her left. A short, fairly built guy with curly black hair, brown freckles spread across his nose, and friendly, slightly wounded brown eyes said, "Hey, John. Come on in."

"John." Not "Mr. Darvelle." Telling Jackie Fuller to call me John must have cosmically clicked me back on track. Or maybe Greer was just a casual guy. One of the two.

We walked into his office and took our seats. Me in front of his desk, him behind it. I looked around. White walls with photos of the marina on them, two windows that provided views of the actual marina, and a nice teak desk, to complete the boat theme, covered in lots of papers.

I looked at Greer. He was wearing a sport shirt with his marina's logo on it, which made sense. He was also wearing a puka-shell necklace, which was troubling. The man was in his early thirties.

"So. What do you want to know?" he asked.

He said it in a way that suggested he would actually be helpful. "Anything you think might help. I have the police case file, so I've read your previous statements."

Greer nodded and said, "So you know what I said before. That Keaton was my big brother, but that he was a really lazy, disrespectful guy who pretty much pissed off everyone he came in contact with eventually."

"Yes," I said. "I'm aware that you said something to that effect before. But let me ask you this. Who was he pissing off right around the time he got shot?"

A concerned look fell over his face. "You know—"

"Yes. You were on a sailing trip in the British Virgin Islands when it happened."

That was Greer's alibi. On a boat. In the ocean. Out of the country. He had left the United States one week prior to the murder. Had flown to Puerto Rico, then to Tortola, and had embarked from there on a sailing trip through the British Virgin Islands and the US Virgin Islands with a college friend who had relatives in Tortola. Delta Air Lines had verified his presence on the flight from L.A. to Puerto Rico. Cape Air had verified his presence on the flight from Puerto Rico to Tortola. On the day of the actual murder, he was in the middle of the ocean east of Tortola, near Anguilla. This was confirmed by his friend, by the first mate on the boat, by the staff at the marina in Tortola they'd departed from, by the friend's family in Tortola. Of course, all this doesn't rule out some kind of involvement in the murder, but on the day of the killing, he himself was in fact a few thousand miles away, roasting in the sun and gliding through Caribbean waters.

Greer's helpful expression reappeared and he said, "You know what, John? When Keat got killed, we weren't very close. At all. We were talking on, like, birthdays and holidays. Maybe. *If* he remembered to call me on my birthday, and *if* he showed up to Christmas at my parents' house. So I honestly don't know who he was pissing off around the time he got killed."

I said, "Sounds like you and Keaton had fallen out a bit. Why did that happen? Was it something specific?"

It was a question that might have offended some people. It implied that even though Greer had a really good alibi, I might still be looking into him.

It didn't seem to bother him. "No. It wasn't something specific, or any one thing, really. You'll have to talk to some of the other people that I'm sure are in your case file to get those stories. His ex–business partner, Craig Helton. Who I like. Craig's a good guy. And I don't think he had anything to do with it. But he does have a specific reason for not liking Keaton."

I nodded.

"For me and Keat, it was just . . . Keaton always let you down. Always. My mom, my dad, me. Everyone. He was just one of those people who don't give a shit about anyone other than themselves. You almost couldn't believe it. If he told you he'd be at your graduation to support you, he wouldn't show up. If he told my parents he'd pay them back for something, he wouldn't. If my dad had a birthday party, he'd show up and get wasted and be really rude to people. Just on and on.

"With me, specifically? No, it wasn't one thing. It was a hundred things. He blew off my high school graduation, which, for some reason, was important to me at the time. And I know that doesn't sound like that big a deal, and it wasn't. But when you add it to all the other stuff . . .

Like, he was rude to some of my girlfriends. He'd borrow money from me and not pay me back. It wasn't just my parents he stiffed. He wrecked my car once and never really apologized. Just kind of said, 'Hey, man, you have insurance.' You know? On and on. And with people like that, if they're your family, you love them and you keep trying. But eventually, something clicks and you just say, 'I'm done.' But what was tricky with Keaton was that he was a really charming guy when he wanted to be. Occasionally he'd apologize for something. He didn't with my car, but for some other things he would. He'd say, you know, 'I'm sorry if I offended you,' playing dumb a bit. But still sort of apologizing. And whether or not he deserved it, I, everybody, gave him lots of chances. But like I said, one day I just said, 'I'm done.' And that's why at the time of his murder we really weren't in touch that much."

I thought, A charming guy with an oily, unctuous smile who lets a bunch of people down all the time. Sounds like a guy I'd like to walk up to and punch really hard in the thigh, then just walk away. And the way he apologized. I'm sorry *if* I offended you. I hate people who apologize that way. *If. If* I offended you. You're not taking any responsibility when you say it that way. You're not acknowledging that *you* fucked up. Have the courage to admit you were at fault. I'm sorry that I was an asshole. I'm sorry that I let you down. I'm sorry that I'm a shitty older brother, Greer. I'm sorry *if* I offended you? Yeah? Well, fuck off, because you haven't apologized yet.

I didn't say any of that to Greer. Instead I said, "Who else was in Keaton's life? I know there's Craig Helton, the guy you mentioned, the guy he started the bar with. And there's the ex-girlfriend, Sydney. I'm going to talk to both of them. You said you and Keaton weren't that close at the end, but do you know anyone else who was in his life? Especially at the time of the murder."

Greer said, "Keaton knew everyone. From growing up, from college, from after college. But *in* his life? At that time? You know, I really don't. I really can't think of anyone in particular. But what I know from having known him my whole life is that, you know, he was a charming guy. He was a manipulator. And you add money to a guy like that . . . It wasn't hard for him to keep finding new people who were willing to hang around him. Give him another chance. Put up with his shit. And it was probably one of those people who decided not to, you know—not to put up with his shit anymore."

Not to put up with his shit anymore. Or, in other words, to kill him.

I looked at Greer. Seemed genuine to me. He had a little bit of that pathos about him that people get when they don't have to fight for their dreams. He seemed just a little *lost*. He'd probably be a different guy if he'd had to earn or raise the money to buy the marina. Yeah, and I'd probably be more likely to want to have a beer with him then too, because he'd have some edge, some bite, some of that energy that comes from eating what you kill. But, I thought, at least he's working. Probably working reasonably hard. The marina looked to me to be pretty successful. Pretty well run. Which probably wasn't that easy to do. Most professional endeavors aren't.

He said, unprompted, "You know, I'm not sure how Keaton got to be the way he was. Was it because our dad worked a lot when he was young, thirteen, fourteen? Keaton was four and a half years older than me. So when he was that age, growing up, our dad was doing whatever he had to do to build his company. He wasn't around a lot. So did Keaton feel neglected? Or was he mad at me? Because when *I* was that age, our dad had sold the company and was more relaxed. Was at home a lot more. Or maybe it was that Keaton felt like he had to compensate because he was the oldest son and we had a successful dad? You know? I don't know. I really don't know. For a long time I felt guilty, like I had it easier or something. But eventually I stopped feeling guilty. Stopped feeling like I had something to do with Keaton being such a dick."

It was honest. It was vulnerable. I admired him for being open. Did anything he'd said help me? Well, I wasn't really sure. But that's okay. I deal with that a lot in my line. Not really being sure.

I said, handing him my card, "Thanks, Greer. Maybe I'll call you again as I get deeper into this thing. And please call me if something comes to you that you think might be helpful."

"I will," he said.

We stood up, shook hands. I took a last look at him as I was walking out his office door. Greer was staring out one of the windows. But it didn't seem like he was scanning the marina. No, he was looking out to sea, to where he'd been when somebody shot his brother.

10

I got to my car and got out my phone. I dialed up the ex–business partner, Craig Helton, nobody there, left a message. With the crowd that's already talked to the police, I wasn't trying to surprise them in any way, pop up unannounced. I was just trying to set up good, old-fashioned, planned-in-advance meetings. Just trying to get my head further around the story I'd read in the case file. I called the ex-girlfriend next, Sydney Scott. Sydney had dated Keaton for years, some in college, some after college, but was now married to a guy named Geoff. I zeroed in on the way Geoff spelled his name. It made me uncomfortable. It made me really uncomfortable.

Sydney, unlike Craig, answered.

"Hi, Sydney. My name is John Darvelle. I'm a private detective."

Before I could continue with my opening spiel, Sydney said, "Yes, Jackie called me. She said you might be calling."

"Great," I said. "Listen, do you have time to talk in person sometime soon?"

"I do. I'm home for the rest of the day. I live in the Venice canals. Would you like to come by today at some point?"

"Yep. I'm in Marina Del Rey as we speak. Close by. Fifteen minutes okay?"

"Actually, can you give me an hour? Geoff and I, my husband, Geoff, and I, were just about to do our workout."

"Sure, that's fine."

Sydney Scott gave me their address.

"All right," I said. "See you in an hour. Bye."

"Love," she said.

"Excuse me?"

"Oh," she laughed. "Right. You don't know me. I say 'love' instead of 'good-bye.' It's not such a fierce ending. It's not so permanent. And it much more represents what I'm about."

I thought: Oh boy.

"Okay," I said. "Got it. See you in an hour."

"Love," she said.

"Right," I said.

We hung up.

I drove from Marina Del Rey into Venice, its neighbor just to the north. These days, Venice was struggling a bit to hang on to its title as the hippest place to live in L.A. It was still tethered to its groovy, hippie-dippie roots, but it was going more mainstream every second. Fighting with too much money coming in and too many hipsters hanging around. Don't get me wrong, it was still in a sweet spot, still a great place to stroll around, have a beer, have a bite, walk out to the ocean, mingle with some truly funky people who had been there a while. But it was just on the verge of becoming played out. L.A.'s version of New York's SoHo. I parked on Abbot Kinney. Went into Abbot's Pizza and got a slice of pepperoni and a slice of barbecue chicken. I ate them, taking intermittent sips of a nice, cold Diet Coke—no Fresca available—then went back outside and watched people walk by for thirty minutes. When I'd burned enough time, I hopped back in the Focus and headed over to the canals.

The Venice canals are right on the south edge of Venice, just inland from the ocean, and were modeled on the actual Venice canals in Italy, only much smaller. So you've got a neighborhood with bungalows and some cool little houses and some really big houses all stacked on top of one another, and all facing and connected by little rivers, with just a few roads into the neighborhood and a few roads out. You can literally canoe over to your neighbor's house. To your neighbor's really expensive house. The canals are high dollar. Overall, it's a pretty unusual, and pretty damn charming, way to exist in Los Angeles. Some depressing, cement-laden sprawl isn't that far away—shit, right over on Lincoln Boulevard—but when you're in the canals, sliding through the water in your canoe with your girlfriend up front and a bottle of wine or perhaps a cold six-pack of Coors Light between your feet, you'd never know it.

I drove down Washington Boulevard, then turned into one of the little side streets that take you into the canals proper. Once you're in the neighborhood, little alleys take you to the backs of the houses. In the small spaces between the houses you can see sections of the water on the other side.

I wound around a couple of these alleylike streets until I found Sydney and Geoff's house. I parked in front of their garage, which faced the alley, then knocked on a door that did too.

No answer. I was right on time, knocking on the door literally one hour from the time Sydney and I had hung up, so getting no answer annoyed me. Sydney and Geoff were probably still doing their workout, maybe even somewhere other than the house, and had lost track of time. They were late.

If you know me, you know I can't stand people who are late. And let me tell you, the thing people always say about people who are late is that they are selfish, and disrespectful of the time of others, and *that's* why they are late. Sure, I guess that's part of it. But I think that's giving these people too much credit. Because I think something else is happening as well. I think people who are late—not all of them, but most of them—are just a little dumb. Look, I'm not saying totally fucking stupid. You know, walking around drooling all over themselves, screaming at strangers, unable to comprehend the simplest of concepts. I'm saying just a little bit dumb. Because to be on time, you have to have the mental capacity and the mental discipline to think into the future. You have to sit there and use mental energy to contemplate some variables, some possibilities, and then make a decision about what you need to do to manage it all. It's a teeny tiny chess match. And you have to figure out your moves. By and large, the people I know who can do this regularly are the same people who can figure out other, bigger, problems. And the ones who can't do that? You're not putting them on the top squad. You're not giving them the big jobs. You're not saying to them: Cut the red wire, not the blue wire, or we're all going to die. Because, you know, they're just a bit dumb.

I walked around to the side of the house, then through the sliver of space between it and the house next to it, and emerged just on the edge of Sydney and Geoff's yard, right on the canal. I could now see all the houses lining the little river on both sides. It was beautiful, wonderful. A breeze put modest ripples on the water.

I moved my eyes over to Sydney and Geoff's backyard. There I saw them finishing their "workout." They were both dressed in, essentially, black karate uniforms, and they were acting out what looked like a karate fight, only they were doing it in slow motion. And they weren't making any contact. One of them would do a slow-motion punch but stop before contact. Then the other one would do a slow-motion chop but, again, stop right before contact. And so on.

They were also humming some sort of chant.

I said under my breath, "What the fuck?"

I walked into their little yard until I caught Sydney's eye. As she did a slow roundhouse kick that didn't come very close to her husband's face, she held up a finger to me. Like: hang on one sec.

I nodded and watched them finish their routine.

An interminable four minutes later they stopped, bowed to each other, and looked over at me. With a smile, Sydney said, "Mr. Darvelle. Hello."

Back to "mister."

I introduced myself to both of them and told them to call me John. Sydney had chestnut brown hair, manipulative light brown bedroom eyes, smooth skin, a rosebud mouth. She had a curvy, sexy body. Really quite fetching, physically. Geoff was in shape—not huge, but it looked like he worked out—and he stood about five-ten. He had a sort of dim, blank look in his eyes. And he had a low hairline, with his dark hair brushed forward. It gave him a simian, Neanderthal quality. But he didn't seem aggressive or mean. He seemed pliant, a pushover. The kind of guy a sexy girl could talk into the whole hippie-slash-fake-karate thing they were fronting.

I looked around. Their yard was on the small side—most of the yards on the canals are—but well kept up. Their house wasn't particularly large, but it had a designed, contemporary-California, state-of-the-art feel. One or both of them had money.

We all sat down on some little chairs they had in the backyard. I couldn't resist: I said, in a genuine enough tone, "So what were you guys just doing? That was your workout?"

"We invented it," Sydney said, a touch defensively. "It's got the beauty of a karate fight without the violence."

She pronounced it "kuh-rot-*tay*." She stared at me with an insecure but defiant look in her eyes, not blinking at all, wondering whether I was going to question it. I looked at Geoff. He didn't roll his eyes. They were barely open, but he didn't roll them. I was impressed. I moved on. "Thanks for talking to me."

"Absolutely," Sydney said. And then, to Geoff, "We should feed Zucchini."

Geoff nodded.

"Dog or cat?" I said. "I love animals."

Now some fire appeared in Sydney's eyes. "Zucchini's our daughter. She's asleep inside."

It got very quiet for what seemed like two hours but was really about ten seconds. I could hear the ripples on the little river. Some wind blowing through some nearby palms. A distant bird.

"My apologies," I said. "Anyway, I know you talked to the police a year and a half ago or so. And I know that at the time of the murder you were with your family in Chicago."

She nodded. "With Geoff, who didn't even know Keaton."

And, like everyone else in the file, Geoff and Sydney had all sorts of corroboration. Confirmation from United Airlines that she and Geoff had flown direct to Chicago two days before the murder and had flown back four days after it. Credit-card receipts documenting essentially their whole trip. Dinner at Gibsons the night before the murder on Geoff's card. Starbucks the morning of—at almost the exact time of—the murder on Sydney's card. Two venti

Caffè Lattes, an Iced Lemon Pound Cake, and a Petite Vanilla Bean Scone purchased at 8:06 a.m. Chicago time . . . Not to mention four of Sydney's family members verifying their day-by-day presence in the greater Chicago area.

Geoff stood up, threw a thumb toward the house, and said, "I'm gonna go . . ." He didn't finish the sentence. He did that thing that people do a lot where they just say half a sentence and expect their audience to fill in the rest.

I *thought* he was going to say: go feed Cauliflower. Or whatever the child's name was. He was probably also heading in because he didn't want to hear his wife talking about her dead ex. Again. I was cool with it. I wanted to talk to her unencumbered by any possible communication barriers that might be created by her husband sitting there.

After Geoff strolled off, I said to Sydney, "I've read the police report. I have the file. As I said, I know you were a long way away at the time of the murder. And also, I've read what you told the police. I read your statements. So I thought maybe we could just talk a bit. At this point in my investigation I'm still trying to get a picture of this guy."

Sydney seemed comforted by the fact that I understood that she'd been halfway across the country at the time of the killing. She still had some sort of defensive thing happening. But she seemed ready to talk.

She said, "Well, I knew Keaton really, really well. We dated, off and on, for almost seven years. We met in college. He went to USC. I went to Art Center in Pasadena to study my passion at the time, photography. Well, I went there for a year, anyway. I dropped out. Too regimented for me."

She looked right at me, staring almost, with her defensive but still sexy eyes. Eyes that said, Are you judging me for dropping out? Do you think I'm a flake?

"Yes" and "yes" would be the answers to those questions. Often when someone says something like "too regimented," it really just means they didn't have the discipline or the stamina to stick it out. Not always, but often.

She continued as she craned her neck and cracked it. "I just think art is more flow-y, more about spontaneity. Not like . . ." Curiously, out of nowhere, really, she started talking like and imitating a robot. "You must take this class. You must learn about this person. Then you must take this class. Then learn about this other person. You must practice every day."

Having lived in Los Angeles my whole life, I knew a few artists. Writers, directors, photographers, even some painters. All the successful ones were very disciplined. They studied what came before them, often possessed an encyclopedic amount of information about the particular field they chose to focus on, and worked on a schedule that they stuck to very seriously. I didn't mention this to Sydney.

She continued with her robot impression, now putting stiff arms out in front of her and moving them robotically as she robot-talked. "Structure, structure, structure. Learn this before you learn that. Do it like we say. Work every day. Practice, practice, practice, practice, practice."

She dropped the robot impression and got back to the other version of herself that she'd let me see. "I'm sorry, I'm just not going to let someone instruct me on how to do my art. I had the same problem with a few of the people I worked for after leaving school. I had stopped taking pictures. I had realized that that actually *wasn't* my passion. I had realized, at that time anyway, that I wanted to get into film. So I worked at a few production companies. And again, it was just all these rules. All these producers wanted me to do it *their* way. And I would always say, It's *art*. I don't just *want* to do it my way. I *have* to. Anyway, I guess it was all for the best, because I realized that film wasn't my passion either. What I'm doing now is. That's why I, well, I guess *we*, invented the workout you saw. I'm going to write a book about it and go on a speaking tour."

I thought, It's amazing what can happen to someone when they don't have to work, or when they are with someone who enables them to not have to. I surmised that in the past she'd leaned on Keaton, and that now it was Geoff who paid the bills. But, boy, entitlement can rear its ugly head quickly. And you combine that with the reality of hard work, and it can just transform and cripple people to the point where the things they say, the excuses they make, the ideas they have, reach an almost comic level of absurdity. My school wanted me to practice? That's your reason for leaving? My boss wanted me to do my job the way he or she told me to? And then, after the dropping out, quitting in a huff, proclaiming that the professionals above you are insane, that's when the entrepreneurial concepts that never actually happen start popping up. A clothing line for pets. An un-thought-through tech start-up. A new form of karate you come up with in your backyard that's going to lead to a speaking tour. Man, it's a sight to behold. And not a pretty one.

Thankfully, she got back to the subject at hand. "Anyway, Keaton and I met when we were both in college, very young, dated all while he was at USC. He lived off campus. I had my own apartment, but I spent a lot of time at his. Then we dated for lots of years after college too."

I said, "And so why did you break up?"

She took a big, dramatic breath and said, "Early on, while he was at USC, he was a handful. So was I. We drank a lot. We went out a lot. You know, that led to fights. Mostly over nothing. He also wasn't the most reliable person. To me or anyone else. We'd have plans, he'd bail. Or we'd have a special night planned and he'd get hammered. We'd break up, but then he'd be really nice and seduce me and I'd come back. But then . . . then . . . the cheating started. This was after college. He'd moved to his house. Where he was . . . where he was killed. His dad got it for him, said it was a good investment. I was still in my little apartment. Keaton and I talked about moving in together, but we never did. But during that time I'd catch him with some bimbo; I'd find phone numbers. Toward the end, he'd basically just disappear. Like, a week would go by and I wouldn't hear from him. That's a long time when you are dating someone. I think he might even have had a second girlfriend. Like, a whole other relationship. That was always my suspicion. It wasn't just catching him in lies. It was . . . I could see it in his eyes. He was somewhere else. I thought so, anyway.

"But the thing is, one day I had a realization. He didn't care. I don't just mean he didn't care about me. I mean, he didn't care when he did something wrong. Like, I'd say, 'You broke our plans,' or 'I haven't heard from you in a week,' and I could tell that he just didn't care. It didn't register. It was almost like he wasn't able to understand that what he'd done was wrong, or that he had hurt someone. He would only be upset because he got caught, or because it was a hassle for him to have to talk about it."

I thought: That's known as a sociopath. "So eventually you ended it?"

"Yeah, or he did. Or we did. I don't remember. But I definitely wanted out."

I thought, It's so hard for someone to say the words, to actually say the words: "I got dumped." Yet hearing someone say those words always makes me like them.

I said, "So how long had you been broken up when he was shot?"

"Several years. Three without any contact."

"Meaning you saw him some even after you had broken up?"

She looked at me, trying to hold on to her challenging visage but showing some shame. "Yeah. A few hookups here and there. I guess to see if there was any hope."

For what, I wanted to say. So I did.

"Recapturing our love," she said defiantly.

Oh, right, that. I moved on. "So do you know whether he ever moved on to someone else? I mean, someone who stuck?"

"I don't know. And after a while I stopped caring. Because a year or so after Keaton and I were done-done, like no hookups, nothing, I found my true love. Keaton in some way led me to Geoff."

I thought: Kind of like how photography led you to film, which led you to fake karate.

And then I thought about Geoff. Another guy with a lot of money, coincidentally. I mean, Geoff had to be the one in this setup with the dough. Right? How did he get it? Who knows? Family money? Luck? One of those jobs you sometimes hear about where you don't have to do much but somehow make a lot of money? Whatever the way, how else could he have gotten this one? She's annoying, but she's beautiful. And Geoff could barely put together a sentence. He had literally not been able to get through an entire sentence when he'd made his exit. Half a sentence had worn him out. I pictured him inside, eyes half lidded, mouth hanging open, staring at the TV in his karate uniform. Yeah, and with this cat, Sydney'd found a guy who was a little easier than Keaton Fuller to handle, to control. Who was willing to buy her a house and play pretend karate in the yard if he got to sleep with her. Well, in his defense, she *was* sexy. I didn't like her. I might go crazy if I had to live in that house with her. But if I didn't have a girlfriend, and I do have a girlfriend, I'd definitely sleep with her if the opportunity presented itself.

Maybe I shouldn't have admitted that.

I said, "So what do you think happened? In terms of his murder? You have any guesses? Any people, situations you saw him get in, anything that could have led to something like that?"

"No. I really don't. All I can say is that it didn't surprise me. Well, when I first heard, it surprised me. No, it shocked me. But it didn't surprise me. People were always mad at him. Always. From the moment I met him. His friends, his family, me. But like I said, in the years leading up to his murder I'd totally lost touch with him. But I'm sure he'd found new people to upset."

I nodded. And for some reason, I have no idea why, I said, "So how'd you meet Geoff?"

She smiled and looked at me with that defensive, seductive stare and started to tell me. Almost instantly I tuned her out and looked over at the nice ripples on the water. I pictured myself walking over to the neighbors' yard, then out onto their little dock, then getting in their canoe and slowly, steadily paddling away.

11

I was back in my car, emerging now from the canals onto Washington Boulevard. As I passed the In-N-Out Burger, I gave the big neon sign a longing look. A look that said, We will dance again soon, friend.

I thought: What next, what next? Craig Helton, the ex–business partner, hadn't called me back, and it didn't look like I'd be able to talk to him today. Hmm. I decided to head home.

I live in Mar Vista, a modest, but to my eye beautiful, neighborhood filled with treelined streets and Craftsman houses just inland from Venice Beach. Mar Vista is under-appreciated, a hidden gem—qualities I love in a neighbor-hood, and in a person. It sits at just the right place in the city too. I can take Venice Boulevard to the beach, or the other way, to the freeways, or all the way downtown, if I need to, say, go talk to a perfect-haired, granite-faced police detective and I don't feel like dealing with the 10.

I pulled into my house, a Craftsman at the end of a cul-de-sac, that I've remodeled over time. I knocked down lots of walls and vaulted the ceiling so that now I have essentially one room, spacious in both square footage and height, that serves as most of the ground floor, encompassing the kitchen, a living-room area, and a dining-room area. A small guest bedroom and a bathroom are the only other rooms downstairs. My bedroom sits above the garage, the only room on the second floor.

I'd knocked down the walls in my house mostly to provide enough room for proper play at my home Ping-Pong table. It occupies, beautifully and perfectly, one corner of the big downstairs room. But I also knocked down the walls because I just like the way a room looks and functions when it's open, with various areas within it, like a hotel lobby.

I got the feeling that my girlfriend was inside my house. After twelve or so years as a detective, you can sense certain things. That, and her car was in my driveway. Oh, and I'd called her and told her to come over as well. And she'd texted me when she'd arrived . . .

Her name is Nancy Alvarez. She's an ER nurse at the Santa Monica Medical Center. She's half Mexican. Her father emigrated from Mexico City, her mother from Kansas City. Nancy grew up in the Valley not far from where I grew up, but I never met her as a kid. I met her when I was in the ER after getting the shit kicked out of me by two heavies who didn't want me to find out what their boss did for a living. Old case.

Nancy has long brown hair and brown skin and brown eyes and a very calm demeanor. But if you catch her eyes just right you can see that underneath that calm demeanor, some kind of storm is raging. But not in a bad way, or an angry way. In a way that is good. In a way that tells you she has intense feelings about things, and an equally intense sensitivity. But her demeanor almost always remains calm, and she's calm in her delivery of statements too. And that, combined with the thoughtful, articulate way she expresses things, always makes me like her more. That's important. The way someone expresses themselves, the way someone says things, articulates things, can have a lot to do with whether you like them, or love them.

I find her really funny too. Sometimes she says things, calmly, that kill me. And of course other times she gives me shit when I deserve it. Which I enjoy as well. Not right when it's happening but later, when I think about it. But back to that intensity-lurking-underneath thing. That quality is connected to something else I really like. She's often serious and is, at her core, quite responsible. I know, so romantic, right? But it's true. There's something about that that I'm really drawn to. When she gets her bills, she opens them up and pays them. When we meet somewhere, she's always there, right on time. Which, obviously, I appreciate. When she has things to deal with at work, she doesn't avoid the problem. She goes in and deals. I guess what pulls me in about this is that it means she respects herself. She's not a mess, some kind of pretty picture with a disaster lurking underneath. And she's not pulling that unimaginative act where people confuse certain types of cavalier behavior with being charming. Nancy cares about doing something right simply because she just innately feels it's the way to go. All of this, for me, heightens her sexiness. Amplifies her foxiness. Makes me think she's even more attractive.

I found Nancy in the big main room. She walked toward me as I walked in and we kissed. But before we could even speak, my phone began buzzing in my pocket. Nancy nodded, like, It's okay, get it. I looked at my phone. Craig Helton, the ex–business partner.

"John Darvelle," I said cleverly.

"Hi, John. This is Craig Helton calling you back."

I explained who I was and then what I wanted, to talk to him in person. He said, fine, come to his office tomorrow. Tomorrow was a Sunday. Craig informed me that he was an insurance agent—health insurance—and he liked to go in on weekends to catch up on things when no one else was around. Needless to say I understood, and I told him that. We made a time. He gave me the address. We hung up.

Later, Nancy and I were having dinner at my little dining table. She'd brought over some chili that she'd made. It was outstanding. Delicious. And I love meals that are all in one bowl, as a general rule, which perhaps made it more delicious.

She said, "A guy came in today who had run over his own foot with a lawn mower."

I said, "I'm working on a case where a guy was walking

out of his house one morning and took a bullet that blew his whole chest open."

Nancy looked at me and said in her calm, sexy voice, with absolutely no smile, "Pass the salt."

I laughed really hard.

After we were finished with dinner, I sat on a chair in the bathroom of my bedroom and Nancy zipped my head down with my Oster head shaver. She's really good at it, better than I am. Makes it even, crisp, perfect. And, involuntarily, she adds a sensual touch, her left hand resting on, sometimes lightly squeezing, my left shoulder. I sat there, closed my eyes, and listened to the buzzer as she moved it all over my head.

BZZZZZZ. BZZZZZZ. BZZZZZZ.

Later, back in the main room, sitting on the couch, Nancy having a glass of red wine, me having a Budweiser, she said, "So you think that taking the case with the old lady somehow led to you getting the case you're on now? Shot-in-the-Chest-in-the-Morning Guy?"

"Yeah, I do."

"Hmm," she said. "You don't think that when you get started on something, literally anything, you're just making yourself busy, so you're not *thinking* as much about what's *not* happening, and that way, when something good *does* happen, it just sort of seems like the initial thing caused it?"

"No," I said. "I don't."

"I don't either," she said calmly and smiled.

And then she asked, "So how do the two guys who came to your office to threaten you fit in to your theory?"

"They don't. That happened because I decided to let Heather Press be."

Nancy thought for a second and asked, "Well, do you think the mean-old-lady case is connected in any other way to the one you're on now?"

"Now that's debatable," I said. "No, that's more than debatable. That's unlikely. Very unlikely. But I guess, like a lot in life, you never know."

"Right," she said. "You never know."

12

At eleven the next morning, I hopped on the 405 North and took it over the hill to a depressing section of the Valley. I'm okay with the Valley. As I mentioned, I grew up in the Valley. There are, in fact, some nice, really nice, downright beautiful, sections of the Valley.

Where I was now simply was not one of them.

I drove the Focus down a bleak, treeless, sun-pelted, low-end-commerce-laden street. One depressing storefront after the next. A forgotten JCPenney. A ninety-nine-cent store. An abandoned building that I'm pretty sure used to be a RadioShack. Too bad, because I was in the market for an enormous Texas Instruments calculator.

And there was traffic, semibad traffic, even on a Sunday.

I found the little parking lot for Helton's building. His office, Teamwork Insurance, was wedged between a sad-looking Italian restaurant and a Laundromat. I parked my car and got out. It was 140 degrees, and still. I walked in through the glass door that had TEAMWORK INSURANCE stenciled on it.

Inside, there were six desks and one guy. Craig Helton sat at the back left desk. As I entered, he stood up and waved me in, waved me back. He was wearing dark, sort of mom jeans and a black sport shirt, tucked in. He had on a braided brown leather belt, and his loafers, which I could see under the desk, were new but cheap.

Fashion did not appear to be his thing.

Craig had dark hair that he'd kind of spiked up a bit and a brown goatee, and he was about five-ten. We shook, and he gave me what I believed was a genuine smile.

He motioned to the chair in front of his desk and said, "Have a seat."

As we both sat down, he said, "So the family's looking back into it, huh?"

I nodded.

"And I'm the guy Keaton burned in business, so you gotta talk to me." He didn't phrase it as a question.

I nodded again and said, "Yeah. So, you know, I read all the police reports. I know the basics of your story with Keaton, the business, the bar, the falling out. And I also know where you were at the time of the murder, and that you were never a suspect."

Craig had been at home with his wife and two kids, not too far away from where we were right then. And he, like everyone else, had all sorts of verification. He had his wife, of course, and his two kids, ages six and seven at the time. All of them were home, awake, eating breakfast at 6 a.m., the time of the murder. This was also verified by a neighbor, a single mom named Sandy Simpson who lived right next door. Sandy had been having plumbing problems at her house, so she and her daughter, Zola, had been using the Heltons' bathroom and shower. And *they* were at Craig's house that morning at 6 a.m. as well. Craig was covered.

I continued. "If you don't mind, can you run me through your relationship with Keaton? How you met, the situation with the bar. Anything else you think might be helpful."

Craig started right in, no problem. "Keaton and I met because he started hanging around some people I knew who were in a band called the Test. They broke up, they're not around anymore, but they were kind of a popular band for a while around here. I knew them from growing up. Keaton knew them from going to their shows and partying with them. And, you know, everyone loves Keaton. At first. So that's how we met. We were twenty-six, twenty-seven. Keaton and I were the same age. We became friends pretty fast. We both weren't afraid of a good time. After a while, I told him I wanted to start a bar. Knew of a great location, thought I could run it well. And let me tell you, you get a bar up and running, you can print money. Print it. Sure enough, a couple years after we met, we ended up doing it together. It was here in the Valley, not too far away, near Laurel Canyon. I took out a big loan—the loan was in my name, but we had agreed, *we're partners.* I'd hire everyone, run the bar, do all the work, but Keaton would make half the payments on the loan."

He gave me a look that said: You know where this story is going.

Craig said, with a heartbroken fire in his eyes, "You get a bar up and running and you can print money. Print it. Anyway, long story short, Keaton started drinking way too much at the bar, giving away a ton of free booze, and then eventually not making his payments. And telling me, 'Hey, man, I told you I'd help you get started, that's it.' Which was total bullshit. We had talked over and over about how you have to keep funding a business, any business, until it catches on. And that you need capital to persevere. And that he was going to continue making the payments for as long as we needed. Two years, minimum. Anyway, eventually he just disappeared. As did all those random people he'd invite to the bar. So then I started having to put too much of the bar's money back into the loan payments, I was stressed out of my mind, some people quit, we had a few bad months in a row, I didn't have Keaton's promise in writing, and, you know, I defaulted on the loan and the bank took the bar. It totally fucked up my credit. And believe it or not, I'm still making payments on that loan. Still, to this day. Some four years later."

"What about the family? Phil and Jackie? Did you tell them the situation? Did they help you out?"

"You know what? I did tell them. And they did help me out. A little. Mr. Fuller wrote me a check one time. Not for nearly what Keaton owed me, but it was nice, I guess. I don't hold it against the family, really. Except for the fact that they didn't instill any values in their son. Maybe they tried. I don't know."

I looked at Craig. A nice, if naive, guy. Probably saw something of a ticket out in his wealthy, fancy friend. Only he didn't know it was a ticket to being a health insurance agent in the Valley wearing mom jeans, a Marathon Bar belt, and morbidly depressing loafers.

I said, "Where'd you grow up? Around here?"

"Yeah," he said. "Right near here."

I said, "I grew up not too far from here too."

Craig shrugged a bit and said, "I'm not from a neighborhood like Keaton's, if that's what you're wondering."

"Do you think that's why he didn't keep his promise to you?" I asked. "Because he thought you were beneath him or something?"

He didn't have to think about my question to answer it. Not even for a split second. He said, "I don't. I think he would have done it to anyone."

He continued, because he wanted to. "It didn't matter who you were. You said you've read the police report. And you've probably talked to other people. I'm sure you've heard similar stories. Not necessarily on this scale, or for money, but he let down all kinds of people for all kinds of reasons. I found all that out too late. And not just people from the Valley, like me. His brother. He was always letting Greer down. Keaton tried to get in with him after his marina started doing okay, and I heard that Greer just said no. No way. I actually heard this story before the bar—Keaton told me, actually. And he convinced me that Greer was jealous of him and didn't want to get outshone at the marina. I bought it at the time. I'll tell you, there's a guy,

Dave Treadway, he was in Keaton's crowd, or from his neighborhood—he was really Greer's friend, I think, and not a prick. A pretty good guy, as I remember. He came by the bar a few times. But then later I ran into him randomly, after all this shit went down. He gave me some good perspective on Keaton. He was the one who made me realize that my getting screwed over had nothing to do with me. Told me a story that Keaton had fallen out with some guys from USC, right after college, some other rich kids, over some movie one of them was trying to get funding for. Over some promise Keaton broke. Point being, Keaton would shit on anyone. And then I heard later that after the bar, Keaton got into the tropical fish business for a while, and *that* didn't work out, you know, for *some* reason. Keaton bailing in one way or another, I'm sure. The guy was just a douche, man. Just a douche."

You could tell that he was still hurt by it all, getting worked up, but that it gave him at least some relief that others had been burned too.

I said, "You got talked to by the cops a lot, even after they determined that you weren't a suspect."

"Yeah, I got talked to a lot. They knew I didn't do it. But they came back to me a few times, I think because I was so open about how much I disliked Keaton. I mean, even more than everyone else. I've calmed down a lot about it. But, man, at the time, I was saying stuff like, I'm glad he's dead, and I *wish* I'd done it. Probably not too smart, but I was still mad. Really mad. Truth is, even now, when I start to get back into it, the anger comes up. It's coming up a little bit now."

He sat there thinking, and the more he thought, the more he heated up.

"Listen to this," Craig began. "One time, he was dating this girl. Some random girl. Nothing serious. This was when we had the bar. And he was out with her, and he met another girl while they were out. So he picks up the new girl and just leaves the first one at the bar with no way to get home. Now, I know that's not the end of the world in the grand scheme. It's not like he killed anyone. But the thing was, he came in the next day and told me the story as if it was a joke. As if it was a story I was supposed to find really funny and, like, laugh at. I remember looking at him like he was from a different planet. And I remember thinking, This guy has no clue that the story he just told makes him seem like a total asshole."

I looked at Craig. Burned, hurt, but on to something with that last story. People often don't know how they really are. Aren't connected to what's really happening with respect to their behavior. This was obviously an extreme example. Leaving a girl at a bar when you're on a date with her is a strikingly clear asshole move. But people do things—lame things, insensitive things—to a much less severe degree all the time, and they often have no clue that they shouldn't be doing them.

Looking back, I know I've committed that crime before.

"You know what else I heard," Craig said, in a way that suggested he wanted to prove to me, if I wasn't convinced already, that Keaton was terrible. "I heard he date-raped a couple of girls in college. Like, forced himself on a couple of girls who were too drunk or too wasted to stop it. I heard this, again, after the bar. I was at a party at a Mexican restaurant in Studio City. Big table. And at the next table over, another big table of people, I see one of the guys who used to come into the bar. So I start talking to him, and the guys with him tell me this date-rape stuff. I didn't know those other guys, and I have no idea if what they were saying was true. And they didn't give me names. They just said they'd heard it. Shit, maybe they knew I was licking my wounds and they were trying to make me feel better by telling me what an asshole Keaton was. But that would be a pretty fucked-up way to make me feel better. I believe it. And, man, think about that. Sleeping with a girl as she's about to pass out. As she's saying *no, stop, don't*. I mean, who would even want to do that? I'll tell you, what's even weirder about that story is that Keaton got girls. When I knew him he did for sure. But I think he always did. Plenty of them. So he just did it for some kind of twisted power trip. What a freak. But I could see it. I could totally see it."

Man, this guy just loathed Keaton Fuller. Loathed him. Greer, Sydney—they didn't have a lot of good things to say. But they at least kept their emotions somewhat in check. Not Craig Helton. His heart was right there on his sleeve. I appreciated it.

I said, handing Craig my card, "I'm not really sure what else to ask you right now. I'd like to know I can call you if I come up with something. I'd also like to thank you for taking the time."

Craig nodded and said, "Call me anytime."

We stood up. We shook hands. And I left.

13

I drove back down that depressing stretch of Valley road toward the freeway, hopped on it, headed south back over the hill. I got back to my office, yanked the slider open, sat down at my desk, and pulled out my MacBook Pro.

I started typing up, in short, crisp bullets, what I knew so far. I do this throughout a case. Basic, brief pieces of information in chronological order. I constantly revise the notes, strip them back to the core nuggets of information. But I add things too, new insights, texture, context. It allows me to go back over the whole case quickly and gives me a simple, written-out narrative that I can print out, hold, and look at. It's interesting, it helps me see where I am, and it often helps me decide where to go. As I was writing out my bullets, I thought, Music, yes, music. I put on Lou Reed's *Street Hassle*, the songs coming out of my new speakers loud and crisp. And then I started to type again. Actually, not true. I started to go insane. *Street Hassle*. Great, inventive record, but the wrong choice for right now. Too weird. Too maddening. I turned it off and sat there. I stopped typing for a sec. I just sat there, thinking. About this guy who nobody liked, getting a big hole put in his chest. About the people in his life at the time of the murder. The sheepish brother, the flaky ex-girlfriend, the burned ex–business partner. And of course the parents. The parents who still grieved profoundly, despite knowing the flaws of their offspring.

So, where to go? You know? The cops had investigated and had ultimately come up empty. Did they do a bad job? Probably not. Look, they don't always do a good job, but they often do, especially when Ott's involved.

So was one of the people I'd talked to hiding something? Sure, it's possible. They all have tight alibis, but that doesn't mean there isn't a nugget buried in one of those stories. Right? Yes, Greer was out in the middle of the ocean, Sydney was in Chicago, Craig was with his family, but any one of them could have been involved *indirectly*. They could have hired someone, or they could know something they aren't telling me. And even if they didn't do it or have it done, they might have been involved somehow in something that maybe wasn't really even their fault. You know? They could have told an unsavory person about Keaton, and then *that* person found a reason to kill him.

The other thought I had was, Okay, the people I've

talked to so far—when I look at them, I don't see it. I don't feel it. I can't see any one of them holding up a gun and firing a hollow-point bullet into the chest of a person they know, or hiring someone else to do it. But the thing is, I *could* be wrong. Because people can snap at any time. Any time. It's such a mystery why and how that happens. Where the rage comes from, and why it comes when it does.

There's a story Ott and the guys down at the station tell about this very subject, and it goes like this. A guy is walking across the street in a really nice section of Santa Monica, Second Street and Wilshire, right by the Fairmont Hotel, right by the Promenade. Beautiful day. A Sunday. So this guy, normal guy, khakis, blazer, is walking across Second Street. And there's a car at the stop sign right there, a guy behind the wheel, waiting for him to cross. Pedestrian's got the right of way, and the guy's walking along, kind of slowly. Just taking his time a bit on a Sunday as he crosses. So the guy in the car honks his horn at him. Not loud. Just a friendly honk. Beep, beep. Let's get moving. And the guy walking across the street? You know what he does? This guy who's never committed a crime in his life, pays his bills, has a family at home? He pulls out a gun and fires three times through the other guy's windshield. Kills the driver. No, more than kills the driver. Unloads into the driver's head until it's nothing but a bunch of blood and brains and bones. Right out of the fucking blue. So where did it come from? The killer's answer was: I'd had enough.

That's what he said.

So, where to go? Where to go?

Do round two on all parties involved to see if they give

me something new, something fresh, something that I can, you know, actually use? See if one of them gives me a reason to believe that they just went off the rails for some reason, like the guy in the story? Or hired somebody else to do it? Or something?

Or maybe, maybe, one of the people I'd talked to had already given me something I could use.

With a case like this, a case that never had a suspect and eventually went cold, you have to really look at the edges. You have to. After all, what choice do you have? The police had come up empty.

I thought about all the things all the people I'd talked to had said. Had anyone given me anything? Had anything stood out as unusual, interesting, weird even? You had a guy running a marina wearing a puka-shell necklace, an ex-girlfriend play-fighting in her yard, an ex–business partner in a tragic insurance office in the Valley, Keaton dabbling in the tropical fish business . . .

The tropical fish business.

I mean, what the fuck is that? I've never heard of anyone being in the tropical fish business. Have you? What does that even mean? Owning an aquarium store? Being one of those guys in really short running shorts and a Hawaiian shirt, with a parrot on his shoulder and a station wagon out back with a bunch of nets and shit in it? Or does it mean breeding and selling expensive fish to weirdo fish people and Bond villains? No clue. But if anything stuck out, *that* stuck out. Right? That's something lurking on the edge of this story. So why not look into it.

Right?

14

I produced the card that Craig Helton had given me just a couple of hours ago. I dialed the number. He answered.

"I didn't think you'd call me so quickly," he said, surprised.

"I didn't either. Have a question, though."

"Yeah."

"You said Keaton went into the tropical fish business. Can you tell me a little more about that? What does that mean, exactly?"

Craig Helton laughed. "I know. Pretty out there, right? Truth is, I don't know that much about it. It was after the bar; we weren't speaking. But I'll tell you what I know."

"Great."

"It was some kind of high-end tropical fish business. Where people spend a lot of money for certain kinds of fish. Not fish you can buy in just a regular old pet store or aquarium place or whatever. That's really all I know. Every time I heard anything about it, I just said, 'Please stop, I don't care.' But like I said, I heard it didn't work out. Keaton left the business, skipped out on them or something. Shocking."

"Did you ever hear who the people were that he was working with? Or did the company have a name that you remember?"

"Never heard anything about the people. But the company, yeah. What was it called? Ugh. I put it out of my mind. Ugh. Man. I can't remember." And then he said, "Let me think. My wife might remember. I'll figure it out and call you back."

"Thank you," I said.

We hung up.

I started looking around the web, doing a cursory investigation into expensive tropical fish. To get my head around what this business might have been about. And, man, I learned quickly that there are indeed some expensive fish out there. With some wild names to boot.

The clarion angelfish. Indigenous to islands off the coast of Mexico. Goes for anywhere from twenty-five hundred to seven thousand dollars a pop. I looked at a picture of one. It was striking, quite beautiful, really. Flat and disk-shaped, bright orange, and sort of see-through, with vertical indigo-blue stripes down its face and side.

The Australian flathead perch. Not as beautiful as the clarion angelfish, to my eye, but certainly interesting looking. Also orange, but not as bright. This one was long, sleek, skinny, minnowlike, with white horizontal stripes rimmed in black. Five thousand bucks.

And look at this. Wow, *really*? The freshwater polka-dot stingray. A black Taiwanese stingray, two little alien eyes on the top of its head, covered in bright white circles, polka dots, of various sizes. One hundred thousand dollars. For one.

And . . . holy shit, you have got to be kidding me. Looks like this might be the top dog. The platinum arowana. Valued at almost four hundred thousand dollars. A big fish compared to the others, looks like two feet long or so. And all white, a bright, glowing white, all over. With a white iris around a yellow eye. I thought: I'm not sure I've ever seen an all-white fish. And then I saw why. There are green, red, silver arowana, and other colors too, found in waters off Africa, Southeast Asia, and South America. But to be white, all white, means a genetic mutation. A rarity. A mistake. I found a video of a platinum arowana moving slowly through a massive aquarium. It had a little bit of an underbite and a slightly smooshed face. Because of the all-white body and the translucent white fins, it blurred a bit as it undulated through the water. It evoked an image of a white Persian cat swimming around underwater, fur swaying as it moved through the water, creating a trailing blur.

Jeez, I don't know if it's worth nearly half a mil, but it's mesmerizing, that's for sure. I watched it some more. Sliding, swaying, blurring.

My phone buzzed and shook. I looked. Craig Helton. I answered.

"Hey, Craig."

"Prestige Fish," he said.

"That was the name?"

"Yep."

"Wow. I think I ate dinner there a couple of days ago."

I heard a stony silence through the phone. Maybe just the slightest hum of a computer or copier in the depressing office where Craig sat.

I continued, "In that Prestige Fish could be the name of a restaurant. It kind of sounds like a restaurant."

"Oh," Craig said. "That was the name of the tropical fish business. Not any restaurant."

I said, "No, I know. I was kidding around. Like, Prestige Fish *could* be the name of a fish place where you could go for a little salmon or something."

Again, no response from Craig. Just that hum in the background. I thought I now maybe heard something being printed. I decided it was time to stop trying to explain to Craig what I had meant. "Never mind," I said. "And thanks, Craig. Thanks for calling me back."

"You bet, John. Call me anytime."

I Googled Prestige Fish, found it, went to the site. It was very simple. No pictures of fish, no pictures of anything. Just a black background and a description of the business, a contact e-mail, and a phone number in crisp yellow type. Interesting. The super-low-tech website, the simplicity of it, suggested confidence, made it seem like they knew what they were doing.

The description of the business read: "We find rare

tropical fish for fish lovers and collectors. Contact us with inquiries or to make an appointment."

Brokers. These guys were brokers. Like real estate agents. Except instead of finding you a high-priced house, they find you a high-priced version of Nemo.

Man, the things that people are into and are willing to pay crazy money for. Cars, sure, but watches, wine, flowers. And fish.

I continued looking around the web to try to make a little more sense of the overall world. I learned pretty quickly that there are people who dive for exotic fish and people who breed exotic fish all over the planet. Hawaii, China, Indonesia, and, like I'd seen in my initial search, Mexico, Australia, Japan. These divers and breeders usually sell the fish to big companies with massive spaces filled with aquariums and pools. Most of the fish have some value, but not insane value, like the platinum arowana. More like fifty bucks a fish, twenty bucks a fish, that kind of thing. The big companies then mass breed the fish and sell them to everyone else—to aquarium stores all over the world, or even straight to customers. The big companies will occasionally get their hands on a rare fish with real value, a fish that is very hard to catch or breed, like a clarion angelfish, and they'll sell it to a high-end fish store or, again, straight to a collector. Prestige Fish, I guessed, just dealt in the high-dollar ones, the rare ones; did the work of finding the fish for you and getting the fish to you.

And how did all these fish get shipped around? Get from a mass breeder to a customer? Get from a diver in

Indonesia to a collector in America? That's what I was wondering. And when I found out, it seemed absurd and almost impossible, but yet it somehow made sense.

They put the fish in a plastic bag with a little water, put it in a box, and overnight it to you.

I sat back and had a thought. Which was: I guess I'm lucky. I mostly just want to work, hit Ping-Pong balls, enjoy cold light beer, and hang out with Nancy. Thank god I don't want to spend a bunch of mental energy, and money, on a bunch of overpriced goldfish.

And then I had another thought, and it was this: If I can get a meeting with the people at Prestige Fish, whoever they are, I'm going to pretend I'm an interested customer.

Why? Why not just tell them I'm a detective and I'm looking into the murder of a man named Keaton Fuller, a man who, I believe, was involved in this business somehow?

Well, sometimes I like to look around, get the feel of a situation, before telling the people there I'm a private cop up in their business. And let's not forget—in *this* situation, it's tropical fucking fish. Just out of the box enough to be something.

I entered a prefix into my phone that made it read "private," didn't want my name somehow appearing, then dialed the number on the Prestige Fish site. I got a recording. I left a message.

"Hi, my name is John Dean. I'm calling because I'm interested in talking to you about acquiring some fish. I'm in L.A. Perhaps I can schedule a time to talk to you soon, in person. Please call me back when you can."

I left my number.

John Dean is a name I use sometimes. One, it's close to my actual name, so I can remember it. Two, if they search for it they'll find a million of them and won't know which way to turn. You give the name Denton Duzenswaddle and they either know you're full of shit immediately, or they find the one guy who's actually named that, call him, and realize pretty damn quickly that he's not interested in buying any Australian flat-head perches.

Nine minutes later I got a call back from the number I had dialed.

"This is John," I said.

"Hi, John. My name is Elana," said a soft, sexy voice. "I'm with Prestige Fish, returning your call."

"Hi, Elana, thank you for calling me back."

"You're welcome," she said.

"You're welcome." You don't always hear that when you say "thank you." You often hear "no problem" or "absolutely" or something. "You're welcome." Something about it felt direct, confident, like the website.

She said, "You'd like to come in and discuss what you're looking for?"

"Yes, I would."

"Great," she said. "How did you hear about us?"

What to say, what to say? Keep it short, keep it simple. I said, "The web."

"Okay," she said. "We don't do orders under five thousand."

"Fine," I said.

"We can do two o'clock Monday, tomorrow."

"Fine," I said again.

She gave me the address and we hung up. Then I closed up my office and went home.

15

When I got home, I went for a five-mile run around Mar Vista. Not too fast, not too slow. Just a nice, steady pace. When I finished my run, I went into my garage. I don't park my car there, ever. It's where I work out. I have a hanging punching bag, a bench press, some arm weights, and some floor mats.

I worked the bag for forty-five minutes. First punches: jabs, and hooks. Then elbows: elbow jabs, and elbow hooks. Then kicks: front kicks, back kicks, roundhouse kicks. At knee level, groin level, chest level. Then a series of knees to the bag. Thigh level. Groin level. For each section of the workout, I'd start slow and loose. Then I'd build to a finish, striking the bag as hard and as precisely as I possibly could.

I learned how to fight from a neighbor I had as a child, an ex–Green Beret by the name of Jim Douglas. Jim's a black belt in karate, but formal karate is not what he taught me. He taught me a more street-style form of fighting that encompasses some karate, some boxing, and some down-and-dirty, do-whatever-you-have-to-to-win bar fighting. Having this skill really comes in handy when I need to defend myself, or hurt someone who just might deserve it. Jim is more than just the man who taught me how to fight, though. He was, and still is, a mentor of sorts to me. And you know what? You're going to meet him later on in this very story.

After working the bag, wiping myself out, I got down on the padded floor mats and stretched for thirty minutes. Then I went inside and drank a freezing Coors Light in four sips.

The next day I woke up early and went for another run. Three miles. Took this one a little slower, just used it as a way to think about the various parts of my case, yeah, to relax a little, see if the old subconscious would throw me any new ideas.

Around noon I showered, put on some jeans and a black James Perse shirt, cut tight. Look the part, Darvelle. Look the part. That's what I told myself. Even though I had absolutely no idea what a guy who spends his life savings on fish is supposed to look like. At one, I was in my car.

Prestige Fish was in Thousand Oaks, one of the really nice sections of the Valley. It's far, far away from that strip of road where Craig Helton sits selling insurance. Both literally and figuratively. Thousand Oaks is some twenty miles northwest of Craig's part of the Valley. A lush, upscale suburban area filled with lots of, you guessed it, beautiful oak trees. It's far enough away from downtown, Hollywood, or Santa Monica that it really seems like it's not connected to L.A. at all, and many of the people who live there act like it, rarely visiting the aforementioned areas.

As I cruised up the 405, I thought: Kind of a strange location for a fish broker. Although I'm not sure why I thought that. Did I think a fish broker should be in Santa Monica or Malibu or Manhattan Beach because those areas are near the ocean? Maybe. Sadly, maybe.

I followed my GPS directions and ended up in a nice town-center area, on a charming street lined with high-end commerce. A polished and pristine-looking Coffee Bean & Tea Leaf, a nice-looking Mexican restaurant with a big outside area and fire pit, an overpriced grocery store. I turned right off the main drag, onto a much smaller side street. About a mile down, I found a lone little building sitting on its own little corner lot. The structure was a fairly new-looking one-story redbrick building with white shutters that could have been a small law office in Memphis. Hmm. Prestige Fish.

I rounded the corner, put the Focus in a spot up a ways, out of sight, walked back around through the little front yard and up to the white door.

I carefully opened it and walked in. A simple, sparse room, a Turkish rug covering much of the hardwood floor. A few sleek chairs in one corner, a pristine glass desk in front of the wall facing the door. Behind it sat a striking, beautiful woman with black hair, pale skin, and bright red lipstick.

The woman said without getting up, "You must be John."

I nodded.

"I'm Elana. We spoke on the phone. Can I offer you a cup of coffee or a cocktail?"

She was like a beautiful stewardess in the first-class cabin of a plane floating above the world.

"Sure," I said. "Thank you. I'll have a cup of coffee. Black."

She disappeared down a hallway behind her, then reappeared with a cup of coffee in a tall porcelain mug. As she handed it to me, she said, "Lee's going to be a few minutes. Lee Graves. That's who you'll be talking to about what you are interested in acquiring."

"Acquiring," the word I had used in my message.

She said, "Would you like to see the fish we have here while you wait? They're not for sale, but our customers usually enjoy seeing them."

I looked at her. Hospitable, but not overly so. She operated with a deft, delicate, and reserved touch. Not an ounce of pushiness. And she spoke quietly and precisely, in a soothing voice. I wanted to close my eyes and just listen to her talk for a while. But instead I said, "Yes. I'd like to see the fish."

"Follow me," she said, almost in a whisper.

"Yes," I said oddly.

We walked down the hall behind her desk, past a shut

door on the left, then a little kitchen on the right. Just beyond the kitchen, we reached what I thought was a closed door. But it wasn't a door. It was the entrance to an elevator. And I knew from the outside of the building that we weren't going up.

We got in the elevator and went slowly down one floor.

We exited into an empty foyer. The lights were very low and the room was cool. We then walked into a room about the size of a big master bedroom, also softly and very dimly lit.

Like the main room upstairs, this one had a beautiful Turkish rug covering a big chunk of the hardwood floor. On the right wall were two large aquariums, bright and beautiful and humming, and there were two more on the left wall. One of the two on the left had multiple fish in it, but the other three contained just a single fish.

We walked over to one of the tanks on the right, one of the tanks with just a single fish inside. It was a wild-looking pink and yellow fish with a large mouth and white stripes running vertically down its body. Not exactly beautiful, but definitely unusual, interesting, exotic.

"Our Neptune grouper," Elana said. "Very rare."

I watched the fish move through the tank. Its big, frowning mouth. Its big, never-blinking eyes. It didn't seem to mind that two large creatures were watching its every move.

As we walked over to the tank next to it, I heard the elevator open. I turned to see a man stepping out of the foyer.

He was probably thirty-five, about six-one, totally

bald—a slick, just-shaved bald head—and in very good shape. Not bulky good shape. Sinewy. Wiry. He had one of those big, expensive watches that people wear these days. Enormous. Just enormous. You could serve dinner on the face of it. For seven. And everyone would have plenty of room. He also wore tight, expensive, but terrible designer jeans and a tight, fitted black V-neck T-shirt with some kind of dragon print on it.

He walked over and said, "Hi, John Dean. I'm Lee Graves."

I nodded, and we shook. He looked suspicious, and suspicious of me.

Elana said, "I showed John the Neptune grouper, and we were just about to look at—"

I interrupted as I walked closer to the tank we stood next to and said, "The clarion angelfish."

It was a risk. But I was pretty sure I was right. Turns out, I was.

Graves said, "One of the most beautiful fish, I think. Pretty rare these days—not *that* rare, but pretty rare." And then he looked at me, gave me a devilish grin, and said, "I can get you one."

Graves had deep-set eyes, and his skin was really tight on his face. He was one of those people who look like skeletons, his clean-shaven head and clean-shaven face adding to the image.

I turned to look at the clarion angelfish. I'd seen a picture of it online, but now I was seeing it for real, seeing it move, seeing it glide. Graves was right. It was beautiful. A small blue mouth, big eyes, a feminine quality. A deep orange with those deep blue vertical stripes that almost looked like gashes in its body.

I turned back to face Elana and Lee Graves. And Graves said, "Elana."

And Elana left. One word, gone. Into the foyer, into the elevator, gone.

Just me, Lee Graves, and the fish now. Graves had an energy that made it seem like he was moving even when he wasn't. And he had a wild, unpredictable look in his eyes. The combination gave the impression that he could strike at any moment. Like a snake. I could see us coming to blows someday—I wasn't exactly sure why. But I was exactly sure that I was looking forward to it.

I'd wanted to get a look at this place before revealing myself as a private eye. I told you that already. Sometimes it's better to do that. You often get a more *accurate* impression of something. I basically told you that already too. And now that I was here, as John Dean, I was glad I had made that decision. There was something strange about this operation. And not just the fact that an entire business was set up around finding people expensive, colorful, gilled creatures. However, when you're in a situation under an alias you can sometimes end up in a spot where you don't know exactly what to say in order to keep up the act. Which, I'm afraid, was where I was. So at that point, it's either tell the people you are lying to who you are, or figure out a way to get out of there.

Before Graves could ask me just exactly what it was that I wanted to acquire, I said, stalling, as I gestured to the tanks, "Who takes care of these?"

"See that door right there?" he said, pointing to a door at the other end of the room, opposite the foyer and the elevator. "That's the door my staff uses. They come in from the back of the building. Down a service elevator. When we moved in, the elevators were already here. A paraplegic stock trader used to work out of this building. This room was filled with screens that he stared at all day. I liked it for my fish. Elevators provide more security than stairs. And I've had some very valuable species in here over the years. My staff comes in twice a day. They keep the tanks clean and temperate, feed the fish, keep them healthy and happy. The clarion angelfish is my baby. She's lived here for three years."

Graves had answered my question, and in doing so had told me blatantly that he knew what he was doing. *I've had some very valuable species in here over the years.* And: *She's lived here for three years.* Now he was ready to get down to business.

He said, "What are you looking for, John?"

I had gotten an idea. I'd decided to go for the get-out-of-there route as opposed to the tell-him-who-I-am route. I said, "Lee. I'm just getting started. So I really don't know exactly what I'm looking for. I know I love exotic fish. I know that when I look at that clarion angelfish it does something to me. Moves me. So I'm going to put an aquarium, a beautiful aquarium, in my new house. When I buy it, that is. I found you on the web, and now that I've met you it's cool to know that when I'm ready to make some purchases you're one of the people I can call."

I could see the slight deflation in his eyes. Just what

I wanted. To him, now, I was a flake. I was a flake who wasn't serious. Who wasn't really going to shell out ten, twenty, fifty Gs. Shit, I didn't even have a tank yet. I didn't even have a house yet. Graves looked, just for a second, like a real estate agent who's just realized that the person he's been driving around the really nice part of town for the last ten days isn't serious and doesn't really have the dough he pretended to. But like any business pro, Graves didn't overreact. He just shot me a sinister smile out of that skeleton head and said, "I'll be right here when you're ready."

And I looked at him, right at him, and said, "Good to know."

16

I think it should be hard to get a gun. Really hard. Much harder than it is. Because too many people get their hands on them who shouldn't. It's that simple. In my business, I have to use a gun sometimes, there's no getting around it. But the truth is, I don't own just one. I own two. When I've got one physically on me, which is pretty often, it's usually my Colt Delta Elite. A powerful ten-millimeter gun that holds eight rounds. I wear it on my hip in a holster, usually under a jacket or shirt. Or sometimes I pin it on my back with my belt. I also have a Sig Sauer P229, which is a powerful gun as well, but it's smaller, easier to conceal, despite the fact that it actually holds ten rounds. I wear my Sig less often, and almost always totally out of view, in a holster on my ankle.

For some reason, my meeting with Graves prompted in me the desire to practice my shooting. There was something about him. He was . . . serious, maybe even threatening. And being in close proximity to that made me want to get *active*, to actively pursue getting better at one of the parts of my job. I've practiced a lot over the years, and I'm a good shot with both guns. But like most things, shit, anything you're trying to do well, you have to keep the sword sharp, you have to do that thing that Sydney Scott hated to do at photography school. You have to practice.

Right then, I had both guns with me in a black canvas carry bag that also houses a few other things I often need. I drove to Northridge, an area of the Valley not too far away from Thousand Oaks. Northridge is a neighborhood closer in personality to the one where I grew up, and closer to what most people associate with the Valley. Look, we're not talking as depressing as where Craig Helton works. No. Not that bad. Northridge is okay. Fine. Bit less upscale than where Graves brokers deals for clarion angelfish and Neptune groupers. Fewer beautiful oak trees. More not-so-beautiful strip malls.

There's an indoor shooting range in Northridge that I've been to a lot over the years, that I like, the Firing Line. I'm pretty sure it was the first indoor shooting range in L.A.

I got there, got a spot for the Focus, went in, bought some ammo, and got another spot, this time for me and my carry bag, in a firing booth twenty-five yards away from a target that looked like the silhouette of the top half of a man.

I fired twenty-four rounds out of my Colt, changed the paper target, and fired twenty rounds out of my Sig.

Afterward, I looked at both targets in the booth. My chest shots and my head shots, out of both the Colt and the Sig, were solid. But not great. I'd improved as I'd continued to fire, but even still, I was a little rusty. Definitely a little rusty. But that's okay. Because I'd be back here at the Firing Line before it mattered. I hoped.

I headed back to my office. Embarrassingly, I hit some pretty bad traffic, but I eventually made it to Culver City, to my space. I opened up the slider and went and sat at my desk.

I put my feet up, laced my hands behind my head, watched a distant UPS truck make a delivery to one of the warehouses across the lot.

Cold. Yes, the case I was on was cold. And now I'd brought another piece, a new piece, into the puzzle, even though I had no clue whether that piece would fit. Why? Because that's what I had to do. I had to shake some bushes to see if anything crawled, or swam, out.

So what next? What next?

Dave Treadway. Keaton and Greer's friend who Craig Helton had mentioned. The one he'd said "wasn't a prick." The one who helped him see the light about Keaton Fuller's character. Treadway was mentioned in the case file along with a few other friends, people who weren't as close to Keaton. Harrier and Martinez had talked to him anyway, shaking bushes just like me. And Treadway, like Greer and Craig Helton and Sydney Scott, had spoken openly about not particularly loving Keaton. And like the rest of them, he had a tight alibi. Talk to him anyway, I told myself. Go to La Jolla, where he lives, that charming coastal town that sits right on top of San Diego, and talk to him anyway.

La Jolla. Hmm. So I was going to go to the greater San Diego area. I realized that this would give me the opportunity to talk to someone else I needed to talk to who lives down there. Someone who might be able to shed some light on my new puzzle piece, Prestige Fish. His name is Marlon Pucci. He's an ex–New Jersey and New York City mob guy who now lives on a sailboat in a marina in Oceanside, California, a great little seaside town north of San Diego and La Jolla.

When he quit the crime business and moved to Oceanside, Marlon had never been to California, had no boating experience, knew nothing about sailing or the sea, literally didn't have a single clue about how to buy a boat, sail a boat, or care for a boat. Much less live on one. He simply had a romantic notion about living on a sailboat in a California marina. So he did it and never looked back. And you know what? He and his wife, Fran, who also had zero prior boating knowledge, are happy as fucking clams. Sitting on their deck in the evenings, going to parties and get-togethers on other people's boats, drinking in the sun, and, of course, just drinking, period. And never, I mean *never*, actually sailing their boat. It doesn't move.

Where did he get this romantic notion? What planted the seed? Well, a murder. Way back when, Marlon whacked a guy and dumped his body in the Atlantic. His mobster buddies nicknamed him Marlon the Marlin. They were razzing him, ribbing him, about his seafaring adventure, but Marlon liked the name. It stuck. What's more, it placed in him—this Jersey born wiseguy—the desire to own the nickname thoroughly and to one day be a full-on boat-living man. Which now he is. And loving every minute of it. And, by the way, getting the last laugh.

I worked a case for Marlon and his wife a few years back. After I found his wife's son, who'd been missing, and everything had essentially worked out, Marlon told me to call on him if I ever thought he could help me. Turns out the old mobster knows a whole lot about a whole lot from his past experiences. And to this day, he still has his ear to the ground. I take him up on his offer not infrequently.

I thought, Well, at least these two puzzle pieces fit together. I could take one trip to San Diego and talk to two people. And, wait, Marlon the Marlin? The fish theme of my story was continuing. Was that a third puzzle piece locking in? A sign saying that talking to my old mobster friend was a necessary element to me getting to the bottom of this quagmire?

Perhaps. Or perhaps it was just a coincidence. That's always the question, right? Is something a coincidence or is it *meant to be*? Because when coincidences happen, you can say: Yeah, makes sense, feels right, there's a certain magic to this, it *should* be happening. Or you can say: Well, nothing like this has happened in a while, and there have been a zillion moments of late that haven't contained any special magic, so this supposedly special thing isn't really special at all. It's only happening randomly, simply because random stuff happens *every so often*.

Right now, I'm going with the former. Because it's all I got. You see what I'm saying?

It was too late to hit the 405 South and head toward San Diego. We're talking stifling, kill-yourself traffic. You know that by now. So I went home, then went to my backyard and took an evening swim in my pool. I'd put a deep rectangular pool in my backyard four years after buying the house. I'd painted the bottom of it a deep, dark blue. In the late evening, when the sun is just about gone, it makes the water in the pool look purple.

It was that time now, the sky just starting to really darken as I dove into the cool, purple water. I closed my eyes and put my hands out and glided the full length of the pool, until my hands softly hit the wall of the shallow end. I came up for air, then turned around, went back down, kicked off the end wall, and shot toward the deep end. This time I kept my eyes open and looked around my liquid purple surroundings like I was a Neptune grouper or a clarion angelfish or a Persian-catlike platinum arowana.

Next morning I called Marlon the Marlin from my house, told him I was going to head down his way, asked him if he had some time to talk.

"For you, Johnny, my boy, I do."

We settled on 3 p.m.

"Hey," he said. "Can you pick me up a bottle of rum? Fran's back East visiting some sick relative, so I can't send her to get it, and I don't feel like going onshore."

Onshore. By that he meant stepping off his boat onto the dock.

"Absolutely. What kind—"

Before I finished my question he said, "Mount Gay. Half gallon."

"You will see me and a half gallon of Mount Gay at 3 p.m."

"I'm counting the minutes," he said as he clicked off.

17

It's a mostly unpleasant drive down the 405 and then the 5 to get to the greater San Diego area. Long stretches of bleak gray concrete, car dealerships on both sides, weird highway-bordering office buildings housing people doing who knows what. And then, as you get near the towns north of San Diego—Carlsbad, Oceanside, Encinitas—the drive starts to take on a different feel. You begin to see glimpses of ocean, of trees, of beautiful cliffs standing tall above a beautiful beach.

And then when you turn off the highway and head due west to enter one of those little seaside towns—that's when the California magic really hits you. That's when you can smell the salt in the air, see the white sand and the big green sea, roll the window down and feel cool air and hot sun simultaneously.

And that's what I did. Off the 5, into Oceanside, and then into Marlon the Marlin's marina. The Oceanside Marina. Before I got out of the Focus I called Dave Treadway, nobody home, left a message on his cell saying I was in the area and to please call me.

Here I was at another marina. Two marinas in four days. Was I in danger of becoming a boat person? Holy smokes, that's frightening. I walked through the lot, then wound my way through the marina toward Marlon's sailboat. I knew my way, had been many times. Right before I got to Marlon's slip, I ran into another marina dweller I'd met a few times while visiting. Hunter Clavana, an Aussie.

"The Darv? How you doing, mate?"

How convenient, he's got two reasons to say "mate."

"Hey, Hunter. What's happening?" I looked at him. I had literally never seen a white man that color. He wasn't tan. He wasn't brown. He was a deep, disturbing, almost charcoal gray. His skin had literally been cooked.

He said, "Oh, all's good. I've felt better, though. Birthday was yesterday. Had too much of that."

He pointed at the half gallon I had in my hand.

"Right," I said. "How old?"

"Thirty-seven."

He looked a hundred. He did. Maybe a hundred and ten.

"Well," I said, moving on, "happy belated."

When I got to Marlon's sailboat, he was on the deck, asleep. Or at least it looked that way—he had his eyes closed. I stepped aboard, walked over, and sat in a chair that was built into the side of the boat. A nice blue cushion. A sly smile appeared on Marlon's face, his eyes still closed, and he said, "How you doing, John?"

"I'm great, Marlon. How are you?"

He opened his eyes and said, "Look at me. I'm fucking wonderful."

I did look at him. Lean and strong into his sixties. With ropy arms, bird legs, and a little old-man gut. A charming shark smile set against dark, suspicious eyes. He was wearing shorts, deck shoes, and an open Hawaiian shirt. And of course, he was tan. Too tan.

I pointed to the silver aviators I was wearing and said, "How do you not wear sunglasses out here, Marlon? It's bright. I mean, the sun bouncing off the water, it's *bright*."

"Fucks with my tan," he said. "If it gets too bright, I just close my eyes. Like I was doing just now when you showed up. I wasn't sleeping. I was sitting, resting, with my eyes closed. And tanning my lids."

"When's Fran coming back?"

"Soon, I hope. Back when I used to play around, I'd love it when my old lady would leave. Shit, back in Jersey, when Fran would go visit her mom, her sister, I'd be looking out the blinds as she left in the cab. And the second that cab left, the second that fucking cab left, I'd run to my car and go to a strip joint. It didn't matter if it was 9 a.m. I'd find one that was open. And I'd have my face buried in some dancer's tits before Fran got to the airport. But now? I don't play around. I don't do that stuff. So I just get bored and lonely. Shit, I'm even glad to see you."

I gave him a smile and handed him the jug of booze.

Marlon said, "You want a rum drink?"

"Yeah, I'll have one. Not too strong."

"I'll make it how I make it."

He had everything he needed right next to him on a little table. He made two drinks at once, going through a careful, meticulous process. Drop the ice in, squeeze the lime, squeeze in the liquid sugar, top it all off with booze. He stirred both drinks up and handed one to me. It was cold, just a little sweet, delicious. And after one sip, one sip, I felt a tiny buzz. I looked around the marina, rum drink in hand, felt the soft breeze coming in off the Pacific, the boats tilting just slightly back and forth, a little sway to the whole world, a little sway to the reality of life.

"I get it," I said.

"Yeah, you do," Marlon returned, taking a big sip. And then, "What can I do you for?"

"You know anything about the tropical fish business?"

"Sure. That's one of the stops people make when they're looking around for a way to get rich without having to do much. You know, think they can get their hands on some really rare fish, sell a few, and make a bunch of coin. Black pearl business is similar. Gold rush mentality. Lottery players. There's this mystery to those trades, like you are going to find some rare fucking gem. Truth is, it's just like most businesses. Like all businesses. A few people do it right, do it well, make money. Most people don't do it very well. Get lazy real quick. Get flaky. Fail."

He closed his eyes and pointed his face to the sun. "Flaky, just like the food they feed those goddamn things."

He laughed at his own joke.

"See," he continued, opening his eyes back up and looking at me. "Above all, like everything, it's competitive. Unless you work hard, work really hard, know what you are fucking doing, commit to doing it for a long time, or have a scam running, you'll lose."

"What do you mean, a scam running?"

He gave me his hard, dark eyes. "I mean like running a business the way we used to sometimes, back East. Where you said to people: Buy this thing from us—whatever the fuck the thing is—or get shot."

I laughed. "Right. That kind of scam."

Marlon took a big sip of his drink, two, three swallows. "Why do you ask, Johnny?"

"Case I'm on. Murder case. One of the many trails I'm following took me to a high-end tropical fish broker called Prestige Fish. In the Valley, Thousand Oaks. The guy who runs it finds rare, expensive tropical fish for people. Guy by the name of Lee Graves. No idea if this guy's up to something or not. I don't like him. And I've got a bad feeling. But I'm not sure. I don't have anything on him. Yet. But, Marlon, you know how much some of these fish sell for?"

"Oh, yeah. Twenty, thirty large. Sometimes more. Especially when two, three of those crazy fucks who buy them want the same fish and there's only one available."

"Yeah. It's crazy. Imagine if you bought one, got it home, and it died?"

"They have insurance for them. That's a whole other business."

Marlon just knows shit. It's that simple.

A nice breeze came through, rocking the boats and

making the little bells hanging off the tops of some of the sails ring, at just the right volume, randomly throughout the marina. I took another sip of my stiff rum drink. The bells, the buzz. It was pleasant.

My cell rang, breaking the moment. Not going to answer it. Not going to take a call while in a conversation with Marlon the Marlin.

He said, "It's okay. You're on a case. I get it."

I sent the call to voice mail anyway.

"That's nice," he said. "People and their phones these days. Jesus H. Fucking Christ. Back in my day, when I was working in Jersey, New York, working for some serious fucking people—you behave the way people do now? Taking calls when you are already talking to someone else? Looking down at the goddamn screen right in the middle of somebody's goddamn sentence? You might get whacked. I'm not kidding. You might seriously get whacked for that."

I laughed. "Might not be a terrible way to handle the problem. It's pretty horrible."

Marlon nodded. "Let me look around for you, put my ear to the ground, see what I can find out about Lee Graves and Prestige Fish."

That's the thing. Marlon had trained himself to listen, to zero in on and remember important information. Sipping his drink, half asleep and half shitcanned on his boat, but he got the name and the company just right.

"Thanks, Marlon."

"Come down sometime just for fun, why don't you. Fran would love to see you. We'll make some dinner, eat it right out here. After the sun goes down, nice and cool, you can see all the lights on the boats."

"That sounds really nice, Marlon. I will."

He said, "Let me show you my new tattoo before you leave."

He held out his right forearm. There was an anchor tattooed on it. I'd seen it before, many times.

"You already know I have that one," he said. He then stood up, took off his Hawaiian shirt, and turned to show me his left side. "Now I got this one too."

It was an octopus, about six inches in height, wearing a captain's hat. I laughed. The choices people make when it comes to their tattoos never cease to amaze me. This girl who lived down the street from me growing up, Lucy Farina. Nice, friendly girl with this big, friendly smile. Always sweet. So sweet. She got a tattoo on her back of a massive flying pterodactyl with blood dripping out of its huge beak. And now? A former mob guy, a former—and still—tough guy, a guy who has killed people, has a googly-eyed, captain's-hat-wearing octopus on his side.

"How'd you choose that?" I said carefully.

"I always wanted an octopus with a fucking sailor hat on my body."

"Yeah?"

"No. Fran and I went into town and got shit-faced, fucking blotto, and I made a mistake. But now he's my friend and I like him."

"There's a lesson in there somewhere."

"I'll call you when I got something, Johnny."

I shook Marlon's hand, hopped off the boat, and started back toward the parking lot. I called my voice mail on the way. Mr. Dave Treadway getting back to me. How nice.

18

Dave Treadway had left me a friendly message saying he was happy to talk and that I should call him back to set something up. So I did.

"Hey, Dave. It's John Darvelle. Thanks for getting back to me."

"You bet. What's happening? How can I help?"

"As I mentioned in my message, I'm a detective—"

"Yes. Sorry to interrupt, but Greer Fuller actually told me you might be calling. So I know the basic gist, his parents hired you . . . you want to talk about Keaton . . . cool, yeah, I can talk."

"Great. Well, as I also mentioned, I'm in the area. I'm in Oceanside right now. Any chance you can meet somewhere to talk in person? I can drive down to La Jolla."

"Um, let me see . . . I'm actually at work now but was planning to go home soon." He thought for a second. "Yeah, we could meet somewhere, or . . . do you want to just come by my apartment?"

I said, "Sounds good."

Now, from Oceanside to La Jolla, that's a drive. Full views of big, dramatic cliffs; deep, forest-green trees lining the highway; and an often not-so-pacific Pacific crashing around out to the right.

I powered my windows down, the air getting a little cooler now, the sky darkening a bit too, making the colors it was holding contrast and pop more, a swath of sherbet orange going into a darker tangerine orange going into a wispy pink sitting right above the horizon.

You could knock San Diego, and the greater San Diego area, as the land of perma-tans and hot tubs and fake boobs—I know, I know, how is that a knock?—but nowhere can you feel the magic of California as strongly as in *this* part of California. Even the airport in San Diego, the one all the surrounding towns use, has a dreamy California energy. Ever been? It's like walking through the Love Boat, in a good way. Beautiful blondes strutting around in pantsuits, golden light cascading across groovy circular bars that look out on the runways. I swear, I think I saw Isaac there at one point.

I drove through Del Mar, then Torrey Pines, then made my way into downtown La Jolla. A little bit of a tourist vibe, but still pretty damn charming, pretty damn California. A little city with a few reasonably tall buildings, a little town center with restaurants and shops I'd never go in, all built around and funneling down to the La Jolla Cove. Lots of those California folks who seem to have plenty of money but no jobs. And some after-work folks too, in their business casual, strolling around, feeling the soft late-afternoon breezes, the big Pacific hanging in the background of the cove, ever present.

Dave Treadway's building was in downtown La Jolla. Near the beach, but not on it. I don't know about you, but when I think of someone living in San Diego or La Jolla, I don't really think of an urban, semi-high-rise apartment building. I think of a light blue clapboard house on the beach, or a Spanish number stuck to the side of a cliff. Not the case here. This was a twenty-or-so-story, sharp-looking building with lots of glass and silver steel. Treadway told me how to park underneath it. I did, and then I was out of the Focus, in a garage elevator, then a lobby, then another elevator up to the fourteenth floor, then walking down a slick, clean hallway.

Right as I got to 14F, the door opened. Dave Treadway was lean and tan and tall, six-three, with dark hair and light eyes.

"Hello, Dave."

"Hi," he said, sticking out his hand and smiling.

He had a friendly smile but a slight underbite to his jaw, giving his traditionally handsome look a little tension.

We walked into the apartment. It was big, with an open feel. It was well decorated, modern but not overly stark or uninviting. Some furniture that had probably been passed down from a parent was mixed in with some sleeker, more contemporary pieces. It all felt very hip, stylish, but also comfortable. You could see hallways heading out of the main room in both directions, more rooms. And, of course, there was the main attraction: big windows lining the whole back wall that held views of downtown La Jolla to the right and the cove to the left, the Pacific sitting, looming, rocking in the distance. There was a balcony outside with some comfortable, stylish furniture, to enjoy it all the more. It all looked good. Either Dave had parents like Keaton and Greer's, or this cat had done well for himself.

Treadway looked at me. "Can I offer you a drink? You want a beer?"

I moved my eyes from the distant ocean and said, "Uh, yeah. Sure."

"Budweiser okay?"

I chuckled to myself. "Yeah. Great."

Treadway went into the kitchen, which was in the corner of the main room, rattled around in there for a second, came back out and handed me a cold, canned Budweiser and a small white cocktail napkin. This young man appeared to have a clue. "Want to sit outside?"

I looked out the big glass wall again and nodded.

Out on the balcony he took a couch, I took a chair. There was a nice breeze, soft sunset light, some faint sounds of traffic. Yeah, it was nice.

"So what's the latest?" he asked.

"What you said on the phone. Keaton Fuller's family has hired me to look back into the case. That's really it. That's the latest. I'm talking to everyone the cops talked to, and some new people too."

He nodded.

I said, "So, how did you know Keaton?"

"Family friend. My mom remarried when I was thirteen. Married a guy in Hancock Park, up in L.A. So we moved there and I became their neighbor."

"You moved from where?"

"Here. Well, San Diego."

"And your dad?"

"San Diego. Never left. He remarried too, by the way, but stayed put. If you were wondering about my dad's love life after he and my mom divorced."

He chuckled. I did too.

"Okay. So you moved to Hancock Park."

"Yeah. Became neighbors with the Fullers. Better friends with Greer, he's my age. But I knew Keaton pretty well too. Really well, I'd say. Spent a lot of time with both those guys over the years. Always at the same neighborhood parties. Always at each other's houses. Same middle school as Greer. We all drifted apart a little as Keaton went off to college, Greer and I went to different high schools and colleges . . . But I still know the family, even now. And my mom and her husband are still their neighbors."

"I know you told the cops this already, but, if you don't mind going over it again . . . what are your thoughts about Keaton Fuller?"

Dave Treadway looked down at his feet, then he looked at me with his blue eyes and his slight underbite.

He said, with some sensitivity, "Keaton Fuller was a guy with some problems." And then, "He wasn't a great guy."

Treadway appeared to be a person who knew how to say things in a way that wouldn't come across as overly crass or offensive or disrespectful to the dead. That said, he had just come right out, in his own way, with a negative assessment.

And why wouldn't he? Ultimately, here was another guy with nothing to hide. Another rock-solid alibi. The building's cameras had Dave getting off the elevator with his wife and child and going into their apartment the night before the murder. At 6:30 on the morning of the shooting, Dave had talked to the doorman from inside the apartment, using the apartment's intercom system, to tell him about a couch delivery happening that day, which was also confirmed by the furniture company. At 7:45 a.m., the building's cameras had Dave leaving his apartment for work, same time as he left every day. The garage cameras had both his cars sitting in the garage all night. Not to mention the fact that the Treadways live in a different city. You're talking about 125 miles of traffic-laden highway between Dave's place and Keaton's place. And, for good measure, on the morning of the murder there were two accidents on the freeways: one on the 5 South, the other on the 405 South, putting the travel time from Los Angeles to La Jolla at roughly three hours no matter which way you went. Of course, like the others, he could have hired someone, could have been involved in some other way, but right now it looked like he didn't have to watch what he said.

I thought Treadway was about to say something else, maybe something a little harsher than "he wasn't a great guy," when the sliding glass door to the balcony opened. A tan, tall, athletic woman with sandy blond hair and very friendly eyes stood there. A blond little boy with wet, just-combed hair stood next to her, holding her hand. Apparently Dave's wife had been in one of the back rooms giving their son a bath.

"Hiiiiii," she said, drawing out the word in a singsongy, charming way.

I instinctively stood up. And then a feeling came over me that was foreign, unsettling. I was intensely dizzy. I felt, for an extreme few seconds, that I was going to throw up or fall down or both. I got a strange, sickening taste in my throat, like that taste you get when you put your tongue up to a battery. I looked around for the arm of the chair or the railing of the balcony, something to hold on to, when the feeling suddenly surged in intensity. I was definitely going to vomit. *Right now.* And then, and *then*, it disappeared. Vanished. Instantly. Went away as fast, faster, than it had appeared. I took a breath, thinking, Holy shit, what *was* that? The height? Being pretty far up in the sky? Realizing, I guess subconsciously, that if I stumbled and the railing gave way I could die? Maybe. But I don't know. I had never been afraid of heights, and I've been on lots of fucking balconies. Was it something about this woman? Did I know her somehow? Had I seen her before? No, I didn't. And I hadn't. I definitely had not.

Dave said, "John, this is my wife, Jill. Jill, this is John Darvelle, the detective."

"Hello," she said, an amiable smile spreading across her face as she extended her hand and we shook. "And this is young David. We call him Davey."

I looked at the child. "Hi, Davey!" I said and smiled, doing my best to talk to a very young kid even though I really didn't know how to. Davey smiled and then his face went blank for a second, that blank faraway look children can get, and then he looked up at his mom and smiled again.

Jill said to Dave, "I'm going to put Davey down and make dinner."

Then she and Treadway shared a brief, very brief, silent communication through their eyes, and then she said to me, "Would you like to stay for dinner? I'm just making some pasta and a salad. Just something simple."

I thought about it. I was hungry. It was a long drive back to my place . . .

"That sounds nice. Yes. Sure."

"Great," she said, like she meant it. And she and Davey slipped back inside and out of view.

I looked back at Dave Treadway. "So, Keaton Fuller wasn't a good guy?"

Something about his wife inviting me for dinner had loosened him up a bit with regard to this subject. Because he said, this time without much sensitivity, "He was, like, the worst guy ever."

And we both laughed. Like he had cut the tension of the moment by just saying what he knew I already knew.

Treadway began to talk, telling me much of the same stuff that everyone else had. That Keaton was a prick, that he let people down, that he could be charming, that he could be the life of the party, but that he fundamentally, at his core, just wasn't a good guy. "Like he just had a chip missing or something. That part of you that tells you not to, you know, be really uncool to a girl. Or break a promise you made to someone in a business deal."

"Craig Helton," I said.

"Yeah," he said. "Not the smartest thing in the world to go into business without a contract, and a lot of people wanted to tell Craig how stupid he had been. But a deal is still a deal. I manage people's money for a living. I study companies all the time. And there are lots of companies out there, huge companies, that started the same way, with a handshake, a verbal agreement. Nike, for example. And I don't think anyone is telling Phil Knight how stupid he is."

Treadway took a contemplative pause, like he was unsure about releasing the next bit of information, then said, "You know, Greer told me that Keaton punched their mom one time."

I said, "Man. This guy. Wow. Really?"

Treadway said, "Yeah. I don't know if he, like, fully beat her up, but yeah, he punched her in the face. When he was a teenager. And Jackie had to make up some story about why the whole side of her face was black-and-blue. Greer told me that, you know, many years later, after too many cocktails."

"Jesus. I'm starting to wish I was the one who killed this guy."

Treadway laughed. "Totally."

We continued talking, Dave now saying that it's almost strange to know someone like that or, more specifically, be a sort-of friend, through family and the neighborhood you live in, of someone who's just kind of despicable.

Eventually I said, pursuing a path of, you know, beating the bushes, "Did you ever know anything about Keaton getting into the tropical fish business?"

Treadway said, "No. That's . . . weird. And kind of cool. What's that about?"

"I don't know. I'm looking into it. I think it was one of the things Keaton got involved with, and then, although I haven't confirmed this . . . it didn't work out. Which reminds me, what's the story with the USC guys who Keaton pissed off? The ones trying to make the movie? Craig Helton mentioned that story to me."

"Right," Treadway said. "You know, that wasn't some major falling-out. That wasn't on the same level as what happened with Keaton and Craig. Some film students were trying to make a short film. Keaton promised them some money, and then when it came time to, you know, actually give them the money he bailed. I really just told Craig that story to help him understand that what happened with *their* business . . . well, that Keaton was just like that. That he would break a promise, that he would fuck over anyone. Some privileged USC guys, or a guy like Craig trying to make it."

I said, "So what do you think happened, Dave? Why do you think Keaton was killed? You knew the guy from when you were thirteen. What's your theory?"

He nodded and said, breaking now a bit from what everyone else had said, "You know, Keaton knew all kinds of people that the rest of us didn't know. He was always finding new groups of people to hang out with, or who would fall in love with him for a while. You know people like that? You just suddenly hear that they are in this new group, kind of out of nowhere? The USC film guys were like that—"

"Or the guys from the band, the Test? The way Craig Helton met Keaton."

"Right, exactly. And I'm not saying the people in that band had anything to do with Keaton getting killed. In fact, I think those guys are all really good guys, and some of them are still friends with Craig. And, shockingly, I don't think they ever fell out with Keaton. The USC guys too . . . They didn't murder Keaton over that film. I mean, I really don't think that happened. But those are both examples of how Keaton just got involved with all sorts of random people. Like, the tropical fish thing you just mentioned. It's like, what? Who? Tropical fish business? Really? But on the other hand, it makes total sense. It's totally Keaton. So I think that somewhere along the line he got in with somebody, or one of those groups of people, and he pissed off the wrong person. You know? I mean, he had a pattern of pissing people off. But it's one thing to let your brother down, or, like, a really sweet guy like Craig Helton, or some rich-kid USC students, but, you know, not everyone is like those people. You piss off the wrong person, just one person, and you never know. There's some crazy people out there."

I thought for a moment about Lee Graves. The way he'd looked at me when I started flaking out at Prestige Fish. His skeleton face had shown some deflation, but there was anger there too. I'd pissed him off by wasting his time.

And then Treadway took a turn I didn't see coming. He said, "You know, I always felt, of all the people Keaton hurt, that Greer somehow took it the hardest. Again, I'm not saying he had anything to do with the murder, like, no way. It's just that thinking about Keaton makes me remember things. And Greer was my friend, *is* my friend, so maybe I paid a little more attention to him or something. But I don't think that's why I feel this way. I really do think Greer was the most disappointed, let down, hurt, something. More than Craig, more than his ex-girlfriend who he cheated on, like, a thousand times. Sydney Frost. Sydney Scott now. Did you talk to her?"

I nodded.

Treadway continued, "There were times growing up when Greer just kind of seemed lost. In a daze. Emotionally scarred or something. And I remember thinking at the time that it was probably Keaton's fault. And now, with more of an adult perspective, I still think that. Some fucked-up thing Keaton had done. Or a bunch of things. Making fun of him, picking on him, not sticking up for him, I don't know. Ultimately, that's why I didn't like Keat. I knew about the whole laundry list of shit he had done to all sorts of people, but that stuff didn't really hit me as much as when I saw in my friend, right up close, the effect of his behavior."

I didn't respond. I just sat there for a second, looking out toward the ocean. Getting dark now. The water taking on a deep blue, almost black color. Lights popping on in the buildings all over La Jolla, and in the lamps lining the boardwalk and the cove. Right then Jill poked her head out, this time sans Davey, and said, "Ready?"

Mid-dinner. The Treadways were quite pleasant to be around, and the food was good too. Simple and good, spaghetti with marinara and a fresh salad with crisp romaine, artichokes, garbanzo beans, yellow peppers, and oil and vinegar. Dave stuck with beer during dinner, which I appreciated. So did I. Jill had red wine. Nancy would have appreciated that. I was enjoying myself.

At one point Dave said, "You know, a private detective is one of those jobs where you could live a whole lifetime and never meet anyone who's actually a private detective. And yet it's a job that every guy is interested in. Every guy would like to meet a PI. I even think every guy wants to *be* a PI, at least a little bit."

I laughed.

Jill said to Dave, "You want to be a private detective now?"

"A little bit, yeah. Every guy does!"

I laughed again.

And then Jill said to me, "Do you think that's true? Every guy wants to be a PI?"

"I don't know. But let me tell you this. It's not always interesting. It can be really boring. Not all the time. But it can be. I'm not sure every guy wants to sit outside someone's house in a midlevel American car for, you know, five hours, waiting for something to happen."

Dave said, "That doesn't sound so bad. It really doesn't."

Again, I laughed. And then I added, truthfully, but also for fun, "It can also be dangerous. Really dangerous."

I looked at both of them, this attractive couple looking back at me and wondering now, basically, if I'd ever killed anyone. That was my guess, at least.

"Don't worry," I said. "I'm not about to pull out my gun."

They gave this nervous laugh.

I added, "I don't think."

We continued chatting. Dave talked a little more about his money-managing life. Turns out he had made it on his own. Cat had done well for himself. Jill talked a bit about her former career as an advertising executive that she might or might not go back to, probably will one day, needs the mental stimulation . . .

When we were finishing eating, just at that moment when it felt like we were all about to stand up and start clearing the table, Jill said, "So, you have a girlfriend?"

"See?" Dave said to her. "You think it's cool to be a PI too." He continued, teasing her, "Do you want me to go into the kitchen or something so you can flirt with our guest in private?"

"What?" she said. "He's cute. I was thinking about setting him up!"

Dave looked at me. "Girls always want to set you up with their friends, and then the friends are never hot enough. It's just that simple."

I laughed. I was genuinely surprised that he said it. He was right, of course.

He continued, "You show up, and you think: Why would someone think this is the woman for me? And you also think: Why did the girl who set me up, set me up with someone clearly less attractive than she is? What does *that* say about her opinion of me?"

I laughed. Right again.

Jill said, "We just want the best for our friends. So we set them up sometimes knowing it might not be the right match, but hoping there will be some kind of spark anyway. That's why that happens." She took a long pause as another thought seemed to occur to her. "Well, we don't always want the best for our friends. We sometimes do."

We all laughed at that. These two were telling it like it is.

I answered Jill's initial question. "I have a girlfriend. Her name's Nancy. She's a nurse."

Jill, ribbing me a bit, said, "So she can take care of you after those *dangerous* situations."

Everyone laughed. No one harder than I.

I said, "That's how we met. Seriously. I got hurt on the job and had to go to the emergency room. She took care of me."

I looked at these two. And I had a thought. A thought I hadn't had in a while: I could be friends with them. You don't have that thought that often when you're in your mid-, okay, late thirties. That you could end up genuine friends with a person, or a couple. I liked them, liked their energy, enjoyed being around them. Don't worry, that didn't mean Dave Treadway was off my list of possible suspects. Nobody was off that list. Not yet. But I liked them.

We got up, cleared the table. I said thank you to Jill for making dinner and thank you to Dave for talking to me. Then I left, got in the Focus, and headed back to Los Angeles in reasonably light, but not too light, never too light, nighttime traffic.

19

Next morning, back at my desk, MacBook Pro open, big slider open, big cup of coffee in my hand. I was revising my case notes, adding what I now knew in crisp, simple bullets. But also looking back over the whole narrative. I looked at the line that first mentioned Prestige Fish.

- Craig Helton tells me Keaton Fuller worked in the tropical fish business, company name: Prestige Fish.

I imagined for a brief second all the players in my story as tropical fish swimming around in an enormous tank.

I saw their faces on the various species. There was Jackie Fuller swimming about. There was Dave Treadway gliding around. There was Lee Graves sliding by.

I think I took too many mushrooms in college.

I was imagining this, eyes no longer on my case notes but instead out the slider, when my phone started once again shaking frenetically, spazzing out, snapping me out of my reverie. Marlon the Marlin.

"Marlon."

"Johnny boy, I had a thought."

As you may have noticed, sometimes Marlon calls me "Johnny boy." I'm not sure I like it, and I've thought about it quite a bit. But I let it go, because it's Marlon the Marlin. Not because I think he's going to shoot me if I tell him to stop, although I guess it's possible. No, I let it slide because *it's Marlon the Marlin*, that's how he talks, that's who he is.

"Yessir," I said. "What's happening?"

"I made some calls. Nobody I know knows anything about Graves or Prestige Fish. But, as I said, I had a thought."

"Right, you did in fact say that."

"Well, here it is. There's always the possibility that this is a Pendella Situation."

"Right, that's very true." And then I took a long pause. "What's a Pendella Situation?"

"Good one, John. Good one. Smart-ass. You realize I'm trying to help you, right?"

"Oh, right, yes. Marlon, please continue."

He calls me "Johnny boy." I tease him a bit. You know, give and take.

Marlon said, "See, I was tired when you showed up yesterday, or else I might have thought of this right then. Lot of sun and booze comes with living on a boat."

"Yes, particularly sun. I ran into Hunter Clavana, the Aussie at your marina, yesterday. He's been essentially scorched by the sun."

"Right."

"Like, he might actually catch on fire at some point."

"Right."

"Like, just be walking along and burst into flames."

"Yeah. Yeah."

"I mean, he's a deep gray. Like slate. He's almost black. He's basically black."

"I got it, Johnny boy. I got it."

"So," I said, recalibrating. "The Pendella Situation."

"Lenny Pendella," Marlon said.

"Lenny Pendella," I repeated.

"Zip it. Okay? Zip it."

"Right," I said, meaning it. Sort of.

"So," Marlon continued. "Lenny Pendella was a guy we all knew back in the neighborhood. He was a short little guy with a little white beard, and he had this homely little wife to go along with his homely little white fucking beard. Her name was Liza. Lenny and Liza Pendella. And Lenny and Liza had a knickknack shop."

"A knickknack shop?"

"Porcelain dolls. Ornaments and shit. Gnomes and trolls to put in your fucking garden. Tchotchkes."

"Ah, okay, right. Got it. I've never been into one of those places. They scare me."

"You and me both, friend. You and me both. Anyway, so Lenny and Liza have this little shop. It's a tiny little place and the rent's pretty low. And there are enough weirdos out there who actually fucking like places like that, so it does okay. Better than okay. It does pretty goddamn well."

"Okay," I said.

"But the truth is," Marlon said with some excitement in his voice, "they are actually running numbers out of Lenny and Liza's Fucking Knickknack Shop. And they are making a shitload of money doing it. But nobody ever looks into them. One, because they have a way to hide the profits—they have a business. But two, the bigger reason—everybody just buys that Lenny and Liza are these fucking fringe characters. So there can't be anything going on there. Shit, Lenny looks like one of the trolls you can buy in his store. So does Liza, for that matter. See, the whole thing's so weird, and even weirdly legit, that it's *got* to be real. Their knickknack shop *can't* be a front for something else. You see what I'm saying?"

I stroked my chin pensively and said, "A Pendella Situation."

"Right," Marlon said. "That's what we came to call stuff like this. A business that's one thing. But a kind-of-strange thing. But a kind-of-strange thing that's actually doing pretty well. Which makes the people doing the strange thing seem like experts in this niche fucking world. But ultimately, of course, it's a business that is, or could be, a front for another thing, a criminal thing, that's more lucrative than the first thing."

"Because after a while, being in the vending-machine business gets too obvious."

"That's right, Johnny boy. But if you sell garden gnomes or tropical fucking fish, you might not be all that obvious. Especially if you know a shitload about garden gnomes or tropical fish. And especially-especially if the fucking garden-gnome or tropical fish business starts doing well. Then you don't just have a business to hide your profits, you've got actual profits to hide your profits. *If* you get looked into, that is, which you won't, because the first business is weird as fuck and it's doing well and you can prove it. Now, I've got no clue if your thing is in fact a Pendella Situation, but, you know, maybe. You said you were on a murder case, a serious fucking case, and if this guy at the fish place is somehow involved in a killing, then in my mind it increases the chances of the Pendella. My guess? Drugs. Blow. Oxy. Maybe heroin, but I doubt it. Not weed, of course. Shit's legal now."

Marlon paused, and I could hear him taking a sip of a drink with lots of ice in it. First big, stiff rum drink of the day. Guy was still nice and sharp.

He continued, "You also said you thought something was happening with this guy. You know, you felt something. And you're good at your job, I'll give you that. A smart-ass sometimes, but good at your job. So I advise you to look around for the Pendella."

"Thanks, Marlon."

"You bet, John. Just tell me what happens, in full, when you have some time. It's the only action I get these days."

Marlon always wants the story. I thought, Well, I'll be happy to give it to him. If I can find it.

We hung up.

I sat there at my desk, now thinking about what Marlon had said set against all the other people and other possibilities in the mix. Again, what next? What next?

I found my answer when a vehicle, a very new-looking Jeep Cherokee, slid in front of my open slider, then parked just around the corner in one of my guest spaces.

I heard the car door shut, then saw Greer Fuller appear. He took in the lot a bit, then swung his eyes over to me, sitting there, looking right at him. I waved him in.

20

Greer Fuller stood in front of my desk. I looked at him, the dark, curly hair, the freckles, the innocent face.

He seemed uncomfortable.

"Greer," I said. "How you doing? What's up?"

"Hey, I was . . . uh . . . I was in the neighborhood. Got your address off your card."

"Cool. That's why I gave it to you. Have a seat."

He sat in one of the chairs in front of my desk.

He still looked uncomfortable.

"You want a drink? Beer? Peach Fresca?"

"It's pretty early for a beer, I think. But . . . Peach Fresca? Are you serious?"

"As a heart attack, Greer. As a heart attack."

I produced a can out of the minifridge next to my desk. And watched with excitement as Greer popped it open and took a sip.

"That's actually really good," he said.

I love turning people on to Peach Fresca.

"Consider your life changed. I buy the product by the case. Peach flavored, that is. It comes in some other flavors too. Original Citrus, of course. Black Cherry. Both are pretty good, but not as good as Peach."

Greer, now with a vaguely confused look in his eye, nodded, took another sip. But confusion wasn't the primary thing Greer was communicating with his body language, his facial expression. He looked like he wanted to talk about something, something that made him, well, uncomfortable.

He looked over at my Ping-Pong table and said, "You play a lot of Ping-Pong?"

"Yeah," I said. "I do. Want to play?"

"Really?"

"Sure."

I grabbed a couple of paddles out of my desk drawer. Not anything advanced. Not like a two-hundred-dollar Killerspin that feels kind of heavy in your hand and has thick, tacky, difficult-to-handle rubber that makes the ball explode off the face with wicked spin. No, nothing like that. I just grabbed a couple of hard bats, basement style, dimples out. Bats that are much, much easier to play with.

I had a feeling Greer wasn't going to be so good.

You know, there are really three kinds of Ping-Pong players. One, people who just have no ability. It's just not in them. They can't even really rally. They miss the ball entirely sometimes. Two, people who have some ability and with some practice can be okay, pretty good, even. These are people you can hit around with, even if they aren't going to give you a particularly good game. But you can put some music on, have a couple beers, hit around, not want to kill yourself. And three, people who have some real innate talent and who, with practice, can become quite good, maybe even great. This third group encompasses a lot of people, because there's a wide gap, a really wide gap, between someone who's very good and someone who's pro-level great. Like, I'm a good player, but I would get killed—killed—by Xu Xin out of China. Or Ma Long, also out of China. Or Vladimir Samsonov out of Belarus. Look, these guys are top ten in the world, but you get my point.

Greer, unfortunately, was in group one. Could not really even hit the ball back. Now, this was a guy I pretty much just innately liked. With his sort of wounded-bird friendliness and all. But it was tough to like him when he made such poor contact, if he made contact at all, with the new orange Halex three-star balls I'd opened just for this occasion. That's another thing about Ping-Pong. The other thing that players don't always share with others. When you love the game and are pretty good at it, watching someone with zero talent kind of makes you not like them. Like, I was literally starting to not like Greer as I watched him flail around. Well, to be honest, I was starting to kind of hate him.

But, as most people do when they play Pong, he was having a good time, and it was loosening him up. So that was good. And it kept my opinion of him just above total disdain. You know? Because maybe Ping-Pong was going to be the conduit to his actually telling me what was on his mind.

I hit a ball with a little zip on it to his forehand side to see what would happen. He took a swing at it and missed entirely, and then, as it bounced around on the concrete floor of my office, he scurried wildly after it, flailing around as he tried to grab the ball. Zero coordination, this one. Zero. He finally got his hands on it, walked back over to the table, and stood there.

He said, "I came by because I wanted to tell you something else about Keaton."

"Okay."

He took a deep breath. "I guess my mom hiring you made me think about stuff again. And the truth is, I want to know what happened as well. I want to help you. So that's why I thought I'd tell you . . . I didn't tell the police this . . . Not many people know about it. My parents do, but I'm not sure if they told the police either. I told them about it, my parents—not when it happened, but later. After the murder. And I know . . . I know they haven't shared this with you. I don't know, you said anything might help you, so . . ."

He was really uncomfortable. This wasn't easy for him. So I said, "Thanks, Greer. Yeah, you never know what might help."

He nodded and said, "Pig Hunt."

I didn't know what to say, so I didn't say anything.

Greer continued. "Pig Hunt. That's what Keaton called

it. When Keaton and I were young, teenagers, we had two pet guinea pigs. Do you know what a guinea pig is?"

"Yeah, sure," I said.

"So ours lived in this cage in our backyard. It was pretty big, pretty nice. They lived there year-round. And Keaton and I played with them all the time. We'd take them out of the cage and hold them and let them walk around, you know, play with them. And see, another thing we used to do is, we had this gun. A twenty-two. A rifle. And when we first got it, our dad would take us on trips to the woods somewhere to shoot it. But after a while, sometimes Keaton and I would shoot it in our backyard, at cans and stuff, when our parents weren't around. You know, they wouldn't have allowed it, probably.

"Anyway, one day, out of nowhere, our parents weren't home, Keaton just started saying 'Pig Hunt.' Walking around the house saying 'Pig Hunt.' Kind of chanting it over and over. Almost turning it into a song, '*Pig Hunt, Pig Hunt.*' Over and over. I just thought he was being weird. And then he stopped. So then later, we go outside with the gun and we're shooting stuff around the yard, like we had a bunch of times. And then he puts the gun down and says, 'Let's go play with the guinea pigs.' So we go over to the cage and he tells me to grab one of them. You know, to play with. And I'm not thinking anything, so I grab one. And I remember, right then, he said: 'Okay, that's the one you chose.' And I didn't know what he meant. So he grabs the guinea pig from me, puts it down on the ground, and yells at it and scares it, so it runs off, runs across our lawn, and hides in the bushes. And then he does what he'd been doing earlier. Over and over. *'Pig Hunt. Pig Hunt. Pig Hunt.'* And then he picks up the rifle and aims it in the direction of the guinea pig. And then, kind of right then, it runs out from behind the bushes. And Keaton shoots it and kills it. I mean, blows its head off. I have no idea why. It was maybe the strangest thing I've ever seen. And I stood there and watched him do it. You know? I guess I let him do it."

I looked at Greer. He looked ashamed, and exhausted.

He continued. "I didn't yell at him or anything. I didn't say a word. I was just shocked. So we buried the guinea pig in a far corner of our backyard—we, well, my parents, have a pretty big backyard . . . We told them we were playing with it and it ran away. Once they realized it was gone, that is, which was, like, two weeks later. Keaton told me never to tell anyone what really happened, and I never did. Until Keat was murdered. Like I said, that's when I told my parents."

Greer wiped at his eyes, the sunlight coming in through the slider catching some smeared tears on the back of his hand. He said, "I just thought, I don't know, maybe knowing that would help you understand him, or help you with your investigation somehow. I don't know anything about what you do, but it seems like the kind of thing that might help." He looked at me with his watery eyes and added, "To know that's the kind of thing he was capable of."

Did it help? Would it help? Not sure. But, man, before Greer arrived, I didn't think I could dislike Keaton Fuller any more. But I was wrong. Guy wasn't just an asshole, he was a sick fuck too. I mean, punching his mom? Roping his little brother into telling him which of their pets to kill? Fuck, I thought, I hate this guy. I'm glad he's dead.

I said, "Thanks for telling me, Greer. I appreciate it."

He took a deep breath and gave me a relieved smile. "Yeah. Thanks for playing Ping-Pong. That was fun."

I walked over to his side of the table and shook his hand. And instinctively, I gave him a little reassuring pat on the back. Which I think he wanted. And maybe needed.

He looked at me, a little mist still covering his eyes, and said, "Bye. See you later."

And then he walked out the open slider, rounded the corner, got in his Jeep, and left.

I stood there and thought, Geez, what a weird story. And I wondered if it was easier for Greer to share that story with, basically, a stranger. As opposed to someone who really knows him, knows his family, his world. Sometimes that's how it works. I also wondered whether Greer realized that—despite the fact that Keaton pulled the trigger in that particular story—he had confessed to me that he knows how to shoot a gun.

21

After Greer left, I decided to go practice my own marksmanship. I drove over the hill to the Valley, to Northridge, to the Firing Line. I got in the firing booth and, just like last time, squeezed twenty-four rounds out of my Colt and twenty rounds out of my Sig.

And again, I studied my targets. Better. I was finding my form. I had the muscle memory from years of practice, but the *active* practice, the *current* practice, was helping. Yeah, the targets looked better. Tighter clusters of bullet holes. Fewer loose shots. Would my shots hold up in a pressure situation? Maybe. Perhaps even probably. But the sword still needed some sharpening.

I'd be back.

I got back in the Focus, put my mind back on the case, and headed back over the hill.

One of the things I've learned as a PI is that even when people ask you for your help and then tell you "everything" you need to know to help them, they sometimes still don't tell you everything-everything. It's the strangest thing. It's like when people go to a shrink and then hide things from the shrink, even though that goes directly against their own self-interest. Is it embarrassment? Fear? Or, more simply, just the fact that certain subjects are difficult to talk about? Shit, is it stupidity? It's probably fear. Most of the things that hinder us as humans funnel back to fear. Greer's story was an example of what I'm talking about. And, look, I understand that that particular story might not help me. But it is an interesting glimpse into Keaton, and it is interesting that Greer had held it back.

With Marlon the Marlin's thoughts still jumping around in my head, I had the idea that Jackie Fuller might have more to tell me. Had more information that might help me, that might lead to me figuring out who murdered her son. So I called her and asked if I could come see her. And she said yes.

This time, it was just the two of us in her living room, no sweater-clad, comb-over-sporting Phil. Well, the dogs were there too. Roaming quietly through the house with those placid, peaceful-eyed expressions. I thought, Man, they're kind of like fish too, just moving silently about. I liked them enormously.

I looked at Jackie Fuller, at her tired, tragic face. I told her generally what I'd been up to, minus the Prestige Fish part. Next thing you know, she or her husband calls them or starts looking into it. Who knows? If you know me, I've told you this before: Most people do not know how to process, how to handle, sensitive information. People so often misinterpret it, or even do something destructive with it. Even if they don't mean to.

"I have a question for you, Jackie."

She raised the brows above her worn-out eyes.

"Was Keaton involved with drugs in any way, at any point?"

"You mean, did he do drugs?"

"Sure. We can start there."

"Yes. We had a few incidents where we caught Keaton with drugs."

"What happened? What kinds of drugs?"

"Well, pot. Coke. We caught him with opium once. We didn't know what it was. Phil took it to someone to find out. Can I ask why you're wondering?"

Again, I didn't want to get into any theories I had. I didn't want to give her that information. That some random fish seller *might* be a cover for some drug operation. And, specific to Keaton, that often people who get into drugs are the ones who want to start making a profit off them. So I just told her a half truth. Or a quarter truth. Or maybe less.

"I'm putting together the people Keaton associated with. And now I'm seeing if they, or Keaton, or both, were into drugs. Drugs can lead to trouble. Not always, but sometimes. And sometimes that trouble can be very serious."

Basically true. A politician's answer, but basically true. Jackie Fuller nodded.

"Keaton had a couple of incidents in high school, a couple in college. It all started with this girl he hung around with a bit during both those periods."

"You're not talking about Sydney?"

"No, no. Not that gold digger Sydney."

I was surprised to see Jackie's fangs come out. Although I thought her analysis was right.

"Then who?" I asked. "What girl?"

Jackie Fuller sighed and said, "A girl named Andrea. Andrea Cogburn."

"And Andrea is someone Keaton dated?"

"Well, not exactly. It was never that official. But he did hang around her. She was a bad influence. I always thought that." Switching gears a bit, she said, "She grew up not too far away from here, actually. Just south of the Pico–La Brea area."

This was Jackie telling me Andrea didn't come from money. The Pico–La Brea intersection is pretty close to Hancock Park, but south of it lies a very different neighborhood in terms of bank balances.

"Okay, so Keaton hung around this girl off and on during high school and college. And they did drugs together? Were they the same age?"

Jackie shifted a bit in her chair and kind of half-nodded, and then added, "Same age, yes. But they went to different schools. Both for high school and college. Keaton went to high school here in Hancock Park. I'm not sure where Andrea went. And then Keaton, as you know, went to USC, and Andrea went to a small community college somewhere. Here in L.A. I can't remember. I knew it at one time. Somewhere small."

I wondered, Is Andrea Cogburn the girl Sydney Scott had meant when she'd said Keaton might have had another relationship entirely? Might have been dating someone else while he was dating her? In a way, Sydney and Jackie talked about her in a similar way. Dancing around her. Downplaying this girl with their words but putting a spotlight on her with their subtext. It's interesting how that happens. When someone or something is on someone's mind and they don't want it to appear that way, they say things and do things with their body language that end up achieving the reverse of their intentions. Jackie Fuller was presenting this girl as an afterthought, but the total communication was that she wasn't one at all.

I said, "Okay. So they went to different schools. But when they were together, high school, college, they did drugs together. And she's the one who got Keaton interested in drugs initially?"

Jackie nodded. "Yes. I think both those things are true."

"Okay. So where is Andrea now?"

Jackie Fuller didn't answer. She looked down and to her right and put her hand on the back of one of the dogs, who had positioned himself near her. And then she looked at me. I would never have thought her eyes could get more defeated than they already were.

Then she said, "Andrea died."

I looked at Jackie and asked, "When?"

"A few years, several years, after college. She and Keaton weren't in touch anymore. But it was still very sad. Keaton, I remember, tried not to show it, but he was upset. And even though Phil and I weren't particularly fond of Andrea, we were upset too. It was very sad."

"And how? How did she die?"

"She overdosed. She'd gotten way more into coke and things. Again, this was after she and Keaton had stopped hanging around together. Well after. Yeah. Yeah. She OD'd. She OD'd on drugs."

"Is her family still here? Do they still live over near Pico and La Brea?"

Some reluctance flickered in Jackie's eyes. I thought, Here we go again. She's asked me to find out what happened, but now she's reluctant to give me the things I might need to do that very thing.

To Jackie Fuller's credit, she forged ahead and said, "Her dad was never around. I think I have an old number for her mom."

22

Back in the Focus. I dialed up Andrea's mom, Eve Cogburn. She answered and said I could come by whenever. She didn't say it in a cheery way: "Sure, come on by whenever!" Nah, the opposite, in fact. Flat. Emotionless. Like, sure, come by whenever, I don't really care. I said I'd be there in twenty.

Well, I was on my way to talk to another parent about a child who had died. Not my favorite thing to do. Think I'd rather get a prostate exam while waiting in line at the DMV. Added to that, this was yet another trail that might not lead anyplace special.

But, I said to myself, the case is cold, Darvelle. Edges. Examine the edges.

Like Jackie Fuller had said, Eve Cogburn lived "not

too far" from Hancock Park. And like Jackie Fuller had implied, and like I told you, it was a very different neighborhood. South of Pico, between La Brea and Highland. I was close to Eve's now, taking in the neighborhood. There was a bunch of run-down apartments stacked too close to one another, some of them right next to a fast-food joint, a gas station, a dry cleaner. Look, it wasn't as bad as some neighborhoods in L.A. We're not talking rampant crime and daily drive-bys. It was just dreary. Lifeless. Depressing. Not a lot of trees, lots of wires in the sky, a sad-eyed dog looking at you from some sad steps leading up to a sad building. I got to Eve's place, parked out front, took the stairs up to the second floor of her beige, beaten-down eightplex, and knocked.

Eve Cogburn answered the door in an unusual fashion. She just opened it, then walked back to her chair. She didn't say hello. She didn't say anything. I guessed I was supposed to walk in. So I did.

I sat down in a chair across from Eve Cogburn and took in the apartment. It was reasonably pulled together, not messy, a couch, some chairs, an antique-looking table or two, a TV. But everything felt beaten down, dead, just like the outside. Yeah, I mean, the old beige carpet, the low popcorn ceiling, the forlorn, forgotten kitchen.

Eve looked at me and lit a cigarette, a Winston, out of a red and white pack.

"Thanks for talking to me," I said.

She took a drag and nodded.

I had already told her on the phone what I was up to, looking into the murder of Keaton Fuller, so I just got right to it.

"So your daughter, Andrea, dated Keaton?"

Eve nodded again.

"I don't know much about their relationship, obviously. But I get the impression it was off and on. More casual. Is that right? What was the situation?"

Eve looked straight at me and said, "It wasn't casual."

Sometimes when people lose a loved one, or lose hope, they talk in a very direct fashion. In its own way, it's refreshing.

"Okay. What do you mean?"

"I mean they were boyfriend and girlfriend. Now, I don't know if Jackie Fuller remembers it that way. She never liked that they were dating in the first place. But they dated for a couple of years seriously and then, to use your words, off and on after that. But even that was serious too. Their hearts were involved."

She blew out some cigarette smoke and looked right at me. Life had done a number on this woman. Her graying brown hair was thinning and dry. Her face showed the damage of smoke and alcohol. She wasn't obese, but she had a stomach. And the legs that came out of her green housedress were white and bloodless. But she was pretty. You could see a pretty face somewhere in there, somewhere back in time. And she had an intelligence about her. And her eyes. Her eyes held a similar feeling to Jackie Fuller's, yet different. They held the tragedy but not the shame. Anger, helplessness, but not shame.

She said, "I guess there's no way to prove to you that my daughter and Keaton were serious because she's dead. And so is he."

I nodded and said, "How did they meet?"

"How far is Hancock Park from here? Two miles? And when you look like Andrea did, the boys from the nice families find you."

She got up, walked into the back bedroom, and came back holding a picture. She handed it to me.

Andrea Cogburn. Blond, with big, slightly wide-set, bluish-green eyes. Stunning. A true beauty.

"Beautiful," I said.

"Yeah."

"And how long did they date? And when did they stop dating?"

"They dated in high school, even though they were at different schools. They dated in college some—he was at USC, she was at Santa Monica College. I don't know when they broke up. Keaton was always breaking up with her. But a few years after college, it finally ended for good."

I really didn't want to ask Eve Cogburn to explain to me in detail the exact circumstances of her daughter's death. I could probably go to a friend of mine at the morgue and find that out. So I asked Eve Cogburn another question, one that I already knew the answer to, that ended up giving me the answer I wanted: "Your daughter and Keaton, were they into drugs?"

"How much do you know about my daughter's death?"

"Not a lot."

"Andrea overdosed." Eve looked at me with those damaged, but direct, eyes. "That's how she died. Was coming down from coke. Took some sleeping pills. Died. But, to answer your question. Yes, she and Keaton did drugs together. That's probably when it all started. In high school with Keaton."

"Did he get her into drugs?"

Eve shrugged. "Maybe. He had the money to buy them. But most of the time people do what they are going to do. He didn't force the coke up her nose. Mr. Darvelle, have you ever done coke, smoked pot?"

I didn't have it in me to correct her and tell her to call me John. I just said, "Yeah. Both."

"Well, did anyone make you do it?"

"No."

She took a drag off her cigarette and gave me a look that said: then you see my point.

"Did you like Keaton, Eve? Like that he was involved with your daughter?"

She answered, again, by asking me a question. "How much do you know about Keaton?"

"Enough to know that most people didn't like him much."

"Well, you can add me to the list. He was an entitled, rude used-car salesman with a big bank account who loved my daughter but was ashamed to admit it when he was on the other side of Pico."

"You have any thoughts on who might have killed him?"

Another shrug, another question. "Who knows what Keaton Fuller got himself into? All I can tell you is, when I heard he was killed it didn't surprise me."

I thanked Eve Cogburn for her time, got up, and headed for the door. Eve stayed in her chair, her back to me, as I walked out and shut it.

23

I still wanted more specific information on Andrea Cogburn's death, so I called my friend at the morgue, guy named Elliot Watt.

"Elliot, Darvelle."

"Yes."

"Elliot, the way you just said 'yes' didn't sound like you were saying: 'Yes? This *is* Elliot, what do you want?' It sounded like you were saying: 'Yes.' Like, 'yes' as a definitive answer to a question. Like, as if I had asked: 'Is the sky blue?' And you had said: 'Yes.' But I haven't asked you a question yet. And you still said 'yes' that way. Do you see what I'm saying?"

"Yes, Detective Darvelle, I do see what you are saying. And yes, you are correct in your hearing of how I said 'yes.' See, I know you are going to ask me for something, to come down and look at something, and I know that if I say no, you'll just pester me until I say yes. So I just decided to go ahead and say yes to the question you haven't even asked me yet—will I pull something for you—even though I'm not really in the mood right now to do it. Do *you* see what *I'm* saying?"

"Yes. And great," I said. "I'm on my way to the morgue now."

"You're lucky, it's a reasonably slow day. For Los Angeles. If we were in fucking Boise, everyone would be going apeshit. But we're not in Boise, so it's a reasonably slow day."

"Please pull the file for a woman named Andrea Cogburn. White. Died between the ages of, I'd say, twenty-six and twenty-nine. Probably six, seven, eight years ago. Drug overdose. Is that enough info?"

I could tell that Elliot was writing everything down. He said, "Yeah, that's enough." And then: "I'm too good to you, Darvelle. I really am."

"I'll bring you a present. See you soon."

It really helps to have a friend at the morgue. Getting autopsy reports, coroner's reports, Elliot Watt's own personal opinions on stuff—it all goes a long way. Sometimes breaks open a case. I have to tell you, Elliot Watt is a bit of a strange cat. That being said, he's the perfect guy to work in a morgue. He's a bit of a loner. He has an analytical mind. He's innately drawn to the macabre. And he *looks* the part. He literally looks like he belongs there. He's got black hair, alabaster skin, big blue bug eyes, a big mouth with too many teeth. Almost like he himself is dead and has been embalmed. You see him walking around in the darkness of the morgue, sort of shuffling along. A bit like a zombie in a movie.

And I think that's a good thing. There are certain jobs where you want the guy holding them to look and act the part. The guy at the morgue is one of them. A lawyer, *your* lawyer, is another one. You want your lawyer to look and act a certain way, because it's your self-interest he or she is usually protecting. But a doctor, that's the top example. A doctor in charge of *your* health. In charge of whether you're going to, you know, die. True story: One time I went to the doctor, new doctor, just for a checkup, and there was music playing in the waiting room. But it wasn't terrible adult contemporary, or classical music, like it's supposed to be. It was the Clash. "Lost in the Supermarket." Great song. Amazing song. One of the best songs ever. But the wrong song for the doctor's office. You know? I mean, at that point I didn't want to go to that doctor anymore. I wanted to party with him. I mean, I definitely wanted to party with him. But I didn't want to have him as my doctor anymore.

I made a stop to buy Elliot a little something. Then I jetted downtown to North Mission Road to visit the L.A. County morgue.

I walked in. There was Elliot sitting at his neat desk, ready for me, file in front of him—Andrea Cogburn's file, I assumed.

"Here's her file," he said, sliding it over to me.

"Thank you, sir. I got you a couple of presents. Some magazines. A little reading for your downtime."

I presented each one to Elliot, pulling them out one at a time from a brown bag. "The new *Popular Mechanics*, because I know you like it. I have no idea why, but I know you do."

"Thank you," he said as he placed it on his desk. "I have not read this one yet."

I pulled out the next magazine. "An *Over Forty* porn mag," I said. "All the women inside are *mature*. Being the twisted bastard you are, I thought you might like this."

"Well, I really don't read that kind of thing, but okay," he said as he slid it carefully into a drawer and then closed the drawer very gently and quietly.

I pulled out the next magazine. "And then I got you this too. *Cranes Today* magazine." I handed it to him.

He looked at it and said, truly confused, "What the hell is this?"

"It's a copy of *Cranes Today* magazine," I said.

"I don't get it."

"It's a magazine all about cranes. The machines, not the birds."

"Yeah, Darvelle, I can see that. There's a crane on the cover. I still don't get it."

"Well, if you're going to be that guy who publicly reads *Popular Mechanics*, then why not take it all the way into true freakdom and read something like this. Just go sit in a park and be the guy who's on a totally different planet from the rest of us."

"I don't understand you, Darvelle. I really don't. Is that an insult? A joke? What the eff? I mean, I'm helping you. I'm giving you material you otherwise couldn't get."

"What the eff." That's what he said.

"I think you might like it. Just read it."

Elliot didn't have any chairs in front of his desk. He had two against the wall opposite his desk, a little coffee table as well, almost like a waiting room. I took a chair and looked through Andrea Cogburn's file. There was a picture of her in her bed, dead. She didn't look dead. She looked asleep. Sometimes when you see pictures of the dead, they look dead. I mean *dead.* Keaton Fuller looked dead. A giant hole in his chest and out his back. But Andrea Cogburn just looked asleep. She was in her nightgown, in her own bed.

I focused in on the details. Andrea died six years ago, at age twenty-nine, with alcohol, cocaine, Valium, and Ambien in her system. Cause of death: She stopped breathing. Just that simple. You stop breathing, you die. Cessation of breathing isn't the only fatal outcome of an overdose, though. Truth is, an overdose can mean lots of things. It can mean you had a heart attack. It can mean you had a brain aneurysm. Or, as in this case, it can mean your lungs stopped taking in air and pushing it out again.

I looked up at Elliot. He was engrossed in *Cranes Today* magazine. *Engrossed.*

"So," I said. "Andrea Cogburn stopped breathing. What does that mean exactly, Elliot? In Andrea's case? What happened exactly? Why did she stop breathing?"

He lowered the *Cranes Today* magazine and peered

over it at me. He then dropped it on the desk and started talking.

"Basically, on the surface, it means that she was drunk and on coke and then took Valium and Ambien to come down. But she took too many and her throat relaxed too much and she stopped breathing and died. Now, essentially, that's how people with sleep apnea die when they die. Sleep apnea. You know it? It's pretty common."

I nodded.

He continued, "When I say that's how people with sleep apnea die, I don't mean the drugs and alcohol part. I'm talking about the throat part. Their throats relax and close up, and they stop breathing. But people with sleep apnea usually don't die. Their brains send a signal to wake the fuck up, and they do. They gasp for breath, then go back to sleep, then do it again. All fucking night. But they don't die. Now, I'm not saying Andrea Cogburn had sleep apnea. Okay? I'm not saying that. But her throat relaxed and closed up *like* someone with sleep apnea. Then, *if* her brain sent the signal to wake up, and I don't know that it did, but *if* it did, she didn't hear it because she was on too many pills. And if her brain didn't send the signal, which is also possible because she was so wasted, then, well, her throat was closed up and she stopped breathing. Same result, obviously, with or without the signal."

He took a deep breath and continued, "But you know what I think, in addition to all that?"

See? This is why I really come down here. Sure, it's great to see the file. But I can read the file back at my desk. What's really great is to hear, in person, the theories of an expert, a guy who lives and breathes this shit, a proper Morgue Guy.

Elliot said, "I think she offed herself. Suicide. Very hard to prove. After all, what is suicide when you're talking about dying from too many drugs? You could say that everyone who ever died from taking too many drugs committed suicide, if we're talking about a somewhat loose interpretation of the word. But this time, I don't think the term has to be taken that loosely."

"Why do you think that?"

"Girl that size, with what she put in her body in one night? All that Ambien and Valium? And apparently, according to the cops and her own mother, a longtime drug user who had to know what drugs do? That's somebody saying: I don't want to wake up."

I looked at Elliot's big blue bug eyes and said, "Yeah." And then I said, "Thanks, Elliot. Thanks for your help."

He nodded and picked up *Cranes Today*. "You know how much a crane weighs? Thirty tons. Sixty thousand fucking pounds. I mean, think about how heavy that is. Jesus."

"See, I told you you'd like it! I told you, Elliot!"

"Get out of here, Darv."

"Yeah," I said. "Thanks again."

I put Andrea's file back on Elliot's desk and headed out. As I was exiting, Elliot's office door swinging shut behind me, I looked over my shoulder through the door's window and could just make out Elliot's right hand going for the drawer with the *Over Forty* in it.

24

I went home, grabbed a canned Coors Light, and sat outside by my pool. Sat on the edge of it, put the lower half of my legs, from the knees down, in the water. It felt good, cool, relaxing. And the visual of it relaxed me too. The last of the day's sunlight sitting on its smooth purple surface.

So, Marlon tells me that the whole tropical fish thing could be a cover for drugs. Okay. I guess. Maybe. So could that connect to Andrea Cogburn? Like, she and Keaton started doing drugs together way back when and then, with or without her, he got more and more interested in them over time, to the point that eventually he got involved with some real dealers? Real dealers who may or may not be the Prestige Fish people?

Again. I guess. Maybe.

Add to that Andrea's death, or maybe even suicide. So where does that fit in?

"John?"

Or does it fit in? Maybe her death is simply a very unfortunate side trail to this story. Which makes me think of Greer's story, the Pig Hunt story. How does that connect? Or does it *not* connect? Is it just a sad, not to mention weird, element that ultimately doesn't have anything to do with Keaton's murder?

"John?"

Or, shit—maybe her death, or suicide, is connected somehow more directly.

"John!"

And then there were the high-dollar fish. The clarion angelfish, the Neptune grouper. And there was that sinister look on Lee Graves's skeletal face. And there was Craig Helton, and Sydney Scott, and Muriel Dreen, and Heather Press . . .

"John!"

I looked over at Nancy. She'd come out of the house a little while ago to join me; her legs were now dangling in the water like mine. I'd seen her come out, of course, and had greeted her with a smile. But I had no idea what she had asked me, what she was talking about.

"Yeah, babe," I said. "What's up?"

"Don't you agree?"

It seemed that we were in the middle of a conversation. Nancy looked at me with some fire in her eyes. It wasn't exactly anger. It was more that she looked disappointed, even betrayed.

She said, "I thought we decided to be present when we're around each other."

"Sorry, I was thinking about—"

"I know what you were thinking about. Your case. I know that."

Balance. Life balance. It's something that people talk about a lot these days. You can't constantly be thinking about work. You can't be overly consumed by one thing. You need balance. I've never been very good at it.

Truth is, I don't believe in it. You know why? Because I don't think it works. I've never gotten anywhere on a case unless I thought about it all the time. But, beyond me, does anyone get anywhere with anything when they're "balanced"? Were the Stones balanced when they made *Exile*? Or were they all in? Was Robert Pirsig balanced when he wrote *Zen and the Art of Motorcycle Maintenance*? Somehow I doubt it.

But, look, I'm not just talking about exceptional artists. Were you balanced the last time you accomplished something you were really proud of? Something important at work? A big physical achievement? A personal project you really cared about? Maybe you were. But I bet you weren't.

Now, does not having a ton of respect for balance fuck up my life sometimes? Well, it sure looked like it right now. I'd made a promise to Nancy that I wasn't keeping. Not cool. And not good. Because I love her.

I said, "Nance. What was it that you were asking me?"

"John," she said calmly, but with some bite, "I could think about my patients, or my career, or a million other things while you're talking to me, and sometimes I'd like to. But I don't. I make an effort not to."

I nodded. "I'm sorry. What did you ask me?"

She said, "The sunlight looks pretty sitting on the pool like that, don't you think?"

I smiled and said, "Aha. You asked me a question simply because you knew I was thinking about my case. And you knew I wouldn't be able to answer it. You didn't really want the answer to the question. You just did it to bust me."

Remember how I said Nancy gives me shit sometimes when she thinks I deserve it? This would be one of those times.

She smiled and said, "Maybe."

"Well, don't you think that's kind of unfair? I mean, you set me up. You didn't even really want my answer. You already know I like the way the sun sits on the pool. We've talked about that a bunch."

"It doesn't matter. You're still not present, and you should be."

"I need to be present for questions that aren't really even real questions?"

"That's right."

I put my arm around Nancy and kissed her on the cheek. She looked at me with her brown eyes. Soft and now forgiving, but I could still see a flicker of that Nancy fire.

And so I said, again, "I'm sorry."

"Let's make dinner," she said.

"Wait, what? I was just thinking about something else for a quick second."

"Not funny," she said.

"A little funny?" I said.

"No. Not at all. Not even a little bit."

"Let's make dinner," I said.

"Oh. So you did hear me," she said as she looked right at me. "I like that, John. I like that a lot. When you hear me."

I nodded. We stood up. I gave her a kiss, this time on the lips, and we walked inside.

25

The next morning I drove over to my office, updated my case notes, waited for the stifling L.A. traffic to subside a bit, then drove over to Prestige Fish. I didn't call them or make an appointment or announce my visit in any way. I just hopped in the Focus, took the 405 North to Thousand Oaks, found my way to the little redbrick building that housed Lee Graves, Elana, and a few really expensive aquarium dwellers.

I drove past the building and parked two blocks down from the entrance. I situated the Focus so I had a view of the front door and the little parking lot to the left of it. There was a black Tesla Model S in the lot, Graves's, and a deep blue Mercedes C-Class, a lower-end Benz, Elana's. Those were my guesses, anyway.

I didn't know what my next move was going to be. I just sat there watching the front door. You do this a lot in my line. You sit. And you watch. I put on Lou Reed *New York*. It's a great record, one that's meant to be listened to start to finish. One that's better when you listen to it that way. Not enough of those these days. One song leading perfectly into the next. And, man, the songs. Some fast, some slow, but all interesting and emotional. The Velvet Underground records get so much love, respect, adoration. And I'm one of the people who give them that. But *New York*? It's better than some of the Velvets records. It is. Don't say it's not. It is.

The record ended. I didn't put anything else on. I just, you know, sat and watched. Over the course of a couple of hours, not much happened. Only one person went inside. About forty minutes after I stopped listening to *New York*, a beautiful brown BMW 7 Series pulled into the little lot where the Tesla and the Mercedes were. A man just beyond middle age got out and walked in the front door, then exited the building about thirty minutes later with Lee Graves. Graves walked him to his car, shook his hand, sent him on his way.

The BMW came my way, drove right by me. I got a good look at the driver. Lean, tan, with a full head of silverish hair. A silver fox, this guy. He was sitting contentedly behind the wheel. You know those guys who drive those sedans, all satisfied, all content? This guy, driving by me, had his eyes at half-mast, his nostrils flared, one eyebrow cocked just slightly, a camel-colored sweater over his shoulders, a smug grin spread across his face.

And that look.

That look that says: Ahhhh, yes. Yes, my life is gooood.

And: I'm reaaalllly comfortable, right here in the quiet cabin of my high-end sedan. Mmmm, smell that leather.

And: Oh, there's one more thing. Fuck off. All of you. Fuck. Off.

I wondered, after he'd disappeared down some side street: Did that guy just pay Lee Graves a bunch of money to find him a fish? Or did he set up a deal to get some really pure heroin? Or was what happened in there neither of those two things?

Impulsively, I cranked up the Focus and drove toward Prestige Fish. I parked in the lot between the Tesla and the C-Class, right where they could see me. It was time to get something going, to jar something loose. I got out, walked over to the door, turned the knob. Locked. Not open like last time. Not welcoming. Locked. I was sure there were cameras on me, didn't need to look around to verify. Good. Fine by me.

The door opened. The red-lipped, raven-haired first-class flight attendant stood there.

"Mr. Dean," she said. "We were wondering if we were going to hear from you again. Please come in."

We walked in and stood in front of her desk.

Elana said, "Have you decided what it is you are looking for?"

"My name's not John Dean. It's John Darvelle. I'm a private detective. I'd like to speak to Lee Graves."

"Oh," she said, her eyes widening but her overall essence remaining calm and steady. "Why don't I tell Lee you'd like to make an appointment with him and then get back to you."

She was a pro. That's a pro's response. Not defensive. Not dismissive either. But a response that would give her boss time to think about whether he wanted to talk to me.

I said, "Why don't you ask him if he can talk now. I know he's here."

Before she answered, a voice said, "I can talk now."

I looked over to see Lee Graves standing outside a door down the same hallway you take to get to the elevator, but on the left. I'd walked by that door before, but it had been closed tight. Graves was giving me that wild-eyed stare out of his skeleton head, but not the smile. Just a stare. It looked like he'd shaved his head right before he popped out into the hallway. It was slick, clean, shining, and reflecting light. He was in tight jeans and cowboy boots and another tight black T-shirt, no dragon. His shirt was so tight you could see his abs. His intention, for sure.

Graves said, "Why don't you come back into my office."

"Great," I said.

He disappeared through the doorway behind him, and I followed his lead and walked down the hallway and into the room.

His office was simple, sleek. A big black desk with a big black leather desk chair behind it. And behind that, one big window with the shade halfway down. In front of the desk sat two smaller chrome and leather chairs. And in the back corner, on the same wall as the entrance, sat a third black and chrome chair, identical to the two others positioned diagonally in front of it.

There was a very large, beautiful aquarium along one

wall, with a single, foot-long, almost black fish in it. The fish had a triangular fin on its back, like a shark's, that seemed a touch too big for its body. And the fish's mouth didn't face outward but instead down, like it could cruise along the bottom of the tank, sucking things up if it wanted to. It wasn't doing that, though. It was moving along fluidly through the water, in the middle of the aquarium.

I took one of the chairs in front of the desk before Graves invited me to.

He gave me a somewhat disdainful look and said, "Have a seat."

"Thanks," I said.

"So what's up, John Darvelle?"

"You heard me tell Elana my name?"

"Yep," he said, finally giving me his demented smile.

I thought: How? His office isn't that close to the main room, and I hadn't said my name that loudly. Was he listening at his door when I walked in? Did he have an audio system set up to eavesdrop on conversations that happened in the front room? Either way, weird. And either way, he wasn't ashamed to admit it.

"Good," I said. "Then the introductions are done."

"What is it that you want, John Darvelle?"

"I'm investigating the murder of a man named Keaton Fuller. Do you know who that is?"

"Yes, I do. But before I answer any questions, I have a question for you."

Before he spoke again, I said, "I wanted to see what a high-priced fish operation was like before I revealed myself as a detective. I'm assuming you know that Keaton is dead. But you may not know this: The cops never figured out who killed him. So the family brought me in, some sixteen months later, and in the course of my investigation I came across your company and, of course, you. And I said to myself, What the hell is a tropical fish business? So rather than come in and ask you about Keaton without any idea of what you do, I decided to come in and take a look at what you do as someone else, then come back and ask you about Keaton as myself. Why did I do that? I'm not sure. I thought it might help me somehow."

"Did it?" Graves said.

"Again, I'm not sure. We'll see. So, Keaton Fuller?"

Graves said, wearing a cocky expression that made it clear that he didn't have to answer my questions but would anyway, said, "Keaton Fuller came to us through the bank. We had some people helping us find investors. Somebody found him. This was a couple years ago now. So Keaton shows up, interested in essentially being an angel-type investor. Give us money for equity but ultimately have very little to do with the business. Like I said, we were looking for capital. We were looking for guys like him. People who have money and need to put it somewhere. The business was doing well, but we were growing. And my business requires capital sometimes to grow. Like most businesses. All businesses. Look, I've got a lot going on. Partial ownership of breeding pools in Indonesia, Mexico, Singapore. I've got divers I pay all over the world. I've got to pay people to bid when a rare fish hits the market. I've got to pay people to *outbid* when a rare fish hits the market. I've got to pay insurers and shippers. Capital.

"So we met with Keaton. Liked him at first. Took some money from him. But very soon after we took his money, we gave it back. Didn't want it if it came attached to him. And that was that."

Lee Graves leaned back in his chair. Then he pulled his lips apart a bit, revealing more of his white teeth and the top of his gums, and said, "He was a fucking idiot. A joke. I remember hearing he'd gotten shot and thinking, That doesn't surprise me one bit."

"Wait, so he gave you money and then you gave it back?"

"Yeah. He gave us an investment and then started asking for it back, profit off it, almost immediately. Just a total amateur. Ignoring the terms of the contract. And ignoring the basic concept of how it works when you invest in a business. He also wanted to be on some of the calls I was making with breeders, divers. He wanted to meet with clients. And that might have been okay, except that everything he said was stupid, rude, incompetent. We gave him his money back with interest and cut him loose. Never saw him again."

"Who's 'we'? Who else works here? I see just you and Elana."

Just the slightest hint of crimson appeared on his face and his slick head. "We have an office that takes care of all our finances. It's in a different location." He then added, a touch defensively, "Lots of businesses do it that way."

He looked at me. Irritated that I was still probing. He'd given me an answer about Keaton and now I was questioning the way he ran his business. He didn't like it. But I did. Emotions are revealing.

Before I could respond, a man entered the office. He was tall, maybe six-two. But not lean like Graves. Big arms. Big chest. Spent a lot of time in the gym, power lifting. I could see his physical form underneath the black suit and black T-shirt getup he was wearing. He was Mexican. He had long hair, down to his shoulders, hard eyes, a mustache that sat over a hard mouth. He sat down in the chair in the corner behind me.

I hooked a thumb over my right shoulder and said, "Who's that?"

"Weren't you just asking who else works here? Well, he works here."

"He doesn't look like one of the guys who crunch the numbers."

I thought: Maybe people's heads, knees, jaws, perhaps testicles. But not numbers. No, definitely not numbers.

Graves said, a little more irritation in his voice, "What else do you want, Darvelle?"

This time I hooked my thumb to the left, toward the big aquarium, and said, "What kind of fish is that?"

We both looked over at the tank, at the large, blackish, brownish, and maybe deep down in there sort of reddish, fish smoothly moving around, with its unusual fin and its circular, downturned mouth.

"It's a Chinese high-fin. They come from the Yangtze River in China. They're endangered and have some value, but not huge value. Nothing like the other fish you saw here. I just happen to love them. When they're young and small, they're more colorful, and they're banded. They have white bands, vertical stripes. And the dorsal is much more pronounced. Much bigger compared to the body. They look like they might tip over. Most people think that's when they're at their most stunning. Even their name refers to this period. But I think the opposite. I think they're more beautiful as adults. When they're adults, they look like a totally different fish. Like this one. You can just see red underneath the black. And no more stripes. Fin's not as big. But still, to my eye, beautiful. But it's a subtle beauty. Harder to see."

I thought: Who is this guy? Who is this motherfucker? What about *him* is harder to see?

Graves looked back at me and repeated his question. "What else do you want, Darvelle?"

"What else do you want to tell me?"

"Well. I can tell you this: You lied to us, said you were interested in our product, came over, lied to us again, snooped around. Then you came back over, and this time you told us who you are, but you came unannounced, demanding to see me. I guess I just don't really like that. Any of it. I think it's time for you to go. I'm running a business, and I'm making a business decision to say that our conversation is over."

He stood up. I stayed seated. The guy behind me stayed seated too. I reached for my wallet, which made Lee Graves focus on my hand very intensely. Actions, like emotions, are revealing. My move for my wallet made the big guy behind me shift in his chair as well. Did these two guys think I was going for a gun? Or maybe the better question, the more specific question, was, Are these two guys familiar enough with the kind of conflict that results in someone going for a gun that they thought I was going for a gun?

The Chinese high-fin didn't seem to react. It just kept gliding around the tank.

I pulled out my wallet and got out one of my cards. I put it on Graves's desk, then turned it around so it would read right when he sat back down. I said, "If you think of anything else you can share with me about Keaton Fuller, anything you think might help me in my investigation, please contact me."

Graves looked down at the card but didn't touch it, and nodded.

I got up and turned to walk out. I said to the guy in the chair, "It was really nice to meet you."

He looked at me. He had no expression at all. And yet I could tell by his eyes, by his face, that he didn't like me. Funny how that works. Good—I didn't like him either. Him or his boss.

I left the office, said good-bye to Elana, then left Prestige Fish.

26

I went back to my office, opened the slider, sat at my desk, called Detective Mike Ott, LAPD. As the phone rang I pictured Ott sitting at his desk, combing his perfect head of hair. Starting at the part and making nice long strokes one way, then nice long strokes the other way. I have no idea why.

"Ott, Darvelle."

"Yeah."

"Wondering if you can run a check on someone for me."

"Yeah. Okay."

"Man named Lee Graves, runs a company called Prestige Fish. White, I'd say thirty-five, lean, six-one, blue eyes, clean bald head now but who knows how recent that is. Curious if you have anything on him. Priors, any trouble in his past."

"Yeah, might be a few Lee Graveses out there, but let me see if I can match something up. Gimme a day. Busy down here." And then he added, "Prestige Fish, is that a restaurant?"

I laughed. "Sounds like one, doesn't it? No, it's a tropical fish business. Graves is a tropical fish broker."

"Jesus Christ. That's where your investigation has taken you? To a goddamn pet store?"

"Not exactly. The fish this cat deals with sell for real money. Five, ten, twenty large a pop. Sometimes more."

"It's a fucked-up world, Darvelle. It really is. I'll run a check on Graves."

"Thank you, sir."

"By the way, my niece got a part in some show. She's over the fucking moon. You made me look good."

"I knew something was up. You were being way too nice to me."

"Don't get used to it. Me running this check? This is thank-you. *This* is thank-you. Then we're back to square one."

"Sounds good. And believe me, I would never get used to it. Because fundamentally, at your core, you don't like me that much."

"That's true," he said. And then he paused, and I could see a pensive look fall over his granite face, even though I couldn't actually see him. "That's very true."

I said, ending the call, "All right, Ott."

"I'll call you when I got something."

After I hung up with Ott, I got online and bought my friend Gary Delmore a present, a new Ping-Pong bat.

I bought him a Butterfly BalsaCarbo X5. I know, not a super-high-end bat, but, truth is, Gary Delmore can't handle a super-high-end bat. The BalsaCarbo X5 is just a really solid—hell, pretty damn nice—paddle. I had it shipped to him overnight. I have to say, giving Ott's niece a part was nice, really nice. And I know it meant a lot to Ott, which, in turn, will help me. Just now, sure, but probably again too. He'd said *this* was thank-you. But I'd get another favor or two out of him as a result of Delmore's string pulling. So Delmore deserves a little love in return. Got to give back, right?

A few minutes after I'd finished my online shopping excursion, my phone started vibrating on my desk. Shaking around, pulling the old spaz move again. My first thought, before I looked at it, was that Ott had forgotten to say something or ask me something and was calling me back. But when I looked, I realized I was wrong. It was Dave Treadway calling.

"Hi, Dave," I answered.

"Hey, John. You've got me in your caller ID. Nice."

"I do. What's up?"

"Well, Jill and I were talking. Wondering if you and your girlfriend wanted to come down for the day, day after tomorrow? Saturday? We're members of a little beach club down here in La Jolla, and we're going to have a beach day. Have lunch, swim in the ocean. Know it's last-minute, and I guess you're in the middle of a case, but we enjoyed meeting you the other day, so I thought I'd throw it out there."

This I didn't see coming. A call from someone I'd talked to about a case that wasn't a call relating to the case but was rather an invitation to do something social with another couple.

Some thoughts quickly hit me. One: I never do stuff like this, I'm always working. Two: If I were on anything other than a cold case there's no way I would, or probably even could, accept. Three: I had just put a fire under Graves, but I needed to let that fire build a bit, see what he would do with a little time to think. And four, the most important thought: the look in Nancy's eyes the other day when she'd said: "I like it when you hear me, John." Saying to me, You are pulling away from me, and I'm hurt by it, and I will eventually pull away from you.

I know, I know, balance doesn't work. But I knew, somehow I knew, that I owed this to Nancy. I had to go against my belief here. I had to work a little at the relationship. I used to hate it when people would say: you have to *work* at a relationship. I used to think, Yes, you have to work at a relationship, but only in proportion to how much you compromised in the beginning. Meaning that if you don't compromise in the beginning, then you don't have to work that much. The relationship just sort of flows, always. But I've learned, I think, that that's not really true. Because I don't feel like I compromised at all with Nancy, and yet I know I have to put in work at times, make a conscious effort at times, to keep the magic alive. Now, is that *work*? Or is it just doing your part, not being selfish? I don't know. I'd say yes. But whatever you call it, I'm submitting that sometimes you have to do things purely in the other person's interest. Now, this? Going down to La Jolla for a little sun and surf? Yeah, that sounds fun for me too. But I'd say no if there was no Nancy in the picture.

But there *was* a Nancy in the picture. So I said, "Dave, that's really nice. That sounds fun. And I think Nancy, my girlfriend, would really enjoy it. So you're making me look good."

I'd made Ott look good. Now Treadway was making me look good. How nice.

Treadway chuckled. "Happy to help."

"Let's do it," I added, not believing that I was actually going to take a day off. Well, I thought, I will be with someone from the investigation, maybe I'll learn something. And maybe a day off will be helpful, will refresh my mind a bit.

"Yeah?" Treadway said. "Great. Cool. Want to meet at my place at noon or so on Saturday?"

"See you then."

27

When I told Nancy our plans, she gave me one of the smiles I love. The one where she can't even pretend she's not excited. That smile made me really glad I had accepted. Made me think that sometimes I can be smart.

Saturday morning, we hit the road at 9:30 a.m. The 405 to the 5, right into lovely La Jolla. At noon sharp, we pulled into Dave Treadway's garage. I had anticipated traffic, even on a Saturday, and I had been right. The traffic, man, the traffic, always.

We went up to the Treadways' apartment, and I introduced Nancy to everyone. Then Dave, Davey, Jill, Nancy, and I went back down to the parking garage, got into Dave's BMW X5, and headed out.

We drove to the La Jolla Beach and Tennis Club, a tennis and golf club right on the ocean and right in the middle of an upscale, but old-school and tasteful, La Jolla neighborhood full of pretty flowers—California poppies and, look, some black-eyed Susans—and Spanish-style houses. The club, too, had old-school charm. It hadn't been redone to look modern and state-of-the-art. It was still sort of a seventies country club. Tennis courts, a golf course, a pool, a couple of restaurants, all organized around a series of low-slung Brady Bunch–style buildings. And, of course, you had a gorgeous stretch of the Pacific running along the whole thing.

I loved it.

We were out by the pool under a parasol, eating salads and club sandwiches, Jill and Nancy drinking mimosas, Dave and I having beers, Davey having some pineapple juice.

Jill said to Nancy, "So, John told us you two met when he came to the emergency room. That's quite a story. Tell us more."

"Yeah. He came into the hospital with some head trauma, claiming he had fallen down hiking, and I helped take care of him, even though I knew he was lying. And so did the doctor."

"What had actually happened?" Jill asked.

Nancy, protecting the privacy of my job, another one of her very sexy qualities, kept it vague and said, "John meets some unsavory characters in his business."

"Like you guys," I said.

Dave and Jill seemed to enjoy that.

"Anyway," Nancy continued, "when John was all taken care of and leaving the hospital, he asked for my number."

"And?" Jill said, totally sucked in to Nancy's story.

"I made him stand there in silence and suffer while I thought about it for a pretty long time."

Dave and Jill howled at this. I just sat there and took it.

Jill said to Nancy, raising her glass, "Good for you, girl."

They toasted.

Later, as we were all sitting on the beach, a big blanket, a cooler, some chairs, all of us chatting, Davey digging away happily in the sand, Nancy said to Jill, "So how 'bout you two? What's the story there?"

Jill said, pouring some more champagne into her and Nancy's plastic glasses, "I think this is a good how-two-people-met story."

Nancy smiled and took a sip.

Jill continued, "I was jogging on a running path in San Diego. Dave and I both lived in San Diego before we moved up here. So I was jogging along one day, it was a weekend, and, you know, it was 9:30, 10 in the morning, and this guy runs past me in the other direction." She pointed to Dave. "*That* guy. Anyway, I barely noticed him. Next thing I know he's behind me, running now in the same direction as I am. And then he's right next to me, running along. I'm like, What is this guy doing? So he introduces himself as we're running along. And then he asked me out, right there, as we were running. It was . . . weird, really. I almost didn't know what to say, so I just told him how to get in touch with me. Gave him my name and the name of the ad agency where I worked. And said, you know, call me at work, I guess."

Nancy loved it, laughed out loud.

I said, as Dave poured a canned Budweiser into a red plastic Solo cup and handed it to me, "See, Dave. That's what you have to do. There's this conventional wisdom, which as a general rule I hate, that you're going to see someone you're interested in in a place where asking someone out is relatively normal, like a bar or a restaurant or whatever. But that doesn't always happen. Mostly you see people you'd like to say hello to in kind of random places. Like when you're jogging."

Dave said, "Or when you're at the hospital."

"Right! And you have to pull the trigger. It's up to us, *the guy*, to pull the trigger. And that's hard. That takes guts."

I looked over at Jill and Nancy and said, "Let me tell you, ladies, what Dave and I did, it's not that easy."

Dave added, "It is definitely not."

Nancy said, a sparkle in her eye, "But look what you get if you go for it."

She motioned to herself and Jill.

Dave and I couldn't disagree. Now we were the ones toasting.

We all went swimming. Nancy and I went pretty far out. Dave and Jill stayed near the shore with Davey. The cool ocean, after a few cold beers, felt refreshing, rejuvenating, amazing. Nancy and I, in about ten feet of water, took turns swimming down and touching the ocean floor, an always exhilarating, and just a tiny bit scary, trip.

A few hours later, Nancy drifting off to sleep on the blanket, Dave and Jill a little ways down the beach playing in the sand with Davey, me sitting in a chair looking out at the ocean, I got the surge of dizziness again, the feeling I'd had on the Treadways' balcony a few days ago. But this time it was even more intense. My head was spinning. The battery taste reappeared in my throat, rancid and burning and strong. Holy shit, I thought, I'm going to throw up. This time, I'm *definitely* going to throw up. I stood up, thinking that might help. Nancy's body was still and her eyes were closed. Jill, Dave, and Davey were down the beach, smiling and laughing. Nobody seemed to notice that I had this crazy, uncomfortable feeling inside me.

I walked off toward the clubhouse, had to find a bathroom. I found one of the restaurants, classic club look, windows lining the ocean, then found the bathroom, walked in, got to the sink, turned the cold water on high. I cupped water in my hands and splashed it in my face. Over and over. It wasn't helping. I looked in the mirror as a fresh wave of nausea and vertigo came over me. I was going to puke. Or fall and hit my head. I dry heaved. And then I dry heaved again. But nothing came up.

I leaned down and drank some water from the sink, took one, two, three swallows, trying to get that battery taste out of my throat and off my tongue. Drinking water seemed to help. I stood back up. Yes, the feeling was fading. Yes, finally. I took a couple of deep breaths. In, out. In, out. I took another big sip of water. Then another big breath. Yeah, it was fading, fading, gone. I was back.

I walked out of the bathroom, through the restaurant, and back outside. The air, the breeze, it felt good. I crossed over to a little grassy area that bordered the sand. I looked out at the beach and found Jill, Dave, and Davey, now back on the big blanket with Nancy. They were all talking, laughing, toasting. I looked at the group of them, at the water everywhere behind them, at the white sand. All the colors coming at me—the sky, the ocean, the bathing suits on the beach—seemed pushed, heightened, surreal. Nancy and Jill and Dave and Davey could almost have been characters in a movie I was watching. And standing there, that's when I knew where the sick feeling was coming from.

In Jill and Dave and Davey, I was seeing a life that I wasn't going to have. I was seeing a family, a normal life. A great, normal life.

A part of me wants it, has always wanted it, and, yet I had chosen a job that brings me in close contact with death. Often. I'd chosen a job where you have to be *willing to die* in order to do it well. Is that just an excuse not to have to face the responsibility of a family? I don't think so. After all, is it fair to a child, to children, to know that when you leave the house, if you're doing your job right, you might not come back?

Standing there, looking at Jill and Dave and Davey, and now Nancy, especially Nancy, I felt a certain longing. Like I was living in a world just slightly apart from them. And that evening on the balcony, and right here on the beach, my body was reacting to this reality in a way I'd never experienced. In a way that made me physically feel it. But I knew, standing there, that the life I'd chosen to live was the one for me. I *could* bring a family into it, but, knowing what I knew, I probably wouldn't.

I'd told Nancy this. And I'd also told her that if she left, I'd understand. But she'd said she was an adult and could make her own decisions. I understood that, I'd made a decision too. And I felt that it was the right one. Because of that, while knowing that I'd never have that *other* life gave me great pain, I knew the pain would be greater if I went into situations on the job and hedged a bit. Gave it less than I thought was necessary. It's a strange irony in a way, the fact that to do a lot of things well you have to put it all on the line. You have to be willing to fail in a spectacular way in order not to fail in a spectacular way. You have to be willing to lose everything to gain everything. Tough choice. And in my line, sometimes—not always, but sometimes—you have to be willing to die to find out what happened, what really went down, and who did it.

Does this mean I have a death wish? I don't think so, but I don't know. I hope not. I do know that what I'm saying is true. And I could feel the need to take one of those risks with this guy Lee Graves. I could feel a situation like that coming. And, yeah, I know that if I don't go all in, I might not find everything out. So I'm prepared to do it. Shit, I like doing it. In a way, my body telling me that I won't have this other life is also my body telling me that something's coming. It's saying: That dream has to die. Know it, feel it, so you can be fully prepared to face the possible nightmare ahead. It's saying: Are you ready? Are you *still* ready to do what you might have to do?

Is that why Dave and Jill and Davey Treadway entered my story? To show me a life I wasn't going to have, but also to say: Are you going to be ready?

I focused again on the beach, then looked beyond it to the ocean, where I could now see some sailboats way out near the horizon, moving steadily, catching gusts of wind. I walked back down to rejoin everyone.

A few hours later we were all back at the Treadways' apartment. We had decided to have dinner together and were contemplating what to do. Make something, go out, order in? Had this day put the four of us on the verge of becoming real friends? Were Nancy and I going to be part of one of those groups of four, or even six or eight, people who were all in reasonably happy relationships, who hung out together, vacationed together, relied on one another? Oh my god, it was terrifying.

I walked down one of the hallways out of the main room, headed for a bathroom, when I noticed, in one of the back rooms of the apartment, a Ping-Pong table. The table sat in a man cave, a study-type room. Dave's hideout. Now, was the room big enough for actual Ping-Pong? Well, no. But the table did not have anything sitting on it. No papers, no pens, no backpacks. So that was good. Respect. And the room was definitely big enough for beer pong. Which the four of us were going to play, if I had anything to say about it. Remember earlier how I said there was some beer pong in this story? Well, it's about to happen.

I walked back out to the front room, introduced the idea. The Treadways and Nancy loved it. We ordered two pizzas and two cases of Bud Light, had them delivered. That's right, *two* cases of Bud Light. Beer goes quickly, very quickly, when you're playing beer pong.

This was shaping up to be my kind of night.

For the record, there are two kinds of beer pong. The kind where you attempt to throw a Ping-Pong ball into a cup full of beer at the other end of the table, and the kind where you are essentially playing a modified form of Ping-Pong, only instead of trying to win the point in the traditional way, you are trying to hit a Ping-Pong ball, with a Ping-Pong paddle, into a cup of beer at the other end of the table. Now, if you are playing beer pong the Ping-Pong way and you are playing doubles, like we were about to, each team has two cups of beer in front of them, and each team has two cups of beer to aim for on the other side of the table. So you start a point, you and your teammate take turns hitting back the balls that don't land in the cups in front of you, toward the cups on the other side, with the intent being to land your shot in one of their cups. When a ball does land in a cup, that's a plop. If you and your teammate get plopped, you both have to drink your beer. If you and your teammate plop the other guys—well, you get the gist.

That's it.

That's all you have to do to have the best time of your life.

Dave put Davey to bed and brought a viewing monitor into the Ping-Pong room. Everyone had a couple slices of pizza, and then we got to it. Nancy and I versus Dave and Jill. I took it easy, intentionally missing a lot, to make sure everyone got a chance to get into it, to sink balls, to feel the thrill of beer pong.

And boy, did everyone feel the thrill.

When Jill sunk a ball, she screamed, I mean screamed. She didn't even say anything. She just screamed a glorious scream.

When Nancy sunk one, she yelled: "Yes! That's right! Yes!"

When Dave hit a plop, he closed his eyes and clenched his fist in an almost primal way.

We had finished a few spirited games and gone through almost a full case of beer when Dave said something I've heard a lot over the years when people play beer pong, either for the first time or for the first time in a while. He looked at me and said, with a real longing, a real desperation, in his eyes, "We're going to play more games, right?"

To which I responded, "Yes. Yes, that's right."

Dave put on some music. The Descendents. *Somery*. A Southern California choice. A great choice. A pop-punk band that I happen to love. Whose lyrics are clever and moving. "Cameage"—one of the great punk anthems ever, for my money. Jill then went into a closet and came back out holding four hats and said that from now on we all had to wear a hat while we played. Nobody objected, not for a second. Jill gave Nancy a black baseball cap with a marijuana leaf on the front. I got a green John Deere trucker hat. Dave got a big straw Vincent van Gogh hat, and Jill gave herself a tiny little cap with a propeller on top. We looked good. We looked ready. It was getting crazy. I was all for it.

We started a new game. I served, got the first point going. (By the way, you don't aim for the cup on the serve.) Dave hit my serve back, missed. Nancy hit the ball back toward their cups, missed. Then Jill hit, missed. Then I hit the ball, going for it, zeroing in—missed. Barely. Fucking barely. Shit. Then Dave hit, his barely missed too. Then Nancy hit one, high, real high, a nice arc to it, and . . . PLOP. Dead center. Right into the cup in front of Dave.

I looked at Nancy in her black marijuana hat and said, "That's why I love you."

Dave grabbed the ball out of his cup and said, "I'm glad you did that. Because I want to do this." He slammed his entire beer in one sip, even though he technically had a minute or two if he needed it.

Then Jill said, "Me too." And she took down her entire beer in one fluid chug.

Professional behavior. I liked it. We kept playing. After two more games everyone had a hefty, hefty buzz.

I said to Dave, "Do you by any chance have any southern rock?"

Dave said, "I can't believe you'd ask me that. Name a Marshall Tucker song."

As I thought for a sec, he screamed, a wild smile across his face, "Name one!"

" 'This Ol' Cowboy.' "

"Coming right up. And I think it needs to be a little louder."

We played a few more games, everyone making shots, everyone loving it, everyone getting even looser, crazier, sillier. Jill was checking the baby monitor and periodically leaving to check on Davey in the other room. I admired her for having fun and still being a good parent.

Eventually and, as far as Dave and I were concerned,

reluctantly, we stopped playing. One and a half cases of beer, down. We all went back into the living room. Nancy and I accepted the Treadways' invitation to stay in their guest room. At this point, let's face it, it really wasn't a decision we had to think too much about. We were pretty wrecked. But now that we were officially spending the night, it was quite easy for Nancy and me to partake of the joint that Dave and Jill had just lit up. We passed it around, each taking a hit or two. Or three. And soon I, and I think everyone, had another kind of buzz on top of the hefty beer buzz. It was giddy, but also dreamy, wistful, even slightly hallucinatory. The lights in their apartment were low. The music was low, too. We all talked and told stories and laughed about, reminisced about, some of the better beer pong points. Then we all went out onto the balcony. The cool, soft ocean air felt amazing. And at night, without the cars and traffic down below, you could hear the ocean too, hear the waves coming in. A lot of the city lights of La Jolla were out, but many weren't. You could see intermittent lights amid the blackness, almost like stars. At some point, I can't remember the actual time, Dave and Jill went off to their bedroom. And a little after that, Nancy and I went off to ours.

Lying in bed, hanging on to consciousness by a thread, Nancy looked at me and said, "That was fun, John."

And I said, "Yeah. Yeah. It was."

And we both shut our eyes and were out.

28

The next morning, up, some coffee, some hugs, some good-byes. Thankfully there wasn't that thing that happens on the last day of a trip, or the next day after you've had a really good time, where everyone turns into a totally different person than they were the days or night before. You know, walking around stressed and weird and short and tensely packing bags while sighing and interacting with everyone in just a totally bizarre way. You know when that happens? You know when that happens. Awful. Weird. Unnecessary. And as I said, in this case, not happening.

Which was nice.

The drive back wasn't too bad either. However, before

we could hit the road for real, we had to stop for gas right outside La Jolla, which was mildly annoying. But, hey, the Focus needed fuel. And this little speed bump gave Nancy and me the idea to indulge in some fast food at a Mickey D's right near the gas station. As you all know, you're allowed to eat fast food when you're on a road trip. You can go to McDonald's or Burger King or Jack in the Box and just go to town, like we did. If you are *not* on the road, if you are in your actual town, and you do what we did, somehow it becomes exceedingly depressing. But because we were away, it was exceedingly fucking delicious. I got both an Egg McMuffin and a Sausage McMuffin, by the way. One or the other just wouldn't have been enough.

Once we got back to L.A., I took Nancy to my house so she could get her car. But when we got there, I had a thought. I gave her the Focus, grabbed my black carry bag out of it, then got in her car, a silver 2012 VW Passat.

Then I drove that car to work.

That's right. On a Sunday. My second-favorite day to work. You're still stealing time, but you can feel Monday tugging at you, so the experience is a little less freeing.

I got to the warehouse lot, but I didn't park in my usual space. I drove right past it, drove across the lot, and parked on the other side, in a guest spot in front of someone else's warehouse, in front of someone else's slider. I backed the Passat in, tucking it behind a white Acura that was parked facing forward. I could see three-quarters of the lot out of my front window, and I could see the rest of the lot, and the entrance to my space, through the Acura's rear window. I scanned the lot. Nothing out of the ordinary. Some trucks moving some things in and out of spaces. Some cars that I recognized, some that I didn't. It was just normal, semislow Sunday activity.

See, I was thinking that it'd been a couple of days since I'd put a little bee in Lee Graves's bonnet. Irritated him. Disrespected him. And I wondered, it being Sunday and all, if he, or somebody he worked with, might come around to look into me. Like I'd been looking into him. To see if I was in on a Sunday. To see what I was doing. To put me in a location. Maybe even to break into my space and look around a little. Or stake out my space to figure out the best time to illegally enter it. He wouldn't send anyone around to tell me to back off—you know, bring some guys by to threaten me, intimidate me. No, he wouldn't do that, not yet; that would imply that he was doing something wrong. No, at this point he'd just want to see whether he could glean anything that might tell him if I was *good*. If I was a good PI. If Graves was involved in something illegal, I thought, *that's* what he would be wondering. Who is this guy, Darvelle? Is he someone I need to worry about? Is he someone who's on to something? Or is he just a hack PI who heard that Keaton Fuller worked at Prestige Fish and came knocking?

Of course, Graves's sending someone today, or coming by himself, might not happen. Maybe that all went down yesterday, while I was in La Jolla. Or not. Maybe he wasn't thinking about me at all. Yeah, this was just a guess, a hunch. A Sunday hunch.

About forty minutes later I watched a van enter the lot. Pretty new, white, nondescript, almost friendly looking. Nonthreatening. It was driving around almost like a cop drives, not when he's in pursuit of something but when he's just making his presence felt, or just very casually and confidently looking around for something. Slow. Deliberate. Steady. It was circling around the other side of the lot, near my space. I noticed two things. One, the van never stopped moving. When you come to a lot with a bunch of warehouses and you're driving a van, you usually, almost always, eventually stop at one. To pick up some stuff or unload some stuff. Or to do something. And two, when I looked at the driver of the van through my field binocs, he looked an awful lot like the Mexican man who was sitting behind me stoically in Lee Graves's office the other day. If the Mexican man who was sitting behind me stoically in Lee Graves's office the other day had his hair pulled back tight and tied up underneath a ball cap and was wearing sunglasses big enough to cover most of his face.

His mouth. That's what it was. That hard line gave him away.

On its third pass by my slider, I noticed the van slow down ever so slightly. One last look, same result. Nobody home. All locked up. And the white Ford Focus, the car I'd let them see the last time I'd visited Prestige Fish—well, that wasn't there either.

So the big Mexican man could now report to his boss that I wasn't around, I wasn't at work. And while he couldn't put a location on me, he could tell Graves one place I wasn't. Maybe he thought I was at home getting psyched up by watching old *Matt Houston* reruns. I hope so.

The van, keeping its slow, steady pace, made its way to the little road that takes you off the lot, then headed out, surveillance done for the day.

I cranked up the Passat and followed.

The van twisted through Culver City and hopped on the 10, headed east. I did too, hanging back, ten, fifteen cars between us.

We took the 10 past downtown proper, then past that warehouse-laden, industrialized section of the city just east of downtown. Smokestacks and drab concrete clusters and the *L.A. Times* building hanging on for dear life.

We kept going east, kept heading out the 10, like we were going to Palm Springs, or maybe farther east, to Arizona, or to Texas, or all the way to the other side of the country. We curved through some unfashionable, more affordable areas outside of L.A., Boyle Heights, West Covina, until we got to Pomona, where we exited off the interstate.

Pomona is where the L.A. County Fair takes place. I'd been a couple of times. Experienced some fried dough, and some wild-eyed looks from some fried Ferris wheel operators. Amazing how when you go to a fair you'll put your life in the hands of a guy who hasn't slept in three days and has never been to the dentist.

Pomona does have a real farm culture, thus the fair. It also has some nice, gentrified, mildly bucolic neighborhoods. It's got some gloomy, poor, strange neighborhoods too. Hoods without a lot of hope.

I stayed on the van, four, five, six cars back now, through a small, charming sort of downtown area that felt like it belonged in a different time: a general store, a bakery, a boot store. We cleared downtown, then wound through a down-market neighborhood that was nonetheless clean, taken care of, people doing their best to make a nice life for themselves.

We kept going, just two, three cars between me and the van now. I was pretty sure the Mexican man hadn't made me, hadn't even registered that there was a Passat in his rearview. Now, though, now that there were fewer cars between us and we appeared to be getting toward a destination, I planned to be a little more careful. But, truth is, I didn't think I'd have to be that careful. He had a different car in mind for me, and on top of that, I don't think he was looking for me. It's amazing what you can get away with when no one's on the lookout for it. Walk down a city street someday and just pick out somebody to follow. And do it, follow them. And watch how far you can go before they notice you, if they ever do. Trust me, you'll end up thirty miles away from where you started, standing in their front yard, right out in the open, watching them head inside their house, unnoticed.

The down-market but respectable little neighborhood gave way to a bleak, treeless section of Pomona: some houses, some commerce, but a nondescript, undefined feeling to the whole area. And then just past that, practically right next to it, we drove into some of that golden, beautiful California farmland.

And now there was just one car between me and the van. The Mexican man might look into his rearview, see the pickup behind him, see a silver Passat behind that. So what. We drove for about five miles, now passing big farms on both sides. Big swaths of beautiful green and yellow-brown land, silos, barns, cattle, Americana.

The van began to slow down, then reached a dirt-road intersection and turned right. The pickup in front of me and I continued straight on. In my rearview, I could see that the van had stopped about twenty yards down the dirt road at a cattle gate. I watched the man get out of the van to open the gate. And I looked to see where he would go once he got through the gate—way down the dirt road to a distant farmhouse.

I drove straight on, passing more big chunks of farmland. The van was now heading down the dirt road to the farmhouse, but it was tiny in my rearview, like a toy. The pickup and I got to an intersection, I'd say about a mile away from where the van had gone right. The pickup went straight. I took a right, down another road flanked by farms. About two hundred yards down, I pulled my car over to a little dirt area just off the road and got out.

The sun was high, it was hot. I looked around, wheat fields and fences and farmhouses in every direction. I looked in the direction of the one the van with the Mexican man had been headed toward. Across two, three, four plots I could just see the house, a brown structure with white trim, in the distance. And now I could see a second structure, a barn, sitting behind it.

I leaned on the Passat, looking over its roof out into the fields. What next, what next?

I got back in and drove farther down the road I was on for about another mile, until I got to another intersection.

I took a right, so I was now on the road that was *behind*, far behind, the farmhouse the van had gone to. I drove down this road, a lonely, desolate stretch, until I thought I'd be roughly behind the farmhouse, roughly in line with it. Two small houses sat right up close to the road, with small backyards that bordered the backs of the big farms. Just two little country houses that looked like they'd been there forever.

I drove three hundred yards past the houses, swung a U, and started heading back toward them. Twenty yards away, I pulled off the side of the road and tucked the Passat behind a wall of undergrowth.

And then I waited. Waited for the sun to drop.

When it did, it got dark, and I mean *dark*. The little houses up a couple hundred yards or so emanated some light, but not much. And there were no streetlights, and just a sliver of moon up in the sky. I unzipped my carry bag. I changed into a black long-sleeved shirt to go with my black pants and black Adidas running shoes. I holstered my Colt on my belt and my Sig on my ankle. Then I put on a lightweight black windbreaker that zipped up the front. In the front right pocket of the windbreaker was a black ski mask. I left it there, for now.

I got out of the Passat and walked up the road to the two little houses, my markers—in line, across a big field, with the farmhouse I needed to go to. I quietly walked behind the first little house, then quietly climbed over the little wooden fence behind it. I stood there in the big field, in the waist-high wheat. I could see a distant light, and as I heard a distant dog bark, I headed toward it.

29

I walked fast and steadily across the field. The farmhouse, the lights on inside, and the dark barn behind it got bigger and bigger as I got closer and closer. When I was about three hundred yards out, I crouched down low, and stayed that way until I was at the edge of the property. Right at the edge, the field gave way to manicured grass. I stayed just inside the field, got down on my chest, parted the wheat, and looked around. The farmhouse was two stories, maybe four bedrooms, and well maintained, nice. Lights on both upstairs and down. The barn behind it sat in near-total darkness, but I could see, with my adjusting eyes, that it was in good shape too. There were no animals around, no livestock; maybe some horses in the barn, but I doubted it. There were two vehicles in a parking area between the house and the barn. The van and Graves's Tesla.

I didn't see any activity in the windows of the farmhouse, so I got up, still staying relatively low, and very quickly and quietly ran over to the house. Glued to it now, in a section of darkness between what appeared to be a lit kitchen window and a dark window next to it, maybe a bathroom. I took the black ski mask out of my front right pocket and put it on. Then, very slowly, I lifted my head up and looked through the kitchen window. A nice, remodeled farmhouse kitchen, but no one in it. I moved past the dark window to a big window with light coming out of it, on the same side of the house as the kitchen window I'd just looked through. I stood next to it, then very slowly moved my head over to look inside.

This is where they were. The dining room. Burgundy walls. A chandelier. An antique-looking rectangular dining-room table. At the table: Graves, the Mexican man, and another man I'd never seen before. A thin, pale, almost sick-looking older man with long gray hair. He wore what looked to be a blue velvet blazer and a crisp white shirt. He was at the head of the table, Graves on his left, the Mexican man on his right.

The three men were drinking red wine. Each man had a glass in front of him, and there were three bottles on the table. They were chatting, smiling, having a cordial conversation. But it didn't look like everyone had an equal voice. The man with the long gray hair was doing most of the talking. And the body language of the other two suggested that they were giving him respect. Long Gray Hair was in charge.

I ducked out of the frame and moved down the side of the house, then across the front of it, then down the other side, looking in windows, taking in what I could quickly. The house was nice, high end, but not lived in. It looked fake. Like a set. Decorated to achieve an effect: a farmer who had done well. Dark colors, chunky wood furniture, big beige couches, a fireplace the size of a small country.

There didn't appear to be anyone else in the house. No aquariums either. Not a clarion angelfish or a Chinese high-fin anywhere.

I was back at the rear of the farmhouse now. I moved away from it and walked between the Tesla and the big empty van back to the barn, which sat twenty yards away, at the edge of the field I'd come through. There were no exterior lights on the barn, but the sliver of moon and the glowing farmhouse gave me enough light to operate.

I began to circle around it. There were three entrances. Front, side, back, all locked up tight. The windows were blacked out from the inside by a dark tarp. I went around to the side of the barn farthest from the house, where one of the entrances stood between a row of blacked-out windows.

I had my lockpicks with me, but the lock at this entrance, at every entrance, was above my skill set. Way too serious.

I looked along all the windows, at each window, until I found what I was looking for. The interior tarp blacking one of them out had stretched, was billowing a bit, giving me a little slice to look through.

I put my eye up to it but found only more darkness.

I pulled a mini Maglite flashlight out of my pocket.

Where I was, I was pretty sure I could turn it on and not be seen. I clicked it on and shone its beam through the sliver in the tarp. I could see a section of the wall opposite me. Neatly lined up in rows were filled glass liquor bottles, looked like tequila bottles. Next to them were rows of opaque white plastic containers that might or might not have been filled with something, I couldn't tell. I was only getting a partial view of what was there, but there had to be hundreds of bottles and hundreds of containers. And if there were as many on the other walls as there were on the wall that I could see, we could be talking thousands.

I clicked off the light and stood there in the darkness.

A dog barked. Maybe the dog I'd heard earlier as I'd walked into the field behind the little houses. The bark didn't come from Graves's property, sounded like it was coming from the field in the next farm over, maybe a hundred yards away. Was it reacting to me? Or was it just a dog doing its dog thing in a field behind a farm on a nearly moonless night?

It barked again. Then it stopped. Quiet again. Good.

I heard the back door of the farmhouse open and shut.

Shit.

I pulled away from the barn, quickly crossed the grass, and entered the chest-high field.

The light at the front of the barn went on. I dropped down to my chest, flat on the earth. The barn light was helping me hide. It put the areas outside its range in black contrast.

Still down on my chest, I made my way back a bit, just a bit, toward the barn, back to the edge of the high stuff, toward the patch of cut grass. My eyes were trained to my right, to the front quarter of the barn that I could see. A man stepped to the side of the barn and faced me. Two hundred feet away, a silhouette. Graves, for sure. He moved his head in a way that suggested that he was looking into the blackness, right toward me, like a bird zeroing in. Focusing. He pulled a gun sheathed between his belt and his back and held it at his side.

I pulled my Colt, held it out in front of me, pointed at Graves. He looked to his right and jerked his head. He was telling someone else, someone I couldn't see, to make a move.

I pulled my Sig and put it in my left hand.

Thirty seconds later, at the back corner of the barn, to my left, I heard a noise. And then a flashlight went on, a big, bright ray of light moving around, searching, searching for me. It was the Mexican man holding the light. He held it in his left hand, because his right hand held a gun.

The light beam swept toward me, then stopped, shining brightly on the grass directly in front of me. If the Mexican man moved the light just a bit deeper into the field, he might make me. And the guns would start firing. Theirs and mine.

I was okay with this happening. I had *felt* that this might happen. I just didn't want it to happen right now. Not yet. I had more information about Graves, but I didn't have a direct line from that information to Keaton Fuller. And that's what I wanted.

The light moved off the patch of grass. Then the Mexican man walked right in front of me, rounding the corner of the barn where I'd found the sliver of undraped window.

Now Graves and the Mexican man both stood in the pool of light just to the side of the barn's front. And now I had two guns pointed at two silhouettes.

The Mexican man clicked off his flashlight and said, "Nothing. We're clear."

Graves didn't say anything, but I could see his silhouette nod. Then the light at the front of the barn went out and the two men walked back toward the farmhouse.

I could hear Graves unlock the Tesla with his key fob, open a door, then shut it. Graves didn't lock it, though, didn't set the alarm with the fob. Which gave me an idea.

Ten minutes after I heard Graves and the Mexican man reenter the farmhouse, I stood up, walked back over to the front edge of the barn, carefully looked around it back at the farmhouse. Nothing doing. Graves and the Mexican man were probably back at the dining-room table, sipping some red, listening to their boss.

I walked over to the Tesla. Made my way over to the side-view mirror on the driver's side. I pulled out my flashlight again, but I didn't turn it on.

Instead I got low, right next to the mirror, and popped it with the butt of the steel flashlight, breaking it, a little spiderweb appearing instantly. It made a noise, but not much of one. It didn't create any action in the house. I slid the Maglite back into my pocket, then slid out of there, back through the big field, back to Nancy's Passat, back to L.A., and finally back home.

30

Next morning, early, I went to my office, got out my computer, and started adding to, and of course refining, my case notes. I then looked at them, at each crisp line, from the beginning up to right now.

So how had my story progressed?

Well, Keaton Fuller was a bad guy, we all know that, it's been confirmed by everyone in his world. And Keaton Fuller was assassinated, probably by a person who does that kind of thing, a person with some experience. And then there's the Prestige Fish folks, who, I had now confirmed, were part of a Pendella Situation. And who almost certainly had access to someone, or had someone in their employ, who could put a bullet in a guy with a Smith & Wesson M&P pistol from seventy-five yards.

So why was I sure Prestige was a Pendella?

Because of the tequila bottles and the plastic containers. That liquid I could see inside the tequila bottles? Well, it looked like tequila, same golden color, but it wasn't tequila. It was meth. Yes. Pure methamphetamine. Dissolved into a liquid solution, put into bottles and containers to disguise it, and carried over the Mexican border.

Okay, I wasn't one hundred percent sure it was meth. In that I hadn't taken one of the bottles to the cops and had them run a test on the liquid. But this was a smuggling technique I was familiar with, so I was ninety-nine percent sure. And that was good enough, by a long way, for me.

So where was the lab here in California where they mixed the liquid with acetone and turpentine, where they iced it, where they turned it into white, sparkly crystals ready for the street? Well, don't know. They could be using a second Pendella business as a cover for that. An auto-repair shop somewhere. A carpet installation company. And how big was Graves's operation? How deep did it go? How far did it reach? Not sure of that either. But I can tell you this: Just from what I saw, all those bottles and containers, their operation was into the many millions. And roles? What was everyone's role? Graves, the Mexican man, the man with the long gray hair? My guess? The guy with the long gray hair was the one connected to the cartel in Mexico. Was the one who'd been in business here in the States a long time, knew how to run it, set up the Pendella businesses, bring in shrewd new people like Lee Graves, who could learn the operation and one day run it on his own and who, most important, was comfortable with really dangerous illegal activity if it meant making a shitload of coin. And the Mexican man? I'd say a lower-level guy who ran between Mexico and the United States and had the trust of both sides. And who, by the way, had probably killed a lot of people.

So, Keaton Fuller? Right, Keaton Fuller. Where does he fit in? Graves had said that Keaton was an investor in Prestige Fish. Maybe that was a version of the truth. Maybe Keaton had given Graves some money to buy equity in the drug operation—"all businesses need capital"—but then did something stupid and got popped. Sure. These guys, meth guys, they don't care that somebody came from Hancock Park. They kill people all the time. They just pull out a gun and shoot you. Punch in, kill guy, punch out, go home.

And you know what? That mentality just might end up helping me.

So what next? What next?

Back to the Valley. I had a few stops to make. I closed up my laptop, closed up the slider, got in the Focus, and headed out.

31

First stop: the Firing Line shooting range in Northridge.

Again I went through twenty-four rounds on the Colt and twenty rounds on the smaller Sig. But this time I took the whole process slower. Not much slower, just a touch, just a second or two longer between shots. And I focused, intensely focused, on my stance, on my breathing. And I took the shots, all forty-four of them, like there was something on the line.

I looked at my targets. A nice, tight cluster of holes at the head and the heart on both the Colt target and the Sig target. Getting really close to being ready—ready for action.

I got back in the Focus and headed toward my second

Valley stop, Craig Helton's office. I pulled into his horrible little parking lot, and just as I was about to get out, my phone buzzed. Gary Delmore.

"Hey, Gary."

"The Darv!"

"You got the paddle."

"I got the paddle. Thanks, dude, like it a lot. Looking forward to using it to kick your fucking ass."

"You know how silly that comment is, right?"

"I've beaten you once."

"That's right, once. How many times have we played, how many games? A thousand? I bet we've seriously played a thousand games."

"Yeah, I know, but that's what makes it so great. Because every time we talk about our Ping-Pong history, whether it's to each other or to other people, that fact comes up. And it puts this little kernel of doubt into the overall story. Like, hmm, Darvelle *is* beatable. Maybe he's not *that* good. That *one* victory does that. It probably affects your sleep from time to time. I bet it really does. I bet you toss and turn every now and then, just lying there in the dark, thinking about it."

I'd never admit it, never, but he was right. He really was.

I said, "Whatever. Listen, thanks for giving Ott's niece a part. Really helped me out."

"You know, she's pretty good, I have to say. Turns out I might have cast her anyway. I was wondering, though—"

Before he finished his sentence I said, "No. Gary, I'm serious. No. Off-limits. Just get it out of your head."

"John. Chill. You don't even know what I was going to say."

"What were you going to say?"

"I was going to say what you thought I was going to say."

I had to laugh.

"All right, all right," he said. "Just thought I'd check one more time. Thanks again for the bat. Let's seriously play soon."

"Yeah."

"Or grab a beer or a bite."

"Yeah. All of the above."

"Hey, actually, some really cute girls I know are getting together soon—I know, I know, you're with Nancy—I'm just saying, come with me, you'll want to just *look* at these girls. Gorgeous actresses. And believe it or not, gorgeous actresses with personality. Fun, funny. Anyway, we're all getting together for, like, a boozy brunch soon. Want to join?"

I could feel an anger rising up within me, just like that. But not because Gary knows I'm with Nancy. For another reason entirely. "Gary, I don't go to brunch, you know that. Brunch? You actually think I'm going to go to one of those places with a line out the door on the weekend? With a bunch of people standing around outside, starving, waiting to be seated in some horrible, loud, bright, hot-as-balls restaurant. To get some poorly made lukewarm eggs Benedict? With tables of couples everywhere, and terrible fucking service. Dude, really? You're really asking me that?"

"Darv, chill. Jesus. I forgot, you hate brunch. Or maybe

I thought you'd calmed down a bit about the whole thing."

"And also, did you say the term 'boozy brunch'? Did you really just say that? Are you going to start saying the term 'foodie' next? Fuck."

I had raised my voice. Involuntarily. I just couldn't control it. I was yelling at Gary Delmore. "You know what, Gary, send me the paddle back. Just put it in the mail. You know my address. Just put it in the mail and send it back."

Now he started yelling. I guess he couldn't control it either. "No, I'm not going to send it back. It's mine now. And you know what else? Go to therapy, John. Just do it. Just, wherever you are right now, just drive to a psychiatrist's office and get started. And go every day for years. You need a name? I'll give you my therapist's name. I might even pay for it. Whatever it takes to help you."

"Send me the paddle back."

"Fuck off."

"You fuck off."

We hung up at the same time. I thought: I love that guy. I really do.

I got out of the Focus and walked into Craig Helton's insurance office. I caught his eye and he waved me back, gestured for me to sit in front of his desk. He was on the phone, telling me now with his index finger and his eyes to hold on one sec. I nodded, looked around the bleak little room now populated with agents, a stark contrast to the empty one I'd experienced the first time I'd been there. Each desk had an agent sitting behind it. Some desks had a person in front of it, like me, only probably an actual customer. At the desk to Craig's left and my right sat a female agent, no one in front of her, working on her computer. She was wrapped in a blanket to fight off the air-conditioning.

I thought: There's one of them. A member of a strange and bizarre club. The People Who Wear Blankets at Work. This member happened to be a woman, but men do it too. How do you become one of these people, I wondered. Do you just wake up one day and say: Today's the day—I'm going to take part of my bed to work with me. You know, I worked briefly for a big detective agency before I left to start my own thing. There were a few members of the club at the agency. And since then, I've been in lots and lots of offices. And there's almost always one member present. If not two. Yes, an adult, at work, fully wrapped in a blanket, a quilt, a duvet. And all you see is a little face poking out the top of it.

Craig hung up the phone and looked at me. "Sorry about that. How are you, John? How's the case? What's happening?"

I said, "The fish people you mentioned."

He produced a snarky laugh. "Yeah. Prestige Fish. What about them?"

"Did you ever hear anything about what Keaton was actually doing? His role?"

"Man, no. Not really. You know, we weren't speaking at that point. So I wasn't going to hear anything from him."

"I understand. But do you know if he really worked with them? Or was it something he was going to get into, then didn't? What I'm asking is, did it fall through before it got started, or did he work with them for a bit and then something happened? Do you know?"

"I think he did work with them. Because when I would hear about it, from people who knew him around that time, they would say he was saying all the usual Keaton stuff. 'I'm *killing* it. *Crushing* it.' You know, that macho shit."

"Right. He indicated to others that he made some real money working with Prestige Fish?"

"Yeah. I think so. I think that's how I remember it. Right after he started working with them. But I have no idea if it's true. Could all just be a lie. Keaton. Totally full of shit."

And then he looked at me and said, "Why? You getting somewhere with the whole tropical fish thing?"

I looked back at him and said, "Maybe."

I got up, shook his hand, headed for the door. Before I left, I looked back, took one last look at the woman in the blanket. She was eyeing me from beneath a swath of plaid. I turned around and left.

My next stop in the Valley was to pick up my old friend and mentor Jim Douglas. The guy I told you about earlier. The guy who taught me to fight. I was headed right to my old neighborhood, where I grew up. A perfectly nice, suburban section for middle-class Angelenos. My family doesn't live there anymore. My dad died, my mom moved to Idaho, my older brother moved to Arizona. I told you before, Jim was a neighbor when I was a kid. I also told you that he's an ex–Green Beret and a seriously advanced black belt in karate. But I didn't tell you that he still lives right where he always has. Right in the old neighborhood. Jim has four daughters who have all left the house. Graduated from college, started lives and families of their own. Nowadays it's just Jim and his wife, Candy. Back in the day, Jim loved it when I used to come down and hang out with his family. He loved his daughters more than anything, but he also loved that I was a boy who he could teach things to. And I loved that he was a man who knew about the things I wanted to know about. Stuff my dad didn't have a lot of knowledge about. It was pretty much a match made in heaven. Or, more accurately, a match made in a middle-class neighborhood in the Valley.

The things Jim taught me over the years I use almost every day in my professional life. And when things start to ratchet up on a case, I sometimes call on him to help me. Like now.

I got to his house, got out of the Focus, and walked up to his door. As I was about to ring the bell, Jim opened it. I looked at him. Jim's black, pretty tall, about five-eleven, and very thick and stout, with thick arms, thick thighs, a thick neck, and a big, solid-as-steel gut. Standing there, he filled up the door entrance almost entirely.

"John, my boy."

"Hi, Jim."

We hugged.

Jim wore a tight white army-style T-shirt and maroon Riddell coaching shorts, the kind Little League baseball coaches wore in the seventies. He also wore army-issue gold aviator sunglasses and a hunter green, un-broken-in baseball cap with a big high front emblazoned with some kind of military logo. Jim seemed to have a number of hats like this. On his feet, lightweight black combat boots and bright white athletic socks.

"That's a fantastic outfit," I said.

Jim didn't answer.

"Where do you even get shorts like that? Do they still sell those? At Big 5 or whatever? Those look pretty new. Or did you buy a bunch back in the day? That's what you did, I bet. You have a stash of them."

"Son, are we going to go look at what you want to show me, or are we gonna stand here and talk about my shorts?"

"I thought we could do both. I mean, I honestly want to know where you get shorts like that. What are they made of? It's, like, stretchy material. Is it rayon? They look flammable."

"You through?"

"I guess."

We got in my car and buckled up. Jim filled up the seat entirely.

"What kind of car is this one?"

"Ford Focus."

"You really can't remember these cars you drive. That was a good idea, John."

"Hey, thanks, Jim. You can move the seat back a little bit if you need to."

Jim said, "Clean in here too. Clean and nice."

Right. I was still in the phase of my car ownership where I kept it pristine. I hadn't reached that moment when you decide it's okay to trash it a bit. That moment, it's a big one. The one where you say to yourself, Yeah, okay, I guess

I'll leave a little trash in the cup holder. Or you look at an empty soda can on the floorboard in front of the backseat, and you think about it long and hard, you stare it down, and then . . . you get out of the car and shut the door, leaving it there.

No, I wasn't there yet, and I was fighting, fighting hard, to never arrive.

Jim said, "Please turn the AC on. Hot as shit in here."

"Balls. That's how you say it now. It's hot as balls. It's no longer hot as shit anywhere. I used the phrase earlier today, in fact. So, you would say: 'Please turn the AC on. Hot as balls in here.'"

Jim looked at me, his gold aviators covering his eyes, and said, "Just turn it on, John."

I nodded, cranked up the Focus, and blasted the AC. A smile stretched across Jim's face.

We headed south, took Laurel Canyon over the hill into Hollywood. We hit Sunset Boulevard and went right until we got to Keaton's old neighborhood, Sunset Plaza. We cruised by clusters of Hollywood glitz, trendy restaurants, bars, and coffee shops.

We saw a very skinny woman walking a very small dog down the boulevard, an iced latte she'd just gotten at Coffee Bean in her left hand, the dog's strained leash in her right. She wore big glasses, cutoff jeans, high heels. Some people would think she was attractive. Not Jim.

"Where's her ass?" he said.

"Not sure."

I turned right off Sunset and went up Rising Glen

Road. You could take a quick right and go to Keaton Fuller's old house, but I didn't. I headed up a bit farther, to the little embankment off the road where you could pull over and stretch your legs. Or get a straight shot right down into the driveway of Keaton's old place.

We got out of the Focus and stood in the little clearing, and I explained the case I was on to Jim. I took him through it, from start to finish. He listened, without interrupting, as I gave every detail. It's a lost art, actually listening. Calmly sitting and really listening. Most people sit in front of you on edge like a dog waiting for a treat, lips and body quivering, barely able to contain themselves, barely able to wait to pounce, to tell *you* something *they* know. Not Jim. He just lit a couple of Benson & Hedges 100's, took long luxurious drags, and listened.

After I finished, Jim walked over to the edge of the clearing, got into a shooting stance, and held up an imaginary pistol. He stayed like that, still as a statue, for about thirty seconds. Then he stood up.

He said, "The guy fired just once?"

"No other bullets found. So, yes. Think so."

"Well," he said. "Then the shooter most likely had training. That's a tough shot. A very tough shot. And the Smith too. Might indicate that they knew what they were doing."

The Smith & Wesson M&P nine millimeter, that's what he meant. Like we talked about, a gun used by lots of police and military forces. And, yes, a gun used by lots of civilians as well. And within that group of civilians were, of course, lots of *ex*-cops and *ex*-military. But also: *pros*.

People who need a gun to be reliable because they use it a lot.

So. Graves was in the meth business. Keaton had worked for Graves, at least for a little while—maybe, probably, in the meth business, because according to Craig Helton he'd told people he was *killing* it. And now Jim had confirmed for me what I had already thought to be true: that the kill shot was the kill shot of a pro.

Jim and I walked back over to the Focus. Jim, who'd put both his smokes out on the bottom of his boots and was holding the butts in his left hand, produced a ziplock bag from the pocket of his coaching shorts and housed the butts in it. Then he put the bag back in his pocket.

"Don't want to leave the butts here, litter. Don't want to accidentally light the Hollywood Hills on fire either, wind comes along, lights one of them back up. And, of course, I don't want to mar the pristine beauty of the ashtray in your Ford whatever-the-hell-it-is."

"Thanks, Jim. Hey, because we're here, let's go down to Sunset Plaza and have a Hollywood lunch."

"You pay, I'll go."

"You got it."

Typically, I choose restaurants by temperature. Not of the food but of the actual restaurant. Most restaurants get it so wrong. It's just scorching inside them so often. Uncomfortable. Not pleasant to eat in. Pay attention to this next time you go to your favorite restaurant. Ask yourself: Is the temperature right in here? Is it *exactly* right? I'll go to a restaurant whose food isn't as good as the next guy's if the temperature is more comfortable.

Today Jim and I didn't have to make that call. We sat outside at a chic Sunset Plaza joint. It was pleasant, always a bit cooler on this side of the hill. Out on the patio with us were skinny, tan people doing shots of wheatgrass, others chatting over strawberry soy smoothies, chickpeas everywhere you looked.

Jim, looking at the menu, said, "What's keeeen-wa?"

He pronounced it correctly. But it took him forever to get it out, like it was the first time he'd seen the word.

I said, "Quinoa. It's—"

He interrupted me. "I know what it is, my man. I'm just having some fun. I actually like some of this shit."

We both got Niçoise salads. As we ate them, I told Jim what I thought might happen with Lee Graves and company. And how I'd like him to be involved.

Jim didn't say anything. He just nodded. Took bites of his salad. Nodded some more.

We finished eating. I paid the seventy-six-dollar bill and we got back in the Focus.

I said, "Want to go get some hot dogs at Pink's? I'm starving."

"Absolutely."

So we did. Two dogs each, with mustard, ketchup, kraut, and relish.

Afterward Jim said, "I feel much better."

"Me too."

I took Jim home. I walked him to his door and said, "I think this is going to get hot, Jim. Soon. I'm going to need you on call."

Jim looked at me, his big, broad face behind the gold aviators, and said, "Phone's never off, boy."

32

After Jim went inside, I got in the Focus and sat there for a minute. I was thinking, I hope Graves calls me. I hope the spiderweb in his mirror gets him to call me.

I decided to wait in the Valley and see if it happened. Because if he did call me, maybe he'd invite me to come see him as well. Or maybe I could get him to invite me. That was the real hope, a face-to-face conversation.

I needed to kill some time.

I drove down the street to my childhood home and looked at it. For quite a while. Just sat there and looked at it. It filled me with a mix of emotions, some happy, some sad, some somewhere in between. The house, this inanimate object, because of my history with it, had an energy to it. As I looked at it, I thought, It's not really inanimate at all. It's *alive*, sending me vibrations, stirring me up.

I looked down at my phone sitting in one of the cup holders. Still no call from Graves.

I drove over to Studio City, to the public golf course right there on Whitsett. I bought a bucket of balls, then grabbed two loaner clubs, a driver and a nine iron, and walked over to the driving range.

I teed up a ball, grabbed the driver, got set, took a big swing, and shellacked the ball straight—280, maybe 290 yards. I looked up, around, down the line of other people at the range. No one had seen my drive.

I thought right then, I really did: Maybe I'll get great. Just practice constantly, and try out for the senior tour someday. I teed up another ball. I got set. I guided the driver back, then swung as hard as I could. I guess I hit just a sliver of the side of the ball closest to me, really hard. Because the ball slammed into the wooden partition in front of me, then ricocheted off it and came back and hit me in the right ankle. It stung. It stung bad. In two ways. The pain way. And the pride way.

I looked up, and then down the line of other golfers. Two men and one woman were staring at me, judgment in their eyes. I stared back for about ten seconds, then teed up another ball.

I finished off my bucket and returned the clubs.

Still no call from Graves.

I went into the little restaurant that bordered the driving range. I got a Bud Light and sat down. I enjoyed it at a very leisurely pace. Then I walked back out to the Focus. And that's when my cell buzzed. Graves.

"Darvelle, it's Lee Graves."

"Hi, Lee."

"When you were here last, you asked me to call you if I thought of anything that might help you."

"That's right, I did."

"Well, I thought of something."

"Oh, good. Stuff that helps me is good."

Before he could say anything else, I said, "You know, I'm not too far from you right now. Want me to come by?"

"Yeah," he said. "Sure. Good."

"See you in thirty."

Thirty-three minutes later I was sitting in front of Lee Graves's desk, his slick skeleton face in front of me, the Chinese high-fin smoothly swimming around to my left.

I said, "So, Lee, what do you got for me?"

He slid a piece of paper across his desk toward me. I picked it up, looked at it. It was a bill for a side-view mirror replacement on a Tesla Model S. It was expensive. I did my best Laurence Olivier. "Is this supposed to be some sort of clue that connects to Keaton Fuller that I'm not understanding?"

Graves said, "You don't know why I'm showing you this?"

"Was I not clear a second ago? No, I don't."

"You broke my mirror."

I said, giving Graves a smug smile, "What are you doing, man? Is this your way of getting back at me because I pretended to be interested in your fish?"

Lee Graves looked at me. He wanted it to be a casual

look, but I could see the intensity. He was trying to tell whether I was lying. Trying to determine whether I had been looking around in the dark out at his farmhouse in Pomona. Trying, still, to determine whether I was trouble.

Graves ultimately had to know that I would never admit it. Why would I? Why would anyone? I would be showing my cards, and admitting that I'd committed a small crime. No, he was using the mirror bill to see whether he could make out the truth under the bluff. That was his game. Which is just what I wanted.

Graves said, "Someone broke my mirror. It wasn't an accident. I didn't run into something, or back into anything. Someone broke it. I don't know when, exactly. But it was yesterday. My car was parked right out there."

He pointed out the window behind him.

Here was my chance to tell him I'd done it, without telling him I'd done it. That was my goal. That and to make him think, through my performance, that I was a little macho, a little small-time, a little green. Somebody he could handle.

I said, with just enough of a smarmy smile, "You sure it didn't happen somewhere else?"

Graves said, "Why would you say that?"

"Well, if someone is going to break your mirror, why would they do it when your car is parked right outside your window?"

"I don't know. But that's when it happened. Because I noticed it when I walked out of here and got in my car. It's not the kind of thing that takes a while to notice. If someone keyed my car, I might not notice for a while. Might not

see it. But because it's the *mirror*, a place I look every time I'm driving, I noticed it right away. And the person who did it knew that. Knew I would know where the car was when it happened. I just think whoever did it wanted to piss me off. Do it right out there in my own parking lot."

I was pretty sure now that he thought I'd done it. That he thought his little game had uncovered the truth. Now it was time for him to back off and start implementing his plans for me.

He continued. "Look, I thought it might be you, as you are the only person who has come into my life lately who I don't trust."

Clever. He's not going to be too nice. Not yet.

I said naively, "You don't trust me? How come?"

"Well, why should I? You've already lied to me."

I sighed. "So is this the only reason I'm here? To talk about your mirror? I didn't break it. I don't know what you're talking about."

"Okay," he said. "You didn't break it. My bad. Maybe it was an ex-girlfriend. My exes tend to know I love my cars. Or maybe it was a business thing. Most of my customers, all my customers, are happy. But sometimes my competitors aren't."

Graves took a breath, reset, and said, "All right, done with that. Truth is, I actually do think I have something that can help you. I want to show you why Keaton didn't work out."

"Okay," I said. "Good. I'd like that."

"See that Chinese high-fin right there? The one looking right at you?"

I looked over at the black fish with its downward-pointing mouth, and it was indeed now facing me, giving me its two black eyes.

"Yeah," I said.

"Well, like I told you, they aren't the most valuable fish in the world. They're just a fish I like. And because I like them, I started breeding them. I have a little house in Calabasas. It's not where I live. I live here in Thousand Oaks. On the golf course. The one where they have the invitational every year. The place in Calabasas is a second home, with some land behind it. I put in a couple of breeding pools. The high-fins aren't that hard to breed because they live in cool water. Some of these other fish, the clarion angelfish you saw . . . impossible to breed."

I nodded along. Graves was trying to charm me. Trying to tell me that he had no clue that I knew anything about him. I went with it.

"Anyway," he said. "I started breeding some koi too. I put the high-fins in one pool and the koi in the other. Eventually, as they got bigger and more colorful, some of the koi attained some real value. Clarion angelfish value. So I took Keaton up to the pools to show him the fish, and . . ." Graves paused like a thought had just come to him and said, "You know what? Why don't you come to the house. I'll show you what he did."

"Okay," I said. "When?"

Graves made a show of looking at his computer, checking his schedule. "I just have one more appointment today. You want to meet me at the house at the end of the day?"

I needed the address. I wasn't going to go to the house that day, no way, but I needed the address.

"Sure, where is it?"

He gave me the address.

And then I said, "Oh, wait. Shit. I can't do it this evening. I've got a tail to do on a husband who might be running around on his old lady. This is supposedly the night he goes out with his boys to drink a few beers. Well, we're going to see about that."

Said by John Darvelle with clueless macho flair. See, Lee? I'm a small-time PI. Nothing to worry about here. Don't let this throw you off your plan.

It didn't. Graves said casually, "Cool. Well, I could do tomorrow end of day too. Around seven."

Just when it's getting dark.

"Sure," I said. "Good with me. See you there at seven."

33

That night at midnight, Jim Douglas and I cased Lee Graves's house in Calabasas. Calabasas is high-dollar, pastoral mountain living just inland from Malibu. It's home to thick sections of tall green trees, horse ranches, and verdant, wide-open stretches of land, all mixed in with gray rock, steep hills, mountains forcing their way toward the sky. Many of the properties in Calabasas have a spooky isolation about them, a Manson-y California energy. Graves's place wasn't an exception.

Through the darkness, Jim and I first established that no one was at the house, just a few lights on to give the appearance of inhabitants. We then moved around the property, analyzing its layout. Off the main road up one of the mountains, a dirt road took you to the entrance to Graves's property, where, to get into the actual property by car, you had to drive through a locked gate.

Jim and I walked through the trees and brush on the west side of the gate to find the house. A small ranch-style house, off-white adobe with a red-shingled roof, one story, maybe two bedrooms. Behind it, where we were now, we could see the two breeding pools sitting in the ground, just visible in the darkness. They looked like rectangular, swimming-pool-sized ponds. Behind the pools was a section of grass, then about a hundred yards of thick woods. Tall California pines. Behind the woods there was a big, wide clearing, a mountain shooting up to the east of it, and the Pacific, a black force in the distance, way, way down to the west.

We spent sixty minutes casing the property. Then we made our plan, figured out where Jim would be positioned, and got out of there.

The next morning, I got up and did a light workout. Took an easy, slow three-mile run. Did a light, loose thirty minutes on my punching bag. Punches, elbows, kicks, knees. Followed by twenty minutes of stretching on the floor mats.

I showered and got dressed. Loose-fitting olive green pants, a loose, long-sleeve brown T-shirt, a loose, worn-in navy blue hoodie, my all-black Adidas running shoes. The colors were a form of camouflage, but I didn't think Graves would notice. The pants were loose to conceal my Sig, and the two layers of upper-body clothing were loose to conceal my Colt. I hoped Graves wouldn't notice that either.

At noon, I drove to my office and updated my case notes.

After a light lunch and some water, I went over the hill to Northridge, to the Firing Line. I got in the booth with my Colt and my Sig. I fired eight rounds out of my Colt and ten rounds out of my Sig. Relaxed, but focused. Loose, but tight. I looked at my targets. They both looked just exactly how I wanted them to look.

I reloaded both guns, hit the safeties, and hit the road.

At six o'clock, I entered the city of Calabasas and went to a nice, well-kept-up little strip mall. Starbucks, Panera, Chipotle. I parked the Focus, killed the engine. Then I put on my ankle holster, nice and tight, and housed the Sig in it. I put the Colt on the passenger seat and covered it with a magazine. Then I leaned my seat back, closed my eyes, and tried to just relax. Breathe a little bit, in and out, in and out.

At 6:35, I left for Graves's house. At 6:50 I was pretty high up in the Santa Monica mountains, parked on the dirt road just outside the gate that let you onto the property. My Colt was no longer on the passenger seat. It was tight against my lower back, with my pants, my T-shirt, and my hoodie over it, concealing it.

At 7:05, I looked in my rearview and saw a new, blue Toyota Land Cruiser pull onto the dirt road, then drive up and park behind me. Graves got out and walked over to my window. I powered it down.

"Pull over and hop in my truck. Road's a little tough to get down. Keeps the house a little more protected."

After he told me that, I suspected, more than ever, that

what I thought might happen here really might happen here.

I moved the Focus off to the side of the dirt road, got out, and got in Graves's slightly jacked-up Land Cruiser.

Graves pressed a button on a little handheld remote and the steel gate slid to one side, opening up.

We drove down a long, bumpy dirt road. Could the Focus have made it? Yeah, easily. The road eventually revealed the low-slung, Spanish-style ranch house that Jim and I had seen last night in the shadows.

Graves and I got out, walked into the house. Inside, it was simple, spare, a typical California ranch. Sparse. Native American blankets on the backs of some couches. Lots of exposed tan tile on the floors. Like the farmhouse in Pomona, it looked unused, unreal, set up for show.

We walked out the back door to the backyard. And although the sky was beginning to darken a bit, everything I'd seen last night was now crisp and clear and laid out in front of me. The two perfectly rectangular breeding ponds, and then the woods, and then the clearing flanked by the mountain to the east and the sea to the west.

Graves and I walked over to a ten-foot strip of grass between the two big ponds.

He pointed to the pond on his right, the one on the east side of the strip of grass, and said, "This pond has the high-fins in it." He pointed to the other pond. "That one has the koi."

From where we stood, the water wasn't that clear in either pond, but you could still see movement, fish sliding around in the water. If you got up close, though, you'd be able to see them clearly. I walked over, leaned down, put my face near the surface of the pond with the Chinese high-fins. Some were about the size of the one in Lee Graves's office. Some were bigger. But there were lots of smaller ones too, fitting the description Graves had given that day in his office. They were more colorful, had the banded, vertical white stripes and of course the high fin. On the smaller fish, the fin looked like a big, oversized triangle, out of balance with the body. I crossed over to look closely at the pond with the koi in it. I'd seen koi before. To my eyes, they were just enormous, wildly colorful goldfish. Not beautiful. They seemed kind of deformed looking at times, kind of disgusting.

As I watched all the colors moving beneath the surface, Graves said, "Like I told you, some of those have some real value. The idea is to breed them so the color patterns are unique and beautiful and striking."

I stood up, turned to Graves, and said, "I'll ask you what I asked you when I saw the fish in your office. Who takes care of them? Where is everyone?"

"Yeah," Graves said, "it's lonely out here, isn't it? The staff is gone. They come in the morning, leave in the afternoon." And then he added with sarcasm beneath a smile, "Thank you for your concern."

He and I stood there in that strip of grass between the two ponds, facing each other. I could feel the adrenaline rising up in my body. I could feel something coming.

I said, "So, Lee. What did you want to show me? What was it exactly that Keaton did here that you wanted to show me?"

Graves flashed me his teeth and pointed at the pond with the high-fins in it. "He took a piss in the pond. The day I took him out here to show him the fish, we had a little party. Just a handful of people. He gets drunk, walks over to this pond, this pond filled with the fish I love, whips it out, takes a whiz. I knew from that moment, this guy is a piece of utter dog shit. Now, it didn't do anything to the fish. It's not like it killed them or anything. The pond, the fish, fine. It was just a blatant act of disrespect. I fired him on the spot. Sent his drunk ass home."

I looked at Graves. "Is that story true?"

"Do you think it's true, John?"

"It's the type of story about him that could be true. But I don't think it is. I think you just made it up."

Graves started clapping his hands, light applause. "You're right. I did just make it up."

"I know why I'm here, Lee."

"Tell me."

"I'm here so you can kill me."

"Now why would I do that?"

"Because of what I know."

We both stood there on that strip of grass, still, tense, neither of us making a move but both of us ready to.

"And what do you know?"

I said, "I know that the fish are a cover for your other business. The one that's illegal. You thought I *might* know about that. Well, now you *know* I know it. Either way, you tell me to come here. Tell me to leave my car outside the gate. That way, you can catch me *on* the property. Trespassing. You have to figure I carry, so as soon as you establish that, you shoot me. Or somebody else does. And then you tell the police that I was going to shoot you. I'm a stranger with a gun on the property trying to get at your fish. Your expensive koi. The cops will identify me as a private investigator probably looking into something, but that doesn't really make a difference. You just play dumb. To you I'm just a trespasser, a trespasser with a loaded gun. On your land, practically in your house. The castle doctrine will cover you. You're *allowed* to shoot me if you're threatened. You're allowed to have guards on your property shoot me. It's smart. Your plan. It's really smart. And, shit, you've probably already made the call to move all the meth I saw, shut down the farmhouse, whatever. And that's it. Once I'm gone, you're back in business. You're just a guy pushing high-dollar fish."

Graves sneered at me, a satisfied look on his skeleton face, and said, "So you *did* break my mirror?"

"Yeah," I said. "I did."

I knew at that point that I was right. I was here to be killed. And Graves wouldn't be relying on just himself to do it. There had to be a man on me. Maybe two.

This. This is the risk, the gamble, the roll of the dice. I thought that this was where the story was heading, and now I was here. I could have called Ott, tried to explain what I'd gotten myself into, tried to get him to set up a cover. One that would be much less dangerous. But I hadn't. Because that would mean meetings, and red tape, and endless complications that would probably result in the whole thing *not* happening. And even if it did happen, it would mean that there would be men involved who I didn't want to be involved. And it might mean the whole situation turning in a direction I didn't want it to go.

But the other reason—the real reason—I didn't call was that I wanted the risk of this situation. I felt that if I took it, if I took the story all the way to the edge, I could get the answer. Who killed Keaton Fuller. That other life I'd seen on the beach that day, the Treadways'—this is why I didn't think I could have it.

Graves reached around to the back of his belt, pulled his gun, and pointed it at me. A Smith & Wesson M&P nine millimeter, now two feet from my face.

I said, "You're not going to shoot me until you know I'm armed. You're pulling your gun so I'll pull mine. If I have one."

"Shit," he said, "these days? I'll just say you were reaching for something and I *thought* it was a gun."

"If you were an innocent man, sure. But you'll take that risk with all you've got going? I doubt it. You've got to *know* that I've got one. That I brought one. Then you shoot me and you got no problems."

He said, "You're a licensed PI. You've got a gun on you."

I said, "Of course I do."

He raised his left hand just slightly, giving a signal to someone, I thought—giving a shooter in the woods the green light—but giving a signal to me too. I ran toward him and at the same time ducked, jerked my head down. I heard a crack from the woods. A bullet whizzed above my head and clipped the corner of the house. I grabbed Graves's right hand with my left, hooked my right leg around both of his legs, and pushed forward. We slammed down on the grass, on the strip between the ponds. I was on top of Graves, making sure to keep contact with him, making it a very risky shot for the gunman in the woods. I pinned Graves's right wrist against the ground so that the gun lay flat on the earth. I was putting all my energy, my focus, there. Graves head-butted me, hard. He went for my nose, to crack it, to make my eyes fill with tears and blood, but I moved just enough that instead he caught the side of my face and my right eye. The swelling started instantly.

With my left hand still pinning Graves's right wrist, his gun hand, I punched him one, two, three, four times in the face with my right hand. Quick, fast, hard shots. I got his nose twice, got the blood flowing. Graves went for another head-butt. Got me again in the same eye. It stung. Killed. My eye was already nearly swollen shut.

I shifted my energy back toward the gun. Into getting that Smith out of his hand. I started slamming my right fist down into his right arm, just below his wrist. Again, one, two, three, four. As hard as I could, with everything I had. Then I did it again. One, two, three, four. Pummeling his arm, trying to kill it. As I punched his right forearm, he got his left arm out from underneath my knee and started going at my face. He got me, once, twice, three times. In my jaw, in my mouth, and again in my eye. I didn't care. I took the hits.

I brought my right elbow up high, put all my weight behind it, and slammed it down on that right arm just below his wrist. Slam. Right on the spot I'd been going at just before. It had to have damn near broken his arm. He released the gun. I reached over with my right hand, grabbed it, tried to toss it into the pond with the high-fins. As I threw the gun, Graves got me in the neck with his left hand and I went backward.

As I fell back toward the grass, I could see that the gun I'd thrown had landed on the edge of the pond. It hadn't made it into the water. Just before my head hit the earth, another crack came from the woods, another bullet zipped over my skull.

Holy fuck.

I pushed myself up and ran for the woods. I zigzagged fast, moving in three directions at once. Straight, then to one side, then to the other side, then straight.

Another crack. Another bullet screaming by my face.

At the edge of the woods, I yanked my head around to look back at Graves. A bloody-faced skeleton, he was now staggering to his feet. I didn't want to pull my gun and fire at him because I didn't want him out of the picture prematurely. I—Jim and I—had to get the gunman in the woods first. I take out Graves now, and the gunman might retreat. I leave Graves, and he, or they, doesn't go anywhere. And I wanted them all.

I disappeared into the woods, into the tall California pines. I ran for ten yards, fast, still zigzagging. I stopped, stuck my chest to a tree, the thickness of the trunk between me and Graves. I looked around it to find Graves. I caught a piece of him through the trees. He was on his feet, on the edge of the woods now, gun back in his hand. He was coming in. Coming after me.

Right then: Boom. The loudest crack yet. A bullet tore

through a tree to my left. The shot had come from the direction of the mountain. The same direction the other three had come from. The gunman.

I moved deeper into the woods, pushing toward the clearing. Both the gunman and Graves were going to have a tough time getting a good shot at me. Too many trees. Too many obstacles. And I was hidden by my clothes, and moving, always moving.

From tree to tree to tree. Telling myself, Get to the clearing, give Jim a chance.

I was close, fifteen yards out.

And then again: Boom.

Another crack, another bullet tearing through bark and tree leaves five feet away from my head. But this one . . . this one came from the direction opposite the mountain. Counting Graves, a third gunman. A third fucking gunman. I had one on each side of me in the woods, and Graves coming from the direction of the house.

Get to the clearing, John. Get to the clearing.

I pulled my Colt. I fired one shot in the direction of the gunman on the mountain side. Then I fired another shot in the direction of the gunman on the ocean side. Then I fired a third shot back at Graves, who had to be closing in now, using the trees just like I was.

Just keeping everyone honest.

I moved toward the clearing. Tree to tree to tree. I was five yards out now.

And then I fired shots in the same three directions as before.

Bam. Bam. Bam.

I got to the edge of the woods, to the clearing, and looked out. At a vast swath of undulating green land spotted with rocks, the mountain shooting up on the right side, the east side, the land slanting down on the left, the west side, falling in on itself as it made its way eventually to the ocean.

I pinned my Colt against my back and pulled my Sig.

Again I fired three shots. This time it was as much for location as for cover. Because I wasn't really going anywhere now. And I wanted these assholes to know where I was.

Okay, I thought, my throat tight, my breathing heavy. Here goes.

I moved out into the clearing, into the open, and looked toward the mountain. And I made one of the gunmen. It was the Mexican man, in full camouflage, pinned behind a tree, an assault rifle up to his eye. I moved back into the trees and fired at him with the Sig, just as he fired at me. We both missed. My shot, again, was mostly for cover. If I hit him, fine, but it was mostly to make him flinch, miss. My bullet tore through the branches above his head; his bullet flew by me, rocketing far down into the clearing.

I moved five yards back into the woods. My heart was pounding in my ears. I was sweating everywhere. I could feel it dripping down my back, my legs. I moved again, not deeper into the woods but instead along the edge of the clearing, away from the mountain. So I could pop back into the clearing in a slightly different location, in case either gunman was setting up on me.

I made another move out into the clearing, looking

first in the direction of the mountain, seeing nothing but firing one shot anyway. Then flipping around to look in the other direction, toward the ocean. I made the second gunman. A middle-aged white man with a trimmed white beard. I'd never seen him before. He was also in cammies, was wearing yellow shooting glasses, and had his assault rifle trained right at me. As I jerked back into the woods I shot two rounds with the Sig, knowing, because I didn't stay with my shots, that my rounds would in all likelihood miss. Cover. Again, cover.

I was back in the woods.

Graves. Where was he? Waiting, back in the woods by the house. Waiting for his men to do the job.

Okay, I thought again. The time is now. The move that Jim and I planned. The time is right now.

The taste instantly filled my throat. The battery acid. The balcony. The beach. Except this time it wasn't the fear of realizing that a path I could take, might even want to take, had to die. It was the fear that *I* might die. That whatever it is that is me might be blasted away forever. It was the other side, the more searing, sickening side, of the same coin. The death coin.

I holstered my Sig and pulled my Colt back out. Two rounds left.

I moved back out into the clearing. I looked in the direction of the mountain. Nothing. I fired one shot. Then I turned my head to look in the direction of the ocean. The gunman with the white beard and the yellow glasses moved out from behind a tree, rifle up. I held the Colt out in front of me and aimed, like I'd done so many times at the

Firing Line. Before he could pull the trigger, my bullet shot through the yellow glass in front of his open left eye, then through his head and out the back. He dropped the rifle, then his body dropped to the grass. Dead.

But now I was exposed in the clearing, my back to the mountain, to the other gunman, a sitting fucking duck. Part of the plan. Part of a very dangerous plan.

I whipped around to face the mountain. And there he was. The Mexican man, at the tail end of his move out into the clearing. Rifle now up, set, ready to fire. But, like me, exposed. I'd drawn him out fully. I looked at him. He looked at me. It was a split second that was also a universe of time. I stood there, defenseless. A dead man. But only a dead man if Jim missed.

The dice were rolling. I floated above myself for that endless split second and tasted and swallowed the battery acid and wondered, really wondered, if I would die, or if I'd already been killed. Standing there, floating, swallowing that rancid taste of death. And watching the scene. Watching very carefully, able to focus so clearly on the Mexican man's hand on the trigger, on his one closed eye, on the totality of his head as a bullet ripped through it and it exploded into a red firework of blood and brains and skull.

Down. Dead.

I got my binocs out of my jacket and scanned the mountain in the fading light until I found Jim. There he was, right where we'd decided he should be. He was behind a rock, his rifle resting on it for balance. He was still in the shooting position, his hands on the gun, his big head and face near it, just shy of where it would be if he were aiming and firing.

He wore a camouflage, baseball-style hat and, like the white-bearded man I'd killed, yellow shooting glasses. His gold necklace with the big gold cross hung down, suspended in the air. Smoke from his shot still lingered in front of his face. His expression was frozen, like he was in a trance. His mouth hung open a bit, his jaw loose, almost like it was detached. A superheightened state of concentration and connection with his body, like a professional athlete in the zone.

There he was, an image in my binoculars, an image I'd never forget. He'd delivered once again. He'd saved my life. In a different way than the way he'd saved it when I found him as a child, but he'd saved it just the same.

Jim Douglas.

He's always been there for me.

He taught me everything.

And he doesn't miss when it counts.

I pinned the Colt against my back and pulled my Sig again.

Graves. Now to find Graves.

I reentered the woods, moving again from tree to tree to tree, moving back toward the house.

Graves had wanted his men to do the job, but now he was going to have to face me and try to finish it himself.

I stopped, listened, looked for movement.

I was still pretty deep in the woods, twenty yards in, but I could see the yard now, and the ponds and the house. And then I heard movement to my right. Graves. I fired. Not to hit him. To once again cover myself. And to scare him. Right now, I wanted him alive.

I darted five yards in the direction of the noise. And

then I made him, caught the side of his body and his arm and his hand holding the Smith, all of it a blur moving behind a tree. He was forty feet away.

I put volume into my voice and said, "Graves. Drop your gun and show yourself."

I heard a maniacal laugh echoing through the woods. And then he said, loudly, just like me, "You have no idea, Darvelle. You have no idea what you've done."

"Your two men are dead. I shot them both. I know that. You want to join them? Come out. Let's talk. I'm not going to shoot you. And you're not going to shoot me."

Jim wasn't coming down. But I didn't want Graves to know that. I didn't want Graves to know about Jim at all. And I don't think he did, given the mayhem of the bullets. No, I wanted Graves to believe that it was just me and him. And I wanted him to think he had a chance to take me down.

I pinned the Sig with the front of my belt and pulled both my hands out from behind the tree. "Here are my hands, Graves. Show me yours and step out. Let's talk."

I kept my hands where they were and moved my head out from behind the tree. I saw Graves's face. He'd wiped the blood off, but remnants of it were smeared into his skin. His nose was an exploded mess, spread all over his face.

"Graves. Show me your hands. And step out. I want to talk to you. Do it, so you don't have to die."

He showed me his hands. At the same time, we both stepped fully out, now facing each other, forty feet apart, with no trees between us. I could see Graves's gun strapped with the front of his belt, just like mine was. Instinctively, we both moved about five feet closer to each other.

"You have two choices, Graves. Let me cuff you and take you downtown. Or get shot, and then go downtown, if you're still alive."

Graves gave me the maniacal laugh again. "I'm not going to prison, Darvelle."

Prison, that's where he'd taken it. Did he mean he's not going to prison because the people he's working for would kill him before he got there, even if I did take him downtown? Or did he mean he's not going to prison because he's going to shoot me? I wasn't sure. He probably wasn't either.

I said to Graves, "Did you kill Keaton Fuller?"

He widened his eyes and pulled his lips back, giving me the skeleton smile once again. "I'll answer the way you answered when I called you out for having a gun on you. Of course. Of course I did. Of course I killed that idiot. You think a guy like that can pull the shit he pulls and get away with it when he's dealing with someone like me? And the people I work with? The guy was a dead man two weeks in."

"Why, though? Why exactly? What did he do?"

"What did he do? What did he do? He got in the way. Just like you."

He went for his gun, the Smith. I pulled my Sig and shot him in the arm that held it. The Smith fell to the ground. Then Graves ran in the direction of the house. I followed. I had him now.

Graves cleared the woods and made his way over to the strip of grass between the two ponds. He was now standing right where we'd started. He was bleeding badly from his right shoulder, wincing in pain.

I walked toward him. I wasn't going to kill him. I wanted him alive. Ott would want him alive too. We'd get more information out of him about Keaton, and then about the drug operation. He'd rat. I was sure of it. He'd rat. A lot of criminals do. No honor among thieves.

Graves dropped to his knees, the pain pulling him toward the earth.

And then, in another half second that seemed like an eternity, I realized what he was doing. The drama of dropping to his knees was a show. He'd left the gun from our initial struggle where I'd thrown it. Right at the edge of the pond with the high-fins in it. The gun he'd just dropped in the woods was his second gun. Same kind of Smith as his first one, same kind of Smith as the one that killed Keaton Fuller. The LAPD has a stock of these weapons. And so did Lee Graves.

Yes, Graves had a gun right there on that strip of grass—one more chance to put me down.

In one quick move he reached for it with his left hand, held it up, aimed it right at me. I shot him in the chest with the Sig.

Graves exploded backward and to his right, and went into the pond with the Chinese high-fins.

I walked over to the strip of grass, then over to the pond, and looked down into it. The water settled and I kneeled down, again putting my face up close to the surface. There was Graves, on the bottom, two feet down. His skeletal face and his destroyed nose and his bald head were enlarged by the water, and through it they looked whiter, paler. His eyes were open, and his now-magnified skeleton smile was frozen on his face, permanently, the last time I'd ever see it. The blood from his chest and arm, pushed by a little ripple in the water, began to drift across his face.

And then the high-fins started moving in. Nipping at, eating, reveling in the blood of Lee Graves.

I sat down on the strip of grass. Darkness was coming fast as I dialed Detective Mike Ott.

34

What we had now was a bit of a mess. Three dead men on a ranch in Calabasas, and a tropical fish business in Thousand Oaks that existed as a cover-up for a drug business run out of, at least in part, a farm in Pomona. As it turned out, Graves's hubris stung him even after his death, because he hadn't bothered to move the product out of the farmhouse.

Once I'd told Ott the story, start to finish, no details left out, standing right there on that same strip of grass between the ponds, he immediately set up a raid on the Pomona house. For that night. Well, technically the following morning, 4 a.m. Because now that Graves was dead, had been killed, Ott would not wait, could not wait, for the people in Pomona or anyone else in the organization to hear about it and make a move, if they hadn't already—and they hadn't.

The LAPD ended up with a pretty large drug bust connected to a pretty large Mexican cartel. The night of the raid, they seized hundreds of pounds of liquid meth and more than thirty weapons. And they made two big arrests: They got the older man with the long gray hair, a man named Louis Delacorte, one of the top guys in the ring on this side of the border, who had a direct relationship with the leader of the family in Mexico. And they got another man who was at the house with Delacorte, a man named Rafael Rivera, the head of a street gang out of Pomona, the top runner of the gang, one of the men who actually physically sold the meth. Not to mention a longtime criminal who'd killed many people and who'd been making a shitload of money illegally for a long time.

Now, would these two give the police information in exchange for shorter sentences? Names of gang members here in L.A.? Names of members of the cartel, of the family, in Mexico? Who knows? My bet was that if Graves had survived, he would have ratted. Something about him. But these two? Who knows? And I guess the bigger question was, did this bust make a big difference in the overall Southern California drug war? Hardly. But it did keep many millions of dollars' worth of meth off the street. So it made a dent.

Which made Ott happy. After the raid, he was much, much less pissed off at me for setting up a possible shootout, which turned into an actual shootout, with Graves on my own.

As for Keaton Fuller, they closed the case on him. Gave me a polygraph that read clean when I said that Lee Graves confessed to me, in no uncertain terms, that he had killed Keaton. You combine my statement with the fact that Graves was part of a lethal drug organization—shit, there were two dead trained assassins on his property the night I called Ott—and the story tracked for everyone. Including Jackie and Phil Fuller.

So a few days later I was at my office, sitting at my desk, now no longer working on an active case but instead kind of mulling over the case I'd just been on, the Keaton Fuller case. Anyway, one of the warehouse owners a few doors down, a cat by the name of Eddie Stanton, has an actual cat, a kitty cat, named Toast. Toast was named Toast because he had been badly burned in a house fire, and as a result, patches of his body have no fur, just charred skin. Toast walks with a wild, wobbly gait and has a bad right eyelid that bounces up and down, basically out of his control. Eddie Stanton often brings Toast with him when he visits his space. Eddie's got a few high-end motorcycles in his warehouse and likes to come look at them or sit on them or something. And when Eddie's doing whatever it is that he does, Toast often weeble-wobbles down to see me. Which I love. Because I love Toast. Talk about a fighter.

So that day, I had Toast right up on my desk. He was ramming his head into my hand as I scratched it. And I was thinking, Here you have this guy Keaton Fuller, who'd done so many people wrong personally, hurt them, disappointed them, let them down, insulted them—shit, mentally abused them with stuff like Pig Hunt. Yeah, so many people. But—but—all the people who he had done this stuff to were essentially, in the most general terms, good people. Not perfect people, obviously. Flawed people, like most of us. Like all of us. But basically good people. People with hearts. So then, this guy Keaton Fuller gets involved with a group of people who also have hearts, but of a different kind. Black. Black hearts. And these people don't have this long history with Keaton. Don't have this knowledge of his family, or of his fine pedigree, to set against his shameful behavior. These people don't have the context to say: "Oh, that's just Keaton." And even if they did, these people don't have it in them to be affected by his address or his lineage. They couldn't give two shits. So when he does maybe just one thing that's out of line, something similar perhaps to the things he'd done to a whole line of people before them, they popped him. Quickly. Heartlessly. Just like that. It wasn't connected to all his previous behavior, it wasn't any kind of punishment for his sins. And yet somehow it was. You know? He got it in the end. Not from the people who had all these reasons over all these years to hate him. To give it to him. But from making the entitled mistake of treating the fish people, the meth people, like he'd treated everyone else. Maybe only one time. Poetic justice essentially did him in.

Oftentimes in life, things make sense, work themselves out, but not in the linear way you think they should. That's true in my line too, in my cases. Things don't always come to me in a linear, logical way. Sometimes I'll have a revelation on a case, but it won't come from methodically looking at or refining my case notes. Or from connecting puzzle pieces that I've laid out in their logical order. Sometimes it will—in fact, lots of times, which is why I do those things—but not always.

Yeah, sometimes I'll have an insightful thought, or I'll realize that my conclusions on something are wrong, totally wrong, while I'm just sitting at my desk scratching the head of a burned-up kitty cat. Or while I'm driving around doing the most mundane and pedestrian of errands.

35

Doing errands. Errands. That's when I had this thought. I carried Toast down to Eddie Stanton's space, said a quick hello to Eddie, then took off in the Focus to do fucking errands. I really don't enjoy doing errands, okay? I know, I know, learn to like the things you're not supposed to like. And I do that, sometimes. But I can't get there with most errands. So I slogged through the drugstore, skulked through the grocery store, went to my house, unloaded everything, then went to one of those do-it-yourself car washes. Now this errand I actually enjoyed. I enjoy making the Focus look crisp and clean and new, like a just-readied rental. Like I said, we were still in the honeymoon phase.

And then, once my car was nice and clean and perfectly unmemorable, I went to gas it up. Get the tank nice and full again. And putting gas in my car made me think. It connected me to something. It threw a line to my subconscious, gave me a feeling not unlike déjà vu. Moments. Moments I'd collected over the course of the Keaton Fuller investigation all started reappearing now in my mind. But with new meaning attached to them. Because something, something didn't feel right. At first the images, the moments, were a little scrambled. I saw Greer Fuller as a kid in his yard standing next to Keaton, who was aiming a twenty-two at an innocent animal. I saw Craig Helton saying: "You get a bar up and running and you can print money. Print it." I saw Sydney and Geoff Scott behind their house in the Venice canals, clad in karate uniforms, pulling slow-motion noncontact moves.

And then, now sitting in my car, just about ready to take off from the gas station, I looked out the driver's-side window and saw the face of Heather Press. The gardener who stole Muriel Dreen's ring. She wasn't actually there, of course, but her face was there, hanging in my window, just like it had that time she'd walked over to my car to tell me that she'd taken the ring to hurt the hurtful Muriel Dreen.

This was the image I needed to see.

Because Heather Press was telling me something this time too. Her face was giving me a rush of thoughts and images and possibilities. Yes, somewhere down inside I sensed that I had unfinished business. Was Graves not my guy? Did he confess to killing Keaton Fuller simply to complete his tough-guy act? To show me, right before he tried to kill me, that he was ruthless, that he wasn't the type of guy Keaton Fuller, or anyone else, could fuck with?

I left the gas station and drove back to my office. Opened up the slider, sat at my desk, called Detective Mike Ott. But not to talk to him about this, no. To get him to connect me to a colleague of his who could get me records from the California Department of Motor Vehicles. Which he did. I spoke to this person, a woman named Janet Falcone.

And then I hung up, and looked around the web for some other information I needed.

And then I left my office, locked up the slider, and drove to an apartment just south of the Pico–La Brea intersection, to visit a sad, nearly broken woman who lived there. I knocked on her door, and she answered by opening it and just walking right to her chair and sitting down with her back to me, not even saying hello.

And I said to this woman, "I want to ask you another question about your daughter."

And then we talked.

And then I left and went to a Home Depot.

And then I left the Home Depot and went to a cemetery.

And then I left the cemetery and drove south.

And then I went to another gas station, my second of the day, a gas station I'd been to before, just last week with Nancy.

And then I drove a little farther south.

36

Dave? John Darvelle."

"Hey, John! How are you, man?"

"Listen, I'm in La Jolla. You home?"

"Yeah, just. We're all here. You want to come by?"

"Well, wondering if you and I could take a walk. Want to bounce something off you. But I really need to use the bathroom. Mind if I park, come up, then we can take a walk?"

He laughed the laugh of someone who doesn't totally know what's happening but is happy to go along with it. "Yeah," he said. "Sure."

"All right, I'll be up in a sec."

I parked in the garage, got out, got my backpack out

of the backseat, and put it on, wore it. I elevator-ed up, walked into Dave Treadway's apartment, said hi to Dave, to Jill, to Davey. Then I went to the back Ping-Pong room, Dave's man cave, used the bathroom, and came out.

I looked at Treadway. "Ready?"

Dave Treadway and I walked down the sidewalk toward the La Jolla Cove. The La Jolla Cove that you could see a nice corner of, in the not-too-far distance, from Dave's balcony. The La Jolla Cove that stood out as beautiful, even in beautiful La Jolla.

As we walked down the sidewalk, I told Dave Treadway the full details of the Keaton Fuller case. It hadn't made the papers yet. And even if it had, what La Jolla resident reads the L.A. papers? For that matter, what L.A. resident reads the L.A. papers?

Just as we got to the cove, I got to the end of my story: the shootout that resulted in the deaths of Lee Graves and his two hired killers.

Dave Treadway and I sat down on a bench that bordered the cove. At this time of day, the end of the day, there were people everywhere. Some sitting on benches like us. Some standing on the beach, at the shore, looking out at the water. And some people, lots of people, snorkeling. That's right, tropical fish were present. Treadway had nothing to do with the fish world, with the fish people I'd taken down, and yet here we were, talking about the same case, and tropical fish, while not visible, were all around us. Swimming and gliding about, my constant companions on this one, my colorful friends, my cosmic thread.

"Man," Dave said. "We were joking around about how you have a dangerous job, but, holy shit, you almost got killed. I mean, you could very easily be dead."

I said, "I want you to listen to me for a second. Okay, Dave?"

He gave me that same laugh that he'd given me when I'd asked to use the bathroom and said, "Okay."

"One of the interesting things that happens when you're on a case, pretty much any case, is that you consider most everyone you meet along the way as a possible suspect. You just can't help it. I mean, basically everyone. On this one, I never looked at Jackie or Phil Fuller as a possibility, but everyone else? Yeah. Obviously, I'm looking at Lee Graves that way when I first met him. Same with Craig Helton, the burned ex–business partner. But I'm also looking at you that way. At Sydney. At Greer, Keaton's own brother."

Treadway nodded.

"Seriously. I'm looking at the guy's brother, at this hurt, innocent-looking guy who was Keaton's own flesh and blood, and in the back of my mind I'm saying to myself, you know, maybe. Doubtful. But you never know."

"Right," Treadway said, his chuckle now betraying a little more confusion.

I continued. "Now, in this case, everyone had a really strong alibi. Airtight—that's what the cop I told you about, Mike Ott, had said. Airtight. So my consideration for people like Greer Fuller wasn't *that* intense, but it was still there a little. As I said, you just can't help it. And so that's part of the reason you want to be sure you're right when you solve it. Because you've *considered* the fact that other people *might* have done it. So being one hundred percent sure at the end eliminates any conjecture, as absurd as that conjecture might be. And that's a satisfying feeling. To know. To know something for sure. And, of course, there are other benefits of that clarity as well. More human benefits. Like knowing that a sibling didn't have anything to do with the murder of his own brother. Stuff like that."

Treadway just nodded. No awkward chuckle this time, but the look on his face that accompanied the nod was enough for me to know that he had no idea where I was going.

I said, "But at the end of this one, even though I had Lee Graves's confession, I didn't totally, totally know. I almost totally knew. But not totally, totally. I had the confession of a man who'd tried to kill me, who'd hired guys to try to kill me, and who almost certainly was a *successful* killer himself. And that's a lot. That's pretty damn convincing. Shit, the cops are cool with it. But I didn't have a murder weapon. I had weapons that are the same make and model as the murder weapon, which strongly suggests this guy uses this particular kind of gun, but I didn't have *the* murder weapon. The actual one. I also didn't have a witness. Someone who could say something like: 'I saw Lee Graves driving up the road to that clearing.' Or: 'I saw him fire the gun.' See? I didn't have any proof. An article of clothing, something. I just had a confession."

Again, an unsure nod from Treadway.

I continued. "And that's why my mind kept thinking about it. Because I wasn't one hundred percent sure."

Dave Treadway now gave me his charming smile, the

one with the underbite. The one that was accompanied by the shine in his blue eyes.

I said, "What's my point, right?"

And now another laugh from Treadway. "Right."

"Okay, stay with me on this one."

"Okay, John."

"Let's say you did it."

His smile shifted into a furrowed brow. A friendly but furrowed brow that said: "But you know, and I know, that's not possible."

I said, "But you couldn't have, right? Like, how would that be possible? You're on the apartment video going up to your pad the night before. You're on the elevator video leaving your pad the next morning, at something like 7:45 a.m. You made an intercom call to your doorman at 6:30 a.m. *from* your apartment. Your two cars, also on video, had not left the building. And even if they had left, which they hadn't, what, you're going to race up to L.A., 120, 130 miles away, shoot a guy, then race back? Not to mention, there were two wrecks on the southbound freeways from L.A. to La Jolla that day. Putting the driving time from Keaton's place to your place at three hours. The whole thing is just not possible."

Treadway, perhaps with some relief in his voice, said, "Right. Not possible." And then, after a pause, "And just for the record: didn't happen."

I said, "Add to that, Dave, why would you do that? That's the really important point. Sure, you didn't like Keaton Fuller, but nobody did. That doesn't mean you're going to figure out a way to kill the guy in cold blood."

Treadway shifted. Moved closer to the edge of the

bench. This just became a story he might be getting interested in.

"So, anyway, now listen carefully, Dave. Today I'm at my desk in my office. I work out of a warehouse, don't know if I ever told you that. And this cat wanders down to see me. Not a guy who I might refer to as a cat. An actual cat. So this cat who came to see me is owned by a guy who keeps a couple motorcycles in a nearby warehouse. I like the cat, so I pick it up and pet it a little bit. Today, I'm talking about. Today I did that. Then, an hour or two later, I'm no longer at my office, I'm no longer with the cat, I go to a gas station to fill up my car, my Focus. And all at once, I have all these thoughts. One of them was—and the cat, I think, led me to this—If you, Dave Treadway, *had* driven up from La Jolla and killed Keaton Fuller, what if you hadn't made the drive in a car, but instead you'd made the drive on a motorcycle? One that you'd parked outside your garage so it wouldn't be seen by the garage cameras? So then the questions were: Would that somehow help you make it to L.A. and back in time? And: Either way, would you be able to make it the whole way on one tank of gas? Or would you have to stop somewhere to get gas, like I had to on the morning Nancy and I left your house after we spent the night? See, that memory, of Nancy and me getting gas that morning, was another thing connecting to all the thoughts I had while getting gas today. That's how the mind works sometimes. You just get this onslaught. Now, before I get to whether or not you would be able to make it in time, and whether or not you'd have to get gas, I want to tell you about another thought I had this morning at the gas station."

Dave, shaking his head, still holding on to his charm, said, "Okay" again. And then he said, "Because I don't know what you're talking about, man. A cat at your office? Motorcycles? It's like: What?"

"Let me finish, Dave. So right there at the gas station today, I have this vision. This vision of this woman who was part of the case I was on before I got the Keaton Fuller gig. This woman is a gardener, and she had stolen an engagement ring from her boss, this rich old lady in Beverly Hills. I got her to admit that to me, that she had taken it, and that she still had it. And I got her to give it back. And after she gave it back, she told me why she had taken it. See, she didn't want the ring. She didn't want the money the ring would bring her if she sold it. No. So why did she take it? Well, she told me, in so many words, why she did it. And here's what she said: to strike back. The old lady was a mean old bitch, mean to her employees, the rest of her staff, mean to this woman, the gardener. And so this woman, the gardener, did something to get back at her. To hurt her. See? The gardener didn't just *think* the old lady deserved it, she *knew* it. Because it was personal.

"And see, this girl was a nice, great girl, and had a certain inner strength and confidence about her. Like you. And she was a bit of a bystander in this other world. She was a bit removed from this mean old lady and the rest of her staff, who had been with her forever. She hadn't been working for her for that long. So she was able to watch the whole dynamic kind of from afar, the distance making clear what was no longer obvious to the rest of the staff who'd been beaten up for so long. Which is also a bit like you, down here in La Jolla, watching Keaton Fuller continue to be himself without any consequences. But the thing is, she was still connected enough to this old lady's world to care. To care about the treatment of the other employees. And to care about how the old lady treated her. And to be hurt by it. So this woman's moral compass told her that she had to do something about it—even if that thing was wrong, or even illegal. So I began to think that in a way, you two sort of occupy the same role in your respective stories. Are you following me, Dave?"

Dave Treadway looked at me and shook his head. "No, I'm really not."

I said, "Let me keep going. See, you know all the players in the story: Keaton's parents, Greer, Craig Helton, Keaton's ex-girlfriend, the whole lot. And you knew how Keaton treated all these people. You knew what a shit he was. Your whole life you've known that. And you're this good guy on the edges of it all. Witnessing it all. Seeing it all happen. So I thought, if you *had* done it, it was probably for the same reason that gardener stole that ring: to strike back. To strike back at Keaton Fuller. Plain and simple.

"But, see, the problem was, when all these thoughts and connections started coming to me, I didn't think you'd do it on behalf of any of those people I've just mentioned. Because from what I've seen, your relationships with these people aren't *that* powerful. Right? With the gardener, she was a witness to all the old lady's crimes, yes. But she was also a victim of those crimes. She was directly affected, directly hurt by her. To my knowledge, with what I had uncovered, you really weren't ever directly hurt by Keaton. You weren't like the others. And your relationships with the people he *did* hurt . . . they didn't seem strong enough for you to react so powerfully. Greer was a friend, but you're not going to kill his brother on his behalf. He wasn't that kind of friend. So I thought, if it *was* you, there had to be a story where Keaton hurt you specifically. Or hurt someone you loved. It had to be personal. There had to have been something where your heart was more involved."

I looked at Dave Treadway. He was listening, his face frozen. He looked tired.

I said, "I went and saw Eve Cogburn today, Dave. Andrea's mother. You were close to Andrea. Really close."

Treadway, some momentary relief coming to his face, said, "Yeah, John, I was. That was a long time ago. It's not like that's a secret. If you had asked me about that before, when we talked, I would have told you. I didn't even know that Eve and Andrea were a part of your investigation. I mean, Andrea's dead, but—you know what I mean."

"You met her when she was dating Keaton. And she was nice to you. And you became friends, even though she was a few years older. Probably like a big sister. And you *stayed* friends with her. You even dated her a little bit, after she and Keaton were finally done, a couple years before her death. And you were good to her. Always. Because you cared about her. Deeply. Eve told me that. Eve appreciated that. And, knowing you, I believe that."

"Yeah, John," he said, with a little bite. "All that is true. Except I don't know if I'd say we dated. More just hooked up a few times. Sometimes that happens when two people who care about each other realize the person who used to be too young isn't too young anymore. I'm surprised Andrea shared that with Eve."

Treadway paused for a second and then said, "And, yeah, I tried to help Andrea when she . . . I'm sure you know this . . . when she got heavily into drugs, when it was getting out of control, toward the very end."

I nodded and said, "Dave, knowing all that I know about Keaton Fuller, I think he was a total fucking scumbag. But I bet you know more about how *much* of a scumbag he was. And I bet you know just exactly how much he fucked with Andrea Cogburn. Someone who was very special to you. And I bet, at the end of the day, you put her death on him."

Dave Treadway's expression reconfigured yet again. What was it? Compassion? Recognition? Sadness? He didn't say anything.

"Right, Dave?" I said. "You thought Keaton essentially took Andrea's life. Right? And you thought he deserved to die for it. Right? And so you figured out a way, years later, to do it. You take the stairs all the way down your building, to avoid the elevator cameras. You make sure to leave the door to the stairs open so you can get back in. You don't go to the garage either, so you avoid those cameras too. You get on a motorcycle at about 3:30, 4 a.m. The motorcycle's parked, I don't know, right up the street from your place? You zip up to L.A. You drive up Rising Glen Road, position yourself, pull out a pistol. You've figured out, by this point, that Keaton works out in the morning. And when he walks out of his house, you pop him. You tuck the pistol away, you hop back on your motorcycle, you get out of there.

"And then you hit major traffic on the way back, due to an accident. But you're on a motorcycle, so you can drive right between the cars that are just sitting there stationary. You can zip right through the clogged section. A legal move in L.A. So it's as if there isn't a traffic jam at all. At 6:30, your wife calls the doorman from your home intercom and plays a recording of you—a quick command to watch out for a delivery. Had to be what happened. Then, right around 7:30, you cruise back into La Jolla. Shit, you can do the 120 miles in ninety minutes if you go seventy-five miles an hour, and you have a way to get around any traffic. Then you park the bike down the street. You walk back up the stairs. You're back in your apartment at 7:40. You walk out your front door at 7:45 and get in the elevator, putting you on camera. Then you go down, get in your car, go to work, get away with it."

Treadway said, "John. You just told me that Lee Graves, a meth dealer, a guy who tried to kill you, confessed. You saw with your own eyes that this guy is more than capable of murder. *And he confessed*. John. Are you one of those people who can't let things end? Like, you'll freak out if you don't have something to focus on? To obsess over? Why are you inventing a preposterous story when you've already busted the guy who did it?"

"I know, it's insane."

Treadway laughed. A laugh of relief. "Yeah. It is."

I said, "Problem—for you, anyway—is that I can prove it. It's insane, but I can prove it. It comes back to the question I was asking earlier: Can a motorcycle make it the whole way on one tank of gas? Well, some could. But the one you were on couldn't. See, I called the cop I was telling you about, Mike Ott. He gave me a name at the DMV. A person police detectives call when they want driver information. And that person told me that you have a license to drive a motorcycle and that you, at the time of Keaton's murder, owned one. A 2010 Honda Shadow. A vehicle that, with a full tank of gas, could only cover 110 of the 120 or so miles you needed to go. Which means you're probably getting off at an exit just north of La Jolla, right off the 5. An exit that coincidentally, or cosmically perhaps, is the same exit I got off to get gas when I left your house with Nancy the morning after we spent the night. Only I was, of course, going in the other direction. Amazing how stuff like that works.

"But let's get back to today. Today, I went and talked to the manager of the gas station closest to the freeway when you get off the freeway at that exit. The same gas station I'd gone to with Nancy. The same one. And the manager allowed me to look at the gas station security video of the morning Keaton Fuller was killed. Sure enough, there's a guy gassing up a Honda Shadow at 7:20 a.m. But you can't see the license plate because the guy is, wisely, standing in front of it. And you can't see the rider because he's wearing a helmet. And then when the driver walks the motorcycle over to a space near the store's entrance, and then walks inside to pay—in cash, of course—you still can't see who it is because the person is wearing a hat."

I opened my backpack and pulled out a green John

Deere trucker hat, the one I'd worn playing beer pong, the one I'd absconded with a half hour ago when I used Dave Treadway's bathroom. "This hat," I said. "The driver of that Honda Shadow is wearing this green John Deere hat when he goes in to pay. Your green John Deere hat. I've got it on tape. Right here in my bag."

Dave shook his head and gave me a dismissive sigh. "That's what's holding your story together? A guy you can't see at a gas station wearing a green hat?"

"That's part of the proof, yes. This is the other part." I pulled the murder weapon out of my backpack. A Smith & Wesson M&P nine millimeter. "See, Dave, the other thing I learned from the gardener was that when people commit crimes to strike back at those who deserve it, the evidence often ends up right where it should. Somewhere people wouldn't necessarily look, but somewhere that makes total sense. Somewhere that somehow adds to the meaning of it all. That rich old lady's engagement ring was hidden in the garden right outside the gardener's apartment. And in your case, the gun was buried at Andrea Cogburn's grave. See, another thing I did today was, I went and bought a metal detector. Yeah, for a few hours I was the crazy fuck walking around with a metal detector. But I was okay with it. Because when I got to Andrea's grave and I put the detector up to the soil, the thing started going crazy. And I dug up the gun. The Smith. A very popular gun. One of the most popular guns. Graves had two of them, at least."

Treadway looked at me. I had him, backward and forward, and now he knew it. He might have suspected it before, but now he knew it.

I said, hitting the nail in deeper, "Eve Cogburn gave me permission to investigate the grave site, and once the grounds manager at the cemetery confirmed this, I gave him my phone and had him film me digging up the gun. And I have him and two people who work for him as witnesses that there was no tampering. I'm sure you cleaned the gun, Dave, but did you *really*? Or did you wipe it off like they do in the movies? These days, the tiniest bit of your skin, the tiniest section of a fingerprint . . . That's all they need. And where'd you get it in the first place? Is the purchase clean? The serial number is still on it. I wonder if it can be traced back to you? I bet it can. Yeah, the gun, the hat, the gas station video, the Honda Shadow that you bought. I'd say that's proof. Rock-solid proof."

I was just about to ask him how he pulled off the shot. But then I realized, *not now*. I would later, but not just yet. Right now Treadway needed to let it settle in, once and for all, that I had him.

Dave's face relaxed now, in the way that someone's face relaxes when they get something off their chest. Even if that thing is devastating, terrible, illegal.

I said, "Dave, remember how I told you that Graves talked to me one day about the Chinese high-fin in his office? How he told me it was his favorite fish? Well, later, when I discovered the meth, I realized why. Because he was a Chinese high-fin. He was the Chinese high-fin of my story. You know why? Everyone thinks of that fish in a certain way, small and striped with a big fin on its back. Even its name thinks of it that way. But that's just its image. A short-lived facade. The fish is actually big, and black, with a shark fin that's actually not too big for its body. That's the truth. And that's just like Graves. Understand? A tropical fish broker is the image. A drug dealer is the truth. But see, then, later, amid that whirlwind of connections at the gas station, I realized that no, Graves isn't the Chinese high-fin. You are. An affable guy. A guy who's happy, cool with most everything. Easygoing. Charming. Fun. That's the image. But underneath is the truth. You're a guy who wanted revenge. And you would kill, and you did kill, to get it."

Dave looked at me. He knew it was now his turn to talk. And to his credit, he was now through with the denials.

"Don't do this, John. Let it go. Let me go. Don't do it."

"Why not?"

"Look," he said. "A big part of your life is trying to catch people who did bad things. But more than that, it's to make people who did bad things pay a price. Right?"

"Sure. Yeah. I think that's basically right."

"And sometimes—you have told me this—you break the rules to make sure it happens."

I nodded. "Yeah."

"Well, isn't it okay, then, if other people break the rules sometimes too? In fact, don't you wish that other people would break the rules a little more often? I mean, wouldn't you basically be glad if somebody just took out one of these horrible criminals you hear about all the time on the news? A guy who has raped a bunch of kids at a school? A guy like that? Wouldn't you be glad if somebody just got rid of him? But instead of that happening, we all have to live with it. Go through the agony. Watch the families of the victims suffer. Endure the media coverage, the opinions about what should happen to him, the inevitable denial that always comes, the trial, the whole thing. And after all of it, the guy goes and sits in jail. Wouldn't it be a service to us all if somebody just took out that child-raping piece of shit? Doesn't he just deserve to be gone?"

I looked at Dave Treadway and said, "You want me to answer that hypothetical question? Well, I can't say I'd be upset if somebody killed a child molester. No. I wouldn't be that upset. I think I'd be able to go on with my day."

"Okay. Then let's talk about Keaton Fuller. He destroyed people's lives. He killed animals. He killed his own pet. He got Greer to choose one of their guinea pigs, just told Greer to pick one without telling him what he was up to. And then he shot it. Killed it. Greer told me that once when he was hammered beyond belief. I don't think he even remembers telling me. But how fucked up is that? He also date-raped a girl. Maybe more than one. Or let me say it the way it should be said: He raped a girl. He beat up his own mother. His own mother. And if you ask me, he killed Andrea Cogburn. An amazing girl. An incredible girl. Who was smart and cool and filled with this . . . *light*. He got her hooked on blow, and then crack. And you know what else he did? Made her fuck his friends, John. Made her fuck his friends. He crushed her self-esteem. Then told her to fuck off. So a few years go by and she 'overdoses.' Wrong. She killed herself. She told me she was going to do it. I begged her not to. But she did it anyway. Which in turn basically kills her mom. You've met Eve. That woman is dead too."

"Well," I said. "What about Jackie Fuller? Didn't your killing Keaton kill her? Ever seen the look in her eyes?"

Treadway said, with total sincerity in his voice, "Jackie Fuller has had that look in her eyes ever since Keaton started shitting on people. That guilt? That pain on her face? That's from creating someone so bad and wondering how it happened. I swear, John, at Keaton's funeral she was relieved he was gone."

"Then why'd she hire me?"

"Rich people don't like it when someone does something to them that's out of their control."

I thought about Muriel Dreen sending Tony Lewis and his big crooked-eyed friend over to see me after she'd gotten her ring back. I'd found her ring, but she'd lost control of the story.

Shit, Treadway might be right on that one.

He looked right at me. He gave me the look a friend gives another friend when he needs a really big favor.

"Don't send me to jail, John. The world is a better place without Keaton Fuller. I'm positive of that. He basically killed— No, he killed two people. Don't send me to jail."

I looked around the cove. At the people walking along the shore. At the snorkels poking up out of the ocean. At the sky as the day ended, turning that amazing shade of Southern California orange-pink-blue.

I looked back at Dave Treadway.

He said, "Don't do it, John. Please. Think about Davey. And Jill. For the record, Jill had no clue what I was doing. Later she did. But when I asked her to play that recording, she just thought I was out of the house really early, surfing. And that I wanted the instructions about the couch to come from me, because some of the staff have the annoying tendency to take me more seriously."

"But when the police eventually came around, you had to tell her the truth. Because talking to the staff of your building from *inside* your apartment, not taking the elevator up and down, all the moves you made to not get caught—that was your alibi."

"Yeah," he said. "Yeah. And Jill was totally shocked at first. Stunned. Obviously. But then I told her everything about Keaton, and I guess she understood in some way. And then, after a little while, we slowly started to move on. And then we *did* move on. It's surprising, amazing, how people can move on from things. Before we knew it, we were just living like it never happened."

He took a moment, a memory registering in his eyes. "When we met you, we wanted to be friends with you. It's crazy, but we really did. I, Jill and I, thought nobody would ever find out what I'd done. I'd covered my tracks so well. But beyond that, we had sort of started believing, and living, like I *hadn't* done it. To the point that we didn't even think it was a risk to reach out to you. Of course it occurred to us that befriending you could help to just totally eliminate your being suspicious of us. But that's not why we pursued the friendship."

I thought about what Treadway had said and wondered if maybe somewhere down in his subconscious I had represented what he'd done, and he'd used me to get closer to it. Like the way people return to the scene of a crime. To experience it again, to feel the sick rush of the sin, even though it makes absolutely no sense to do so.

Treadway switched back to the bigger issue and looked at me with a combination of seriousness and hope. “Don't do it, John. Don't do it to my family.”

I said, “I'll tell you what, Dave. Let me think about it. Give me a night to think about it. Don't make any moves. Don't call your lawyer. And don't try to make a run for it, either. I'll be watching, and I will catch you. Just like I caught you now. Just go home, and stay in your apartment with your family. Okay?”

“Okay, John.”

We walked back to his building. He went up. I went down to the garage, got in the Focus, and left.

37

I wasn't worried about Dave Treadway doing anything stupid. In my mind, he trusted that I was going to think about it overnight and get back to him. Plus, I'd told him I was going to be watching. But I wasn't even going to do that. I really didn't think I needed to. In his mind, he makes any kind of move I can see, and I call the cops. He makes any kind of move I can't see, web searches, phone calls—it just makes him look guilty later. The guy was trapped. And not going anywhere.

So why had I done what I'd just done? Good question. Truth is, I wanted to put everything on him and see what happened. See what he would do, what he would say. See if he'd give me his side of the story. Well, now he had.

And now I needed to think about what I was going to do about it.

Yeah. I needed to think. To go somewhere and think this through a bit. I found my way over to the Pacific Coast Highway and took it north for five miles, past the cliffs of Torrey Pines, then went another five to Del Mar. Del Mar is a beautiful, and very high-end, beach town. It's one of those places about which people always say: It's got the most expensive real estate in the country. You know those places? Paradoxically, there are a few of them. Del Mar is one. That said, it's got a lovely *public* beach. Which is where I went. I parked in the lot, then got out and walked down to the sand.

I sat down, took a deep breath, looked around. Night was just starting to fall over the sand and the ocean and sky. There was a warm beach breeze. Some gulls were gathered up high, swaying, getting pushed around by the wind. No one was near me—there were just a few people on the beach, some dots in the distance. I leaned back, put my back against the sand. I was totally flat, looking straight up at a now deeper orange, a fiercer pink, and the very last of the blue.

I was thinking, People don't go to the beach enough in the late afternoon, or at night, even. It's so nice. And when it's sparsely populated like this, it's such a break from the tension of daily California life, especially in L.A.

And then I thought, looking up at the last bit of light in the sky, the colors hanging on, just about to be usurped by darkness: I'm so tired. I closed my eyes. I listened to the waves. I could see them in my mind as I heard them. Rising up, breaking, pushing toward me on the sand. Then getting sucked back out. I fell asleep.

I woke up to a beach totally devoid of people. I was alone out here. A half-moon hung in the sky, and it, along with the stars like pinpricks in the blackness, provided enough light for me to see clouds sitting up there too. Big, wispy gray clouds moving slowly by. You don't think of clouds at night, and I lay there contemplating them, admiring their beauty.

I sat up and I had a thought. *What do I know about right and wrong?*

I walked down to the shore, looked out at the ocean, the moon and the stars putting highlights on the white water when the waves broke.

What do I know about right and wrong?

I stood there looking at the water, and that transported me to another time I was looking out at a big body of water. A time a few years back, when I was working a case in Florida. When I'd finished the case, because I was in Florida I thought: I should go look at the Everglades. Ever been? It's incredible. Incredible.

So I drove down to Miami, from Jacksonville, where I'd been on the job, and hung a right until I got to the largest swamp in the world. There I paid a guy, a guy of Seminole Indian descent, to take me out into the middle of it on his airboat. At one point, he stopped the big fan and we just sat there, deep in the Everglades, in silence. I looked around. There were vast sections of grass coming up through the swamp. Trees coming up out of the water too. And there were prehistoric-looking birds with colossal wingspans soaring around.

And alligators. Everywhere, alligators.

One surfaced right by our boat. His whole body, all fifteen feet of it, appeared all at the same time. I looked at the coarse, thick, seemingly impenetrable skin on his back. I looked at his head, at his exposed teeth, at the two black marbles that were his eyes. I was locked on him, transfixed by this lethal-looking creature floating six feet away from me.

The Seminole man said, "You know how long they been around?"

I let him answer instead of guessing.

He said, "Thirty million years."

I looked back at the alligator. Thirty million years. I stared at it. And I swear I think it was staring at me. Thirty million years. Sitting there on that boat, looking at those black dots sitting in that violent-looking head, thinking, We've been around, what, a few thousand? And we're supposed to know what's really happening? What's really fucking going on? *I'm* supposed to be able to get my head around just exactly what's right and what's wrong?

That's what I was thinking then. And that's what I was thinking now. In Del Mar, at the edge of the ocean. Should I put Dave Treadway away? Should I put him away for gunning down a total scumbag who spent his whole life shitting on others? And, if you go by Dave Treadway's assessment, who killed a girl and rendered her mother a zombie basket case?

That was the question.

Yep, that was the question. Should I put him away, or let it ride? After all, nobody would ever know. As far as anyone was concerned, we'd gotten our man.

I took off my shoes, socks, shirt, pants, and underwear and carried them up to where the water wouldn't take them away even if a big wave came in. Then I walked back down to the water. I got in, up to about my knees. The water was cold. But it was late summer, so it wasn't too bad. I went for it. Ran through water, through white water, toward a distant, black horizon line. I reached a wave that was just about to break and I dove right into the heart of it. I glided through it and popped up on the temporarily placid other side.

I swam farther out, past the point at which I still felt somehow anchored to the shore, still felt comfortable. Where I ended up, the waves weren't close to breaking. They just came in as big black mounds and I'd float up, then down, as they moved through me.

I lay on my back, floating, looking up at the sky, at the stars, at the clouds. Thinking: What should I do about my friend Dave Treadway?

Ten minutes later I swam back to shore, got my clothes, jogged over to the Focus. I had a towel in the trunk. Grabbed it, dried off, got dressed, got in, cranked up the car, cranked up the heat till I was warm. Then I turned off the car, reclined the seat, and fell asleep again.

At 5:30 a.m. I woke up. I was tired. I was exhausted. I got out of the car, used the public bathroom, then got back in, cranked her up again, and drove back to La Jolla.

38

Life is gray, decisions are black and white.

I found a spot on the street right beneath Dave Treadway's building. I got out of my car, walked around the front of it to the sidewalk, leaned on my roof, and looked up at the building, counting the balconies, trying to figure out which one belonged to Dave and Jill and Davey. Got it, recognized the furniture. I could see the cove down a ways to my right, and, down a ways to my left, yet another gas station. I walked over to the gas station and did something I hadn't done in five years. I bought a pack of smokes. Marlboro Lights. I know, not the coolest brand. But the brand that gives me the most satisfying hit. People used to say to me: Marlboro Lights taste like chemicals, like tobacco mixed with chlorine or something. And I'd say to them: Right, exactly, that's why I like them.

Look, cigarettes are disgusting. But once they get their hooks in you, they're amazing. Incredible. Taking a drag is like inhaling heaven. But they kill you, so you have to figure out how to quit, which I did. Except for the one I was about to smoke.

I walked back over to my car, packing my smokes on the butt of my left hand. I got back to the sidewalk, leaned on my car the way I was before, opened up the smokes, lit one, took a big, hungry, powerful drag. The smoke hurt, but it was a good hurt. I blew the smoke out my mouth and my nose. I knew, I really knew, that I could be a dedicated smoker again by the end of the day. I could be a pack-a-day smoker by the end of tomorrow. And I could be a full-on prisoner by the end of the week.

But I wasn't going to let that happen. I promise.

I took another drag, then scanned Dave Treadway's building again until I got to their balcony.

Standing out there now was Jill Treadway, holding Davey, looking down at me. I couldn't see her eyes and she couldn't see mine, but we were looking right at each other. And I could feel her eyes. I could feel in them a look that said: Don't take my husband from me. We stayed like that, locked on each other, as I smoked my cigarette down. I took one final drag, one final drag, then put the butt out on my shoe. Like Jim Douglas had done. I had the butt in my hand. I looked down the sidewalk and spotted a trash can about thirty feet away. I flicked the butt at it, it went high in the sky, it looked like it was going to sail over the trash can, way over, but then a little gust of wind came in off the ocean and slowed it down, put the brakes on it. The butt dropped right into the can.

Luck. Total luck.

Jill Treadway wouldn't have been able to see what I'd just pulled off, the butt was too small, but I looked up to see if she was still watching me anyway. She was gone. The balcony was empty.

I pulled out my cell and dialed Dave Treadway. He answered.

"Let's talk," I said.

Five minutes later he pulled out onto the street in his X5, right in front of me. He pushed open the passenger-side door for me to get in.

"Where are we going?" I said.

"Somewhere we can talk."

I got my backpack—wasn't going to leave that in the Focus, no way—and got in. We drove ten minutes north, to Torrey Pines. Same road I'd taken the evening before. But we didn't continue on to Del Mar. We went just past the Torrey Pines resort to the nature reserve, a beautiful sprawl of wilderness, trails, and pine trees that sits high up on stunning cliffs overlooking the Pacific.

We parked in the public lot, then walked a trail straight west, through the pines and the brush, until we were at the edge of the cliffs overlooking the ocean.

"Let's walk down," Treadway said.

We did. Down a dramatic precipice that deposited us onto a secluded beach below.

Six-thirty a.m., nobody around, a two-hundred-foot

natural wall on one side, the ocean on the other. This would be a private conversation.

"We can definitely talk here," I said.

"Yeah. And I wanted to get one last look at all this in case you decide to turn me in."

I looked at him. I liked him. And the thing was, he had a point. He did. His child molester example? I couldn't really disagree with it. Put terrorists and crazy gunmen who level movie theaters on that list too. It would be a whole lot easier if some of those people just got taken out. We wouldn't need to know who did it, it would just happen. Snap. Gone. For the sake of the victims, the future victims, for everyone else walking the earth as well. Everyone else just trying to live their goddamn lives. So Keaton Fuller—did he belong on that list? A guy who shot animals, raped women, assaulted his mother, broke every promise he ever made. And then there was Andrea Cogburn. Did he kill her? Yeah, kind of. Kind of killed her mom too. Does Keaton Fuller belong on that list? I think he belongs on that list.

Dave Treadway said, "What's it going to be, John?"

"You're going to jail, Dave."

He shook his head and backed up. "Don't do it."

"I'm doing it."

Treadway pulled a gun from his jacket and pointed it at me. It wasn't another Smith. It was a Ruger SR9. Another popular pistol. I looked at him and, involuntarily, I laughed.

"You don't think I'll do it?"

"You might," I said. "But if I walked into your office and started telling you how to move people's money around, you'd laugh, right?"

"What are you talking about?"

"You have to have experience to do stuff like this. You're on my turf. You're not going to win this battle."

"I think Keaton Fuller would tell you differently."

"That wasn't a confrontation. That wasn't a standoff. That was you hiding and deciding to kill a guy. You know, I never asked you—how'd you pull off that shot? That's a tough shot. Did you practice? Are you a good shot?"

He looked at me and answered my question honestly. "I've fired guns over the years. The camp I went to as a kid had a shooting range. I even shot guns once or twice with Keaton and Greer. In their backyard. More recently, I've gone to shooting ranges and played around. Basically, I'm a decent shot. But that shot? That day? That was luck."

Luck. I pictured my cigarette butt flying high in the air, the gust of wind catching it and dropping it right in the trash.

He continued, "Keaton walked out. I'd decided to do it. I aimed, pulled the trigger one time, and he just dropped. A perfect shot, right to the chest. If I had missed him, or gotten him in the arm or something, I probably would have left without finishing the job. But I didn't miss. I got lucky. It was a perfect shot."

And then Treadway jumped right back to what really mattered. "Change your mind, John."

"You can't just kill people, Dave. I agree with you—the world won't miss Keaton Fuller. But that's not your decision to make."

Treadway said again, in almost a monotone, "Change your mind, John."

"Can't do it. I thought about it, but I can't do it. I had to pick one way or the other, and I decided against you. You know, you never know where the line is. It's case by case. The gardener who took the ring? I decided to let her off. Much smaller thing, but she did break the law. But you? Not going to happen. Put the gun down, Dave."

He shook his head no. "You send me to jail for life, you might as well kill me. And my family too. I can't let you do it, John."

"I'm going to do it," I said. And then, "What are you going to do about Jill? You going to lie and say she never found out about any of it? Tell them why you had her put the recording up to the intercom, so the staff would think it was you, but then lie and say she somehow never found out what really happened that morning, so she's completely free of any blame? No way the cops could prove it. That's what I'd do. There's a line I'd cross. Put the gun down, Dave. You're not going to get away with this."

He said, "I got away with Keaton. Almost. And I don't think you've told anyone about me, about what you discovered. Have you?"

"Nope," I said.

"You end up dead on the beach, who's going to bring that back to me? I'll have the evidence. And there are probably plenty of people who'd like to see you dead. Past cases. Shit, you just busted a drug ring. How many people up that chain want you gone? Lots of reasonable doubt. *If* it ever got back to me."

Dave Treadway was a smart guy. He was. If he shot me right here on the beach, he probably *could* get away with it. It would be hard, like he'd said, for someone to bring it back to him. Eve Cogburn knew I was going to visit the grave site, but she didn't know exactly why. Didn't realize how it was connected to the question I'd asked her about Treadway. Or whether it was at all. The cemetery guys saw me dig up a gun, but there'd be no film of it. Treadway would have that, because he knew it was on my phone. Janet Falcone at the DMV knew I'd wanted to know whether Treadway owned a motorcycle, but, again, she didn't know why I was looking into that. The gas station manager could come forward with another copy of the tape, if he discovered somehow that I was dead. But Treadway would have the hat that he was wearing in the tape. Beyond that, what was the tape without everything else?

And, of course, there was the big one: the gun. Treadway would have the gun. The truly incriminating evidence. Not to mention the other big one: Treadway would be the only one with the knowledge of how all the pieces connected together to put the Keaton Fuller murder on him. Yeah, he probably could get away with it.

"All right," I said. "Let's say I change my mind."

And then, like that brutal evening in the woods of Calabasas, I was faced with another split second that lasted another eternity. Dave Treadway thought about that notion, about me changing my mind. I could see it in his eyes. And in that split second, my left fist came down hard on his right hand. As the Ruger fell toward the sand, I hit him in the nose, square. He staggered backward but, before he went down, I spun him and shoved him forward so he face-planted in the sand. I put my knee on his spine, then yanked both his hands back toward me. I cuffed his wrists. Then I pulled out some plastic restraining straps from my jacket. I wound them around his ankles and cinched them tight.

Then I called Detective Mike Ott.

When he picked up, I said, "Mike, you're not going to believe this shit."

Life is gray, decisions are black and white.

39

Ott had a lot to deal with. First I gave him the top line. That while Lee Graves did in fact run a deadly, and highly illegal, drug operation, he had not in fact killed Keaton Fuller. The man I'd bound on the beach had. David Treadway, successful businessman, loving husband and father.

And then I gave him the details of the story. And then the evidence. The tape from the gas station, the hat, the Smith, the video that the cemetery grounds manager had taken of me digging up the gun in front of two of his employees, two more witnesses.

I also gave Ott the more macro responsibility of dealing with it all. Working with the La Jolla police, pushing through the paperwork that would eventually bring Dave Treadway to trial and then put him in prison.

And after that? Well, I drove home. And on that drive home I thought, you know, I bet Lee Graves had initially told me the truth about Keaton's involvement in his operation. In a way, at least. Graves had probably told Keaton that through the fish business, and just maybe some other stuff too, he could grow Keaton's money. But before telling Keaton the *whole* truth, he'd gotten glimpses of his personality. And then, Graves gave the money back to Keaton, along with some walking papers, before Keaton caused him any real trouble. Which he would have. For sure. Now, was I right that that's what happened? Well, I'd never know exactly.

Happens sometimes.

The next evening I was sitting on the edge of my pool with Nancy, our feet dangling in the cool water, the fronds on the palms above us moving just slightly, pushed around a bit by a late-afternoon wind.

Nancy said with a real melancholy in her voice, "It's too bad. You know?"

"Yeah. It was kind of a tough call. Keaton Fuller was a terrible guy. A guy who nobody's going to miss. But I had to do it. Treadway had to go."

"That's not what I meant. He definitely did. You had to put him in jail. You can't go around killing people you don't like. I mean, there have to be some rules in life. Rules are kind of fun in a way. Because you obey most of them. But then you break some of them sometimes. The ones that are *breakable*. And it's fun. Kind of liberating, in a way. But you don't break the ones *you just can't break*. And killing people you don't like is one of them. If that's allowed, you know, just because you feel like it, then we're just like that alligator you always talk about."

"Which is ironic, because thinking about that alligator was what made me consider *not* sending Treadway away."

I looked at her. She wasn't smiling, but there was just a slight upturn at the corners of her big full lips. I said, "So what did you mean when you said 'it's too bad'?"

"Oh," she said. "I said that because we don't get to play beer pong and smoke pot with the Treadways anymore. And that was fun."

I laughed, genuinely surprised by the joke she'd laid on me.

She stayed with it. "Seriously. It's really hard to find other couples to be friends with. Good friends. Real friends. Where you like the dude and I like the chick. You know?"

"Yeah," I said. "It really is."

"Oh well. It was fun while it lasted. Even though we were playing beer pong and smoking pot with, you know, a murderer."

"Ha," I said. "Right again."

Nancy said, "Well, I'm going to go make us some dinner."

She got up and walked inside.

I took off my shirt and slipped into the pool. I was down under the water with my eyes open, looking around. I pushed off the deep-end wall and shot through the water.

And I thought, You know, Graves was the high-fin, and then Treadway was the high-fin, but life can be the high-fin too. So much of life possesses the high-fin quality. The duality. Where you think something is one thing and then you realize it could be, might be, maybe even *is*, something else.

Was Dave Treadway a ruthless killer—or is he a guy who avenged the death of a young girl driven to suicide by Keaton Fuller and, who, in doing so, ridded the world of a sick, awful soul? Is it morally wrong for me to have a child when my going to work means I might die—or is it just fine, something that a kid could deal with, even if I did die? Are coincidences random—or are they *meant to be*? Are we all really here, walking around, playing Ping-Pong, drinking beer, going to Starbucks, going to work, going on vacation, mowing our lawns, stubbing our toes, shopping, seeing movies, visiting with friends, getting sick, getting better, looking for answers, falling in love—or is it all just an illusion created through a chip stuck in our brains by aliens two hundred million years ago?

I swam down to the bottom of the pool and put my feet right in the center of the deep end. And then I pushed off and shot straight up toward the surface, headed for oxygen, for life. Which answers are right? Which answers are real? To those questions? To lots of questions? Well, I guess that just comes down to how you decide to look at it.

THE END

ACKNOWLEDGMENTS

Thank you to Hannah Wood and Erica Spellman-Silverman for all your great work. Total pros, both of you.

Also, thank you to Julie Hersh, the cover-design team at HarperCollins, and Tara Carberry.

Finally, thank you to my family. My mom, my sister, Priscilla, and my brother, Rich. You guys are the best.

ABOUT THE AUTHOR

Michael Craven is an advertising writer and creative director, and is the author of two previous books, *Body Copy* and *The Detective & the Pipe Girl,* nominated for both the Nero Wolfe and Shamus Awards. He lives and works in New York City.